Mrs Hudson & She

IN
SHERLOCK'S
SHADOW

LIZ HEDGECOCK

WHITE
RHINO
BOOKS

For Stephen—
I got there in the end!

He sat down just as Billy knocked on the consulting-room door. I could see the gleam in Sherlock's eyes even from my hiding-place. 'Come in!' he called, and though he looked almost bored, the note of excitement in his voice was impossible to miss. He was on the hunt, ready for the chase. I looked down at my crossed fingers, hoping that he would not be disappointed.

***

Our visitor – Sherlock's visitor – was a stout, red-faced, middle-aged man, whom Billy announced as Mr Higgins. Sherlock's face had fallen a little on his appearance, but a casual observer would not have noticed. 'Take a seat, Mr Higgins,' Sherlock said, waving a hand at the high-backed armchair.

Mr Higgins did as he was told, gripping the arms of the chair as if he were about to embark on a fairground ride. He had placed his bowler hat in his lap, and Sherlock's gaze rested on it for a moment. 'May I introduce my friend and colleague Dr Watson. If you don't mind, he will take notes of our conversation.'

'Oh no, I don't mind, I don't mind at all—'

'Excellent. Now, why does your wife want you to come and see me? Is it something to do with your shop, or another matter?'

Mr Higgins's mouth dropped open. 'I – well!' A chuckle escaped from him as if it had been a hiccup. 'How did you do that?'

'It was simple,' Sherlock replied. 'Your demeanour on entering the room – your apprehension – indicates that you would rather not be here. More precisely, that you do not think you should be here. Therefore, someone whom you cannot refuse has sent you. The most obvious person is a wife, and since your hat has been brushed and you appear well-fed, I took the gamble.'

'But – the shop?'

Sherlock took up his pipe from the table, filled it, and pointed its stem at a region around Mr Higgins's left knee. 'When Billy showed you in, I perceived that you had a magazine protruding from your coat pocket. While it is upside down, I recognise the typeface as that of *The Grocer.*'

'Oh!' Mr Higgins leaned round and scrabbled at his coat pocket, pulling out a crumpled periodical. 'Well, well,' he said, gazing at the paper as if it might have changed in his pocket. 'That's very clever, to know that.'

'Is it a financial matter?' Sherlock lit his pipe and sat back, breathing plumes of smoke. I was glad to be in a different room.

'Oh, no.' Mr Higgins frowned. 'The shop is doing well, as a matter of fact.'

'I am sure it is.' Sherlock blew a smoke ring. 'Do you have anyone staying with you at the moment? Relatives or acquaintances, I mean. Not lodgers.'

Mr Higgins stared again. 'My wife's nephew is with us at the moment—'

'In that case,' Sherlock leaned forward, 'I advise you to examine your books carefully, to change the locks on your shop, and to have a word with your nephew. The strange phenomenon that has brought you here – whatever it may be – is either a distraction technique or a signal to accomplices. I fully expect that if you take no action you will either find a steady trickle of money escaping from your profits, or you will be burgled. You buy trade magazines, you are a careful man; that is plain for anyone to see, including your nephew. Your shop will be insured. Perhaps he sees it as a victimless crime; perhaps he does not care, or he is in the grip of others. At any rate, if you do as I suggest I predict that the strange phenomenon will cease.'

Mr Higgins pulled out a large handkerchief and passed it over his forehead. 'I – I don't know what to say.' His eyes were round as buttons. 'You think that Maisie – my wife – knows?'

'Strongly suspects, I believe.' Sherlock took another puff at his pipe, then regarded it critically. 'I was hoping for a three-pipe problem, but as it turns out that was barely half. If you have nothing else to discuss, Mr Higgins—'

The grocer rose, fumbling in his trouser pocket. 'Your fee—'

Sherlock pulled out his watch and glanced at it. 'I do not charge for the first fifteen minutes, and your case occupied five and a half. Good day to you, Mr Higgins.' He extended a hand, and the grocer pumped it up and down, beaming, before bowing low and taking his leave. His exclamations of wonder grew fainter as he descended, until the front door closed.

Sherlock turned his head, and looked directly at me. 'How did I do, Nell?' His smile was broad.

'I'll come through.' I got up, returned the cushion and the books to their places, and extinguished the lamps.

When I entered the consulting room both men turned to me. Dr Watson was beaming, his notebook forgotten. Sherlock's smile had faded a little.

'Did you spot him, Nell?' he asked.

'You were so quick that I barely had a chance,' I said. 'I noticed the hat and the magazine, but of course I couldn't tell which it was.'

'Study pays off,' Sherlock said around his pipe.

'It may,' I countered, 'but waiving your clients' fees doesn't. We have bills to pay.' I sat in the armchair that Mr Higgins had recently vacated.

'Free advertising, Nell.' Sherlock took the pipe from his mouth and used it to emphasise his points. 'Mr Higgins will marvel all the way home. He will congratulate his wife for her idea of consulting me. Together they will probably tell their whole acquaintance that I am the man to visit.'

'Brilliant, Holmes!' Watson closed his notebook with a snap.

'Not if they come expecting a free consultation.' I smiled to try and take the sting from my remark, but a tiny twist of Sherlock's mouth told me that I need not have bothered. 'You did brilliantly, as always. You know that.' My praise was genuine, but had come too late.

'I am trying to build my practice, Nell. You know that.'

Dr Watson coughed, and rose to his feet. 'I think I'll go and write this case up in my room. Quite a heavy dinner, and I mean to be in early tomorrow. Goodnight.'

'Goodnight,' we echoed.

I waited until the doctor's feet had reached the landing above, then got up and sat on the arm of Sherlock's chair. I

Sherlock fetched a magnifying glass. 'Printed in block characters, using a Cross stylographic pen. Black ink, I think Stephens, very common. Ha!' He dropped the note on the bureau, then frowned and picked it up again, bringing it close to his face.

'Can you see something?' I asked.

'No...' Sherlock responded. He closed his eyes. 'Nell, take the note. What do you smell?'

He handed me the note. I closed my eyes, inhaled, and my mouth twisted at the hint of dung, the rotting meat smell, and... My eyes snapped open.

Sherlock was staring at me. 'What did you smell? Not the obvious, the other.'

I shook my head to try and clear it. 'Jasmine. I smelt jasmine.' I looked up at Sherlock. 'But – what—'

There was a loud knock at the door. 'Not now, Billy,' snapped Sherlock.

'Sir, it's important!' Billy shouted. 'A telegram for Inspector Gregson; they've sent it on from Scotland Yard.'

The inspector jumped up, flung open the door, and snatched the telegram from Billy's hand. We watched him rip it open. His face sagged, and he stood motionless, the telegram in his hand, staring into space.

Sherlock crossed the room. 'What is it?' He took the telegram from the inspector's unresisting hand and scanned it. 'Oh my God.' He passed it to me and I read:

Emmett Stanley vanished from Wandsworth STOP Cell empty.

CHAPTER 4

'There is not a moment to lose,' muttered Sherlock, gathering up his necessary belongings – a magnifying glass, his pipe and tobacco, a notebook – and looking round for his coat.

'It's in the hall,' I said, 'shall I bring it?'

'Please.' When I returned, carrying his coat and my own, Inspector Gregson had moved closer to Sherlock and appeared to be having a quiet word, since both looked up rather guiltily at my entrance.

'Did I miss something?' I asked, keeping my tone neutral.

'Not at all,' said the inspector, as I handed Sherlock his coat. He shrugged it on and filled its pockets. 'I hadn't realised you dabbled in detective work.'

I considered how best to respond to that. 'I used to do analysis for Inspector Lestrade,' I said. 'When I met Mr Holmes, he needed an assistant.'

'I take it you're quite observant, then.'

I surveyed Inspector Gregson, from his polished black shoes to his neatly-parted hair. 'I think so.'

'Are you seeking work at present, Mrs Hudson?' He raised an eyebrow.

'I have some time available,' I replied, after a pause. Inside, though, I was jumping up and down, desperate to know what the inspector had in mind.

He looked down at me and smiled. 'You're a cool hand, Mrs Hudson. Here.' He reached into his pocket and handed me a card. 'I said I'd send someone their way.'

The card was a thick white pasteboard: *Debenham & Freebody, Wigmore Street*. The name above had been scratched out, and *Mr Turner* added, in slightly shaky capitals. 'I'm not sure I understand, Inspector,' I said, looking up at him.

Inspector Gregson put a fatherly hand on my shoulder. 'If you pop along and see Mr Turner, he'll explain it to you.'

'But I—'

'This doesn't need three of us,' the inspector said, firmly.

'Expect me when you see me, Nell,' said Sherlock, and leaned down to peck me on the cheek. 'I'll wire.' And he was gone, his feet thundering downstairs.

'Good luck, Mrs Hudson,' said the inspector. 'I'll see myself out.'

***

I knew Debenham and Freebody well, having visited the department store many times to purchase stockings and gloves. It was no more than fifteen minutes' walk from

25

Baker Street. It had also, once upon a time, been the haberdashers I had used as a front for my various secret expeditions. I had no idea why the inspector would require me to go there, though.

'Good afternoon, ma'am,' cooed one of the assistants, as I walked in. 'What can I interest you in today?'

I approached the counter and drew out my card. 'I wish to see Mr Turner, please.'

The assistant looked down her nose at me. 'What would that be concerning, ma'am?'

'Inspector Gregson advised me of some work,' I said, trying not to blush. However, the word 'Inspector' had acted as a tonic on the assistant, who was already hastening away. She reappeared a minute later, her shoes clacking on the parquet floor. 'He will be with you directly, ma'am.'

Mr Turner was a small, neat, elderly man, his hair suspiciously black. I had put on my most businesslike hat and gloves, but he still eyed me with suspicion. 'This is not what I had in mind,' he muttered. I was unsure whether I had been meant to hear or not.

'Mr Turner?' I said, stepping forward and extending a hand. 'I am Mrs Hudson. Inspector Gregson mentioned that you were looking for someone.'

'Yes, yes, indeed.' He frowned. 'Come this way.'

Mr Turner held open an elegant door at the side of the shop, and I followed him down a narrow corridor to a small office, the desk stacked with papers and ledgers. 'Do take a seat, Mrs, er—'

'Hudson.' I sat in the chair he had waved at, and he

took the chair behind the desk. When he was seated I could just see the top half of his face above the piles of paper.

'Yes, yes,' he said, irritably. 'So did the inspector explain?'

'He said you would,' I replied, feeling foolish. I suspected Inspector Gregson would not have sent Sherlock into a situation without briefing him.

'It's simple,' said Mr Turner. 'Pilfering. Our merchandise is small and easy to steal. People come in, browse, wander about, perhaps buy a metre of ribbon, and all the time they've got three pairs of gloves in their muff. I compare the stock inventory to the receipts, and it's obvious.' He swung from side to side on his chair, gripping the desk. 'I thought it might be one of the staff, but nothing turned up, not after several searches.' I blushed at the thought. 'So.'

'So…?'

'So I need someone to stop 'em.' Mr Turner glared at me. 'I must admit I was hoping the inspector would send a policeman round. That would make them jump!' He smacked the desk and I jumped.

'I don't suppose that would be good for business,' I replied, when I had recovered myself.

'I'm not having it!' Mr Turner bounced in his seat with indignation. I waited until he had composed himself before asking what exactly it was he wished me to do.

He looked at me doubtfully. 'Catch 'em, of course. Pretend you're shopping, watch 'em, and catch 'em. I don't care how. It's all the same to me if you call the doorman, or make 'em put it back. So long as the thieving stops. We're losing money, you know.'

'Speaking of money, what salary do you have in mind?' I felt a little embarrassed to introduce the topic, but as money was pressing I felt obliged.

Mr Turner swivelled in his chair and sucked his teeth. 'Well, it's not as if you're a real policeman, madam. Our assistants are on eight shillings a week.'

'Mr Turner, do you expect me to do a policeman's job for eight shillings a week?' I began to rise from my chair.

'Wait, madam.' Mr Turner flapped a hand at me to resume my seat. 'Perhaps we can work something out.'

In the end, after negotiation on both sides, we settled that I was to start the next week on a trial basis, working in the afternoons, and receive a full assistant's salary. Mr Turner got up and stretched across the desk to shake my hand.

'There's just one more thing,' I said. 'I can't do it as myself.'

Mr Turner sank into his chair and stared at me. '*What?*'

I folded my hands in my lap. 'Consider, Mr Turner. If I frequent your store always looking more or less the same, then the people who steal from you will learn to spot me. And I do have my other work to think about.' I chose not to add that I did not particularly want anyone of my acquaintance to know that I was working in a department store.

Mr Turner's expression changed from incredulity to something like respect. 'You make a good point there, Mrs Hudson.' Then his face grew suspicious. 'Make sure you report to me when you arrive each morning. I don't want any mistakes.' I wondered what sort of mistakes he might mean, before realising that an unfamiliar woman loitering in a department store might find herself being escorted from the premises, if not worse.

Mr Turner got up, came round the desk and held out his hand again. 'Good day to you, Mrs Hudson. I will expect you in my office at half past twelve on Monday.' His eyes burned with the zeal of a responsible shopkeeper. 'A week's trial.'

I shook his hand. 'A week's trial.'

Mr Turner escorted me down the corridor and left me on the shop floor. I surveyed the scene while pretending to examine a display of hats. The store was busy. Women strolled and stood and chatted, in twos and threes, while turning over stockings and trying on gloves. In contrast to the relaxed shoppers, the assistants bustled around, offering reels of ribbon, hurrying to the stock room, urging their customer to try the blue silk. The opportunities for theft were obvious.

I waited until the assistant I had first encountered was free, and approached her. 'Yes, madam?' I was not convinced she recognised me.

'We spoke earlier. I have met with Mr Turner, and I am to start on Monday.' I felt a little foolish as I said it, but it seemed important to make contact with someone I would be working alongside.

'Right you are, ma'am.' She seemed unimpressed at the prospect. 'I'll look out for you, then, on Monday.'

'About that,' I said. 'I might have red hair on Monday.

29

The rest I'm not sure of, yet.'

She took a step back. 'Red hair, ma'am?'

'Yes.' I smiled at her. 'Till Monday.'

I strolled off feeling a little more pleased with myself. Admittedly, Inspector Gregson's tip was not precisely what I had envisaged, but I had secured paid employment, hopefully to become regular, which would supplement Dr Watson's contributions to the household income. How exciting or dull the work would be, I was as yet uncertain, but it was work. It might lead to more opportunities. And with a pleasant sense of a job well done, I built castles in the air all the way to Baker Street.

CHAPTER 5

Sherlock had not returned when I let myself in to 221B Baker Street. I had not expected him to. I busied myself in planning meals for the coming week, since my free time would be compromised for at least that long.

I took my menu downstairs, where I found Billy peeling potatoes and Martha shelling peas. I had been worried they might not get on, but my fears were unjustified. Billy treated Martha as a much older sister, while Martha regarded Billy with an almost maternal eye. Billy joshed, Martha nagged, and they chatted constantly. I spent less time in the kitchen than I had before Martha's arrival, partly because I did not need to, but also because their easy relationship stirred a pang of regret in me. Billy and I had been close, in the days before Sherlock Holmes and Dr Watson had come to Baker Street. He had looked after me at my most vulnerable, and we had become firm friends, working together to keep the house running. I knew things could not be the same now, and I was glad that those dark days were gone, but that didn't stop me regretting the increasing remoteness of our relationship.

They both looked up at my entrance, and waited for me to speak.

'I have taken a job,' I said, feeling rather foolish, 'so I have planned next week's meals early. Martha, will you go through this with me, and see to the orders?'

'Yes, ma'am. In here?'

I looked at the bright fire. 'Yes, in here.'

'What sort of job is it, ma'am?' Billy had put his knife down, a puzzled expression on his face.

I considered how to explain. 'It is something that Inspector Gregson put my way,' I said at last. 'A case of thievery. It might not take long.'

'Ah,' Billy's face cleared and he returned to his potato. 'I thought for a moment—'

'Thought what, Billy?' The words came out perhaps a little more harshly than I had meant.

'I thought you might mean . . . a regular job,' he faltered.

'We shall see,' I replied. 'Martha, the menu.'

Once the menu had been discussed and approved, and the tradespeople's orders agreed, I went upstairs and opened the wardrobe. My dresses hung in a row on the left-hand side: lilac, navy, grey. Any of them would do; they were all of much the same conservative style, since I had had them for half-mourning, although I had removed the black trim as soon as I decently could. I fingered the lilac cotton. That was the dress I had worn when Sherlock had first noticed me, a day when I was feeling positive about life.

It was also the dress I had worn on a much darker day, not so long ago.

I pulled the dove-grey dress from the wardrobe and changed into it. Then I went through to the dressing room, where I kept my own small stock of 'professional equipment'. If I remembered correctly, the auburn wig was in the third hatbox, on a mannequin head to keep its shape. I lifted the box down. My various shawls were folded in the second drawer of the tallboy. I selected a bright Paisley in red and blue. A small black handbag, low-heeled boots, and simple jewellery completed the outfit.

Laden down, I returned to the bedroom, put the small heap of accessories on the bed, and sat at the dressing-table. First I pinned my hair tight to my head. A stocking-cap would have been more convenient, but I hated the constant pressure on my scalp. I settled the auburn wig on my head, drawing it into a simple knot at the nape of my neck. Its colour would be eye-catching enough without an elaborate style, and I had a little black hat with a half-veil which would sit well. I opened the top right-hand drawer of the table, drew out my black box, and set to work.

A few minutes later I pushed my chair back a little and examined myself in the mirror. I had powdered myself quite pale, added a small sprinkling of freckles across the bridge of my nose, and my eyebrows were now reddish-brown. I pinned the hat on, settled the veil, and nodded to myself. For a first day, that would do.

I gasped as the bedroom door burst open. Sherlock strode in, loosening his necktie. He pulled it off and threw it on the bed, then twitched his silk dressing-gown from its hook.

'How was it?' I turned towards him on my stool.

'I need to think,' he snapped. 'I'm going next door. Get someone to bring up a supper tray, will you.' The last words were flung over his shoulder as he disappeared into the consulting room, and the sentence was ended with a slam. I doubted he had even seen me.

I turned back to the mirror. I knew what Sherlock would be doing. He would arrange the cushions in a heap, fetch his tobacco-jar and pipe, and sit cross-legged, puffing away, his mind whirring, until things clicked into place. At first I had thought that the ritual was purely for effect; one of the little tricks he played, quite consciously, to make himself seem more impressive. However, having now seen his rage when disturbed from his reverie, I believed in it absolutely.

I had better warn the household. I got up and went down to the kitchen. 'Mr Holmes is thinking in the consulting room,' I announced. Billy and Martha both started slightly at my change in appearance. 'He doesn't want to be disturbed.'

'Will he be down to dinner, ma'am?' asked Martha, her eyes fixed on my hair. While Billy was comparatively used to my occasional disguises, having seen me in various costumes over the past year, Martha had seen me in disguise just once or twice, paired with Sherlock, and usually with considerable notice.

'I doubt it; a supper tray outside the door will suffice.' I grinned at her stare, smoothing the side of my hair. 'I shall take it off shortly, Martha; it is for the job. I did not want to delay in telling you about Mr Holmes, so I came straight down.' I heard a faint creak from above me. 'Is Dr Watson in?'

'He returned with Mr Holmes, ma'am, just now,' said Billy.

'I shall go and change.' I ran upstairs before my voice could betray me. All the time I was taking off my hat and wig, cleaning my face and redoing my hair – even when I climbed the stairs to Dr Watson's rooms, the phrase *He sent for Watson, not you* ran through my head. I pushed it down, deep down, before knocking on the sitting-room door.

'Enter!' said an irritable voice. Dr Watson was in his shirt-sleeves, a large notebook open on the writing desk, his pen poised. He had already filled a page. 'What is it, Mrs Hudson?'

'I believe you accompanied Mr Holmes today, Dr Watson.' I tried not to let the words sound accusing.

'Yes, I did.' He did not put his pen down. 'I am writing up my account.'

'Could you tell me what happened?'

Dr Watson sighed, looked sadly at his pen, and set it on the blotter. 'Briefly, I set out for Wandsworth Prison as soon as I received the telegram. The cell appeared undisturbed. There was no clue how Stanley got out, and no evidence of a struggle. Nothing untoward whatsoever. Lestrade and a couple of men are interviewing the prison guards who were on duty at the time. From Wandsworth we travelled to Mrs Stanley at their house in Ealing. She was hysterical, barely coherent, and I had to sedate her for her own good. The parcel Mrs Stanley received, and its contents, are presently being examined by a police surgeon. I expect it will be released to Mr Holmes shortly afterwards. Now, if you will excuse me, Mrs Hudson—' He looked pointedly at his notebook.

'Of course, Dr Watson.' I descended the stairs far more slowly than I had ascended, musing. Dr Watson's bald account was no more than I had expected, but it suggested that this would be the sort of case that Sherlock loved: baffling, opaque, and with an element of horror. I would probably be sleeping alone that night, while Sherlock's brain ticked and tested in the room next door. Perhaps he would be ready to talk about it in the morning.

It was odd, I thought, as I unclipped my earrings, that Dr Watson and I were not better friends. We were still Dr Watson and Mrs Hudson to each other, never John and Nell. I had thought that he might mellow in time, and become a little less formal with me, but no. In fact, I suspected that he disapproved of me, which was why I had removed my disguise before visiting his rooms. Admittedly our situation was unconventional, but my suspicion dated from much further back, from when he had opposed Sherlock's idea that I assist him on cases—

My mouth dropped open, and the earring clattered on the dressing table.

Dr Watson was jealous of me.
And I was jealous of him.

CHAPTER 6

By Monday, little had changed. Sherlock had been either out or incommunicado for most of the weekend. The only significant pieces of information he had managed to gather were that the foot sent to Mrs Stanley had been cut from a living person, almost certainly male, and that Mrs Stanley had had no inkling that her husband might disappear. 'I'd stake my life on it,' he said on Sunday night. 'I've seen enough of Effie Stanley to know that she's telling the truth.'

Given the seriousness of the case, my own news took a back seat; indeed, having made my preparations, I put it out of my mind until late morning on Monday, when I made myself a sandwich and went upstairs to get ready. It was the work of a few minutes, since I had left the wig dressed. I checked myself in the mirror, caught up my gloves, and went to say goodbye to Billy and Martha. It was an unwritten rule that, when leaving the house on business of this kind, Sherlock and I would tell someone where we were going and when we expected to return, and show ourselves in case a description became necessary. It never had, so far, but it made me feel a little safer.

I was walking across the hallway to the kitchen stairs when the front door swung open. Sherlock and I stared at each other. He looked exhausted. There were dark shadows under his eyes, and he seemed even thinner than usual.

'What are you doing, Nell?' His brows knitted.

'I am going out,' I replied. 'I have work to do for Inspector Gregson.'

He didn't move. 'What sort of work?'

'Undercover.'

'Well, obviously.' He stepped towards me and lifted my chin with the tip of his finger. 'Where?'

The question I had hoped he wouldn't ask. 'A department store,' I snapped, lifting my chin still higher and meeting his eyes.

'A department store.' A little smile played around the corners of his mouth. While that normally made me want to kiss him, today it was having the opposite effect. 'What, are you going to be a shopgirl?'

'No, I am not. What I shall be is late, if you don't step aside.'

He held the door open for me, his eyebrows raised. 'Or you could come with me and work on the Stanley case, as my assistant...'

'I made a commitment, and I intend to honour it. I should be home by seven.' I swept through the door and marched off down the street with great purpose. When I dared to turn, some way down the road, Sherlock was still in the doorway, watching.

I arrived at Debenham and Freebody five minutes early, and the commissionaire at the door touched his cap to me. 'Good afternoon, ma'am. Are we shopping today?'

'No.' I smiled. 'We're working.'

The assistant I had spoken to was on the handkerchief counter today; her smooth dark head nodded as an elderly lady in tweed explained what she wanted. I waved on my way to Mr Turner's office and she gave me a broad grin, which vanished immediately the customer looked up from the tray of handkerchiefs.

'Come!' Mr Turner barked in response to my knock. I pushed open the door and he stared at me for a second or two before checking his watch and wishing me good afternoon. We exchanged a few pleasantries, but Mr Turner's eyes kept straying to the door, keen for me to begin.

'Is there anything I should know before I start?' I asked.

'I don't think so.' Mr Turner stood, clearly glad that I had taken the hint. 'You should probably let Alphonse know who you are.'

'Alphonse?'

'Yes, on the door. Oh, and introduce yourself to one of the assistants. Once one of them knows who you are, they all will.' Mr Turner nodded his head in dismissal. I felt his eyes on my back as I left the office.

When I emerged onto the shop floor the lady in tweed had made her selection, and the assistant was wrapping them in tissue paper. I waited until the lady had departed with her package, and then walked over.

'It's a good thing you said about the hair,' the assistant said, leaning in confidentially. 'I wouldn't have clocked you otherwise. Although when you said red, I thought you meant carrots.'

'I don't think carrots would suit me,' I said, laughing. 'Anyway, Mr Turner said I should introduce myself...' My voice trailed off as I realised this would mean giving my name. Why hadn't I thought of it before? I could have conducted the whole business under an assumed name, and no one would have been any the wiser. *A lesson for next time, Nell*, I told myself. Then a smile came to my face. 'You can call me Mrs Hudson. Nell Hudson.'

The assistant's round blue eyes became wider still. 'So that isn't...?'

I leaned forward and lowered my voice. 'That's the name I go by, here.'

'Oh!' she exclaimed, her eyes shining. 'Well, I'm Miss Blanchard in front of customers, and Evie the rest of the time.'

'Nice to meet you, Evie.' Around me the store grew busier, as post-lunch shoppers came in. 'I had better get started...' I turned away, but as I did, Evie cleared her throat.

'Um . . . there's just one thing.' She looked terribly nervous.

'What is it, Evie?'

'I hope you don't mind me saying...'

'Oh no,' I muttered, hand moving automatically to check my wig was on straight. I imagined smudged freckles, or a lock of brown hair falling down my back.

40

'What is it? Do I need a mirror?'

'No, no, it's nothing like that,' Evie soothed. 'It's just that—'

'*What?*' I mouthed.

Her words came out in a rush. 'You're all businesslike. You look as if you're here to work, not shop.'

'Oh!' My relieved smile faded as I saw her point. 'What should I do?'

'Wait a moment.' Evie waved at two assistants chatting on the haberdashery counter, and the shorter of the two came over. 'Will you cover me for a few minutes, Gladys? I'm helping Nell out.' She whispered in Gladys's ear. Gladys gawped at me and put a hand to her mouth. 'Come along, Nell.'

I followed Evie through a side door. 'Where are we going?'

'Just to the staff cloakroom,' said Evie. 'Don't worry.'

Behind the next door was a white-tiled washroom with a row of pegs by the door. Evie fetched a battered chair and sat me down. 'Do you mind if I take a few pins out?'

I could feel her hand hovering over my head. 'No, that's all right. So long as my hair stays on.'

Evie laughed, and took off my hat. I closed my eyes and hoped for the best.

'There,' she said two minutes later, settling the hat. 'Just a couple more things. Give me your shawl.' She disappeared round the corner and returned with a little fur collar which she pinned on with a sparkling brooch. 'You can borrow this for the afternoon. Oh, and—' She drew a little jar of salve from her pocket. 'Pout for me. I'll only put a bit on.' I did as I was told. 'There. Your hat needs a flower, really, but you can look now.'

I stood up and went to the looking-glass on the wall. Evie followed, grinning, but I only had eyes for me.

I was something I had never been before in my whole life.

I was *chic*.

***

I hummed to myself as I browsed, drifting from section to section, making a slow circuit round the shop. I affected to be absorbed in details of trim and buttons, but under my eyelashes I watched and waited.

Two girls hurried past, ribbons fluttering. *Perhaps they were in a rush*, my calm, sensible self thought. But I had already caught a whiff of something . . . *illicit*. I couldn't have said what, exactly; but I put down the button card I was holding and wandered in the direction they had taken. Their heads were together, and I heard the *pss-pss* of their whispers.

The pair had stopped at the lingerie counter, towards the front of the shop. The store had quietened and they were examining a selection of silk stockings. One of them asked the assistant a question. She walked to the shelves behind her and scanned them, running her hand down the trays. I was still some distance away, but I saw a quick, convulsive movement from one of them. I strolled forward and paused at a mannequin, affecting to admire her scarf. Now I could get between them and the door.

The assistant brought out a tray and one of the girls shook her head. The shopgirl, her shoulders bowed, picked

42

up the tray and turned to slot it back in, and there it was again, the arm jerking forward. While the shopgirl had her back turned, I heard the words 'I'm sorry, we have to go,' and they hurried off, arm in arm.

I was right next to the quickest path out of the store, twenty feet from them. They had to pass me. They were looking ahead, towards the door. Their cheeks were flushed, their eyes sparkling. I felt almost sorry as I stepped out in front of them.

'Give them to me,' I said. I hadn't seen which girl had taken the stockings, but the one on the right was trembling.

'Excuse me?' said the girl on the left.

'You heard me,' I said. 'Give those stockings to me now, or I'll raise the alarm.' I let my gaze flick to the commissionaire, who was a few yards away, and watching with interest.

'I don't know what you're talking about.'

'I mean it,' I rapped out.

The girl on the right fumbled a bunched-up pair of stockings from her sleeve and slapped them into my palm.

'And the other pair, please,' I said, nicely, ignoring the hatred in her eyes as she fished in her sleeve.

'I didn't know she'd done that, honest—' the girl on the left began.

'Of course you did,' I snapped. 'I shall walk you to the door, and if I catch you again it'll be names, addresses, your parents, and the police. Do you understand?'

They nodded, gulping.

'Excellent.' I strolled behind them. 'Don't think it's just me watching out for you,' I said, as the commissionaire opened the door. 'I'll be letting my colleagues know too.'

They hastened away, still arm in arm, not looking back. I suspected I, and the store, would never see them again.

'I take it you're the, um, detective,' said the commissionaire, surveying me.

'That's right,' I said. 'Good afternoon, Alphonse. I'm sorry I didn't introduce myself earlier.'

'Alphonse!' He wheezed with laughter. 'Alf will do nicely.'

I examined the stockings as I returned to the lingerie counter. They were the finest cream knit silk, with embroidered clocks. I owned nothing so extravagant. 'Here,' I said to the assistant, laying them on the counter. 'Watch out for those two girls.'

The assistant gasped. 'Oh my heavens! The best we have!' She looked from the stockings to me, terror in her eyes. 'You won't tell Mr Turner, will you?'

'No, no,' I said. 'Just put them back on the tray.'

I roamed the store for the rest of the afternoon. I caught no more thieves, possibly because it was Monday, and quiet, but I had a growing sense of unease. As I fingered skeins of wool, and compared embroidery scissors, and tried on gloves, the faces of the two girls swam into my mind, first blurred, then becoming more distinct. Not the girls as they had been when they were caught, but when they had been on the point of getting away with it. Flushed, excited, alive. I knew where I had seen that vitality before. In my own looking glass, as I got ready for work. The only real difference between us was that I was on the right side of the law.

CHAPTER 7

As was my custom when returning to Baker Street disguised, I rang the doorbell and waited. After the sound of the heavy bolts sliding back, and the grind of the key in the lock, the door opened to reveal Billy.

'Good evening, ma'am,' he grinned. 'How did it go?'

'Well, I think.' I stepped in and Billy went through the rigmarole of securing the door. 'My employer seemed happy.' I had returned home by a roundabout route, partly in case anyone was looking out for me, but mainly because it would allow me time to think. By the time I turned into Baker Street I had made peace with myself. The thrill I got from my work was merely the satisfaction of a job well done. It was pride in my work, which was laudable, surely. With the matter resolved to my liking, I was restored to equilibrium. 'Is Mr Holmes in?'

'He is,' came a voice above me. Sherlock was leaning on the banister. 'And he is impatient for his dinner.' The last was delivered with a laugh in his voice.

I curtseyed to him. 'I shall make haste, then.' I mounted the stairs, unpinning my hat as I went.

Sherlock sat on the bed and watched me remove the hat. 'How have you managed to return home smarter than when you left, Nell?' His tone was light, playful, but there was genuine curiosity beneath.

I smiled at him in the mirror. I had wondered if he would notice. 'You should have seen me earlier,' I said, shrugging off my shawl and draping it over the back of my chair. 'I have a personal dresser, and I have been a fashionable shopper all afternoon.' I studied my hair, debating whether I should take down the complicated arrangement of curls and pins, or lift the wig off and hope the hairstyle would be preserved. I decided to risk it, but as my hands went to my head, Sherlock sprang up and took them in his own. 'Let me take it off,' he said, and gently but firmly, he moved my hands away.

'No, I'll do it, you'll disturb the pins—'

'I didn't mean the wig,' he murmured into the nape of my neck, as his hands made their way to the buttons of my bodice.

'I thought you were hungry for your dinner,' I gasped, as the hands worked down.

The hands paused. 'You're right. Please excuse me.' Sherlock straightened up and walked to the door. He grasped the doorknob and doubled over in silent laughter. 'Nell, my dear, you need to take lessons in hiding your disappointment.' Chuckling, he turned the key in the lock. 'But you are right. I find myself with a voracious appetite, and a tempting hors d'oeuvre for the taking.'

I stood, and walked towards him. 'If you talk too much, the dish will grow cold.'

***

When we entered the dining room, very neat and respectable, Dr Watson was already at table, drumming his fingers on the cloth. He looked away as we took our seats.

'Are we late?' I glanced at the clock on the mantel, which suggested that if we were, it was a matter of minutes.

'A trifle,' said Dr Watson, rather shortly.

Presently Billy's footsteps announced the arrival of dinner. I made a good meal, for the hours of wandering around the department store had piqued my appetite. The gentlemen ate well, too. The sudden peal of the doorbell rang out with startling clarity.

I raised my eyebrows at Sherlock. 'I didn't know you were expecting a caller.'

'I'm not.' We both looked at Dr Watson, who shrugged. 'We have one, nevertheless.' Sherlock put his knife and fork together and stood.

I rose too. 'Is the consulting room in order?'

Sherlock snorted. 'Hardly.'

A knock at the door was followed immediately by Billy. 'Sorry to disturb you, but Mr Poskitt's here.'

'Oh!' I exclaimed, smiling. 'Show him into the drawing room, Billy, and we shall join him shortly.' I had not seen Mr Poskitt, Mycroft Holmes's secretary, since my visits to Somerset House to arrange my new identity, but I counted him as a friend.

'I wonder what he wants,' mused Sherlock.

'Oh, Sherlock.' I smoothed my hair and took his arm. 'Is it so impossible that this could be a social call?'

Sherlock snorted. 'Unannounced, on a Monday evening? I think not.'

Dr Watson was on his feet too. 'I'll go and fetch my notebook.'

'Don't bother, Watson,' said Sherlock, as he opened the door. 'This will be off the record.'

***

'I do apologise for disturbing your dinner,' Mr Poskitt said as soon as we entered the drawing room. 'I had thought you would be finished, but—'

'That's quite all right, Mr Poskitt.' I smiled at him, to try and put him at ease, but I was disturbed by the change in his appearance. To a casual observer he was the same neat clerkly figure he had always been; his trousers sharply creased, a flower in his buttonhole, his immaculate bowler hat on his lap. And yet it was as if a film of ash had spread over his countenance, as he sat perched on the edge of the settee. 'Billy will bring coffee shortly, or would you prefer tea?'

Mr Poskitt shook his head; a quick nervous movement. 'A glass of water, perhaps.' He darted a look at Dr Watson. 'May I ask that – I understand that you make a record of Mr Holmes's cases, but I must request that this meeting goes unminuted.' My mouth twitched at Mr Poskitt's use of office language, but any amusement was smothered by my sympathy for his obvious distress.

'How can we help you, Mr Poskitt?' I asked, once Billy had left the room.

Mr Poskitt's eyes darted from one to the other of us, as if unsure where to start. Then they settled on Sherlock. 'May I ask… You may already know, although I suspect you do not…' He twisted at the brim of his hat. 'Mr Holmes, have you spoken with your brother lately?'

'With Mycroft?' Sherlock seemed puzzled. 'I can't say that I have.' The crease between his eyes deepened. 'Is something the matter with him?'

'Er, well, not exactly the matter, but…' Mr Poskitt seemed to be searching his mind for the right phrase. 'There is something the matter,' he declared, at last, 'but not necessarily with Mr Holmes. Though he is affected,' he added hastily.

Sherlock moved forward in his chair. 'Mr Poskitt, you are talking in riddles,' he said.

'I do apologise,' said Mr Poskitt, his neck reddening. 'It is so hard to be precise, when the matter is not.' He reached for his glass of water and took a sip. 'If he knew that I had come here—'

'He won't hear it from us,' I said. 'Suppose you tell us about it just as it comes, and we can ask questions when you are finished.'

Mr Poskitt looked from one to the other of us again, but already his movements were less abrupt. 'And it stays within this room?'

'Of course,' Dr Watson and Sherlock said, together.

Mr Poskitt leaned forward. 'Information is finding its way out of Whitehall,' he said, in a low hoarse voice. 'Valuable information. I am not privy to what it is; I am not senior enough for that, and it is not my department . . .

49

as you know, I work at Somerset House.'

I nodded, feeling a little sick. Mr Poskitt, despite his clerkly air and his position as Mycroft Holmes's secretary, was a senior civil servant in his own right. The fact that he was in the dark underlined the seriousness of the matter.

'Do you know the nature of the information?' Sherlock muttered, even though the servants were downstairs.

Mr Poskitt hung his head. 'It is related to defence and security – and it has been leaked overseas.'

'Good Lord!' exclaimed Dr Watson. The sudden loudness of his voice was almost as shocking as if he had sworn.

Mr Poskitt looked utterly woebegone. 'It is a bad, bad business,' he muttered.

'How do you know it has gone overseas?' Sherlock asked. 'And how is my brother implicated?'

Mr Poskitt sighed, and crossed one leg over the other. 'I shall begin with the easier question. You are aware of the current, er, unrest in Egypt?'

Sherlock smiled a wintry smile. 'Anyone who reads the papers is aware of it.'

'There was a plan to bring things to a head. We had a force ready to advance from Alexandra to Cairo; but the Egyptians were more than ready for us. Later we received word from a neutral source that the plan had been leaked to the Egyptians. I happened to be in the room when Mr Holmes opened the communication,' he added hastily. 'Our source hinted that there was more.'

'So this is pretty high-level stuff, then?' asked Dr Watson.

'It is. A mere handful of men operate at that level, and Mr Holmes, while junior, is one of them.'

'Is he under suspicion?' Sherlock's eyes were like gimlets, though his voice was level.

Mr Poskitt studied the carpet. 'Everyone is under suspicion; but some of Mr Holmes's more, ah, unorthodox methods have been noted. Nothing has been said, but there is an undercurrent, a distinct undercurrent. Mr Holmes usually attends the Wednesday briefing in the Prime Minister's office, and we received a message that the last one had been cancelled. I discovered later that it had not.' He chewed his bottom lip. 'I have not informed Mr Holmes as yet. The atmosphere of suspicion is already having an effect on him. That is why you must not tell anyone I have been here,' he added, the nervousness returning to his voice. 'This is too secret to involve the police, and if it were discovered that you, a lone operator and Mr Holmes's younger brother, were privy to the matter…' He gulped, and fell silent.

'Mr Poskitt, what would you like me to do?' Sherlock's voice was unexpectedly gentle.

'I'm not sure,' Mr Poskitt said miserably. 'Keep an ear open, use your information networks . . . I don't know.' Suddenly he put his head in his hands, knocking his hat to the floor. 'I didn't know where else to go.'

CHAPTER 8

'What am I supposed to do?' Sherlock cried as he paced. 'To dangle a wonderful juicy case in front of me, and then virtually prohibit me from doing anything in connection with it . . . it's inhuman!'

We were alone in the drawing room. Dr Watson had retired to bed, citing an early start in the morning, but I suspected he wished to be out of the way of Sherlock's frustration.

'Mr Poskitt needed to share the burden,' I said, gently. 'And Mycroft is your brother…'

'I know, I know…' Sherlock pushed his hair back with both hands. 'It's not as if we're that close,' he said, stopping suddenly. 'It isn't like your family.' Sherlock had been amazed that I visited my parents and my sister Susan regularly. Then again, they couldn't visit me at Baker Street, given my ostensible role as housekeeper… Sherlock mumbled something.

'I'm sorry, I didn't quite hear,' I said, moving to sit

beside him.

Sherlock pushed a hand through his hair, and sighed. Then he gave me a strange, sidelong glance. 'Were you the clever one in your family, Nell?'

I thought it over for a moment. 'I suppose I was.' Certainly I had been excused various chores on pleading study, which had annoyed Susan no end; but I had made it up to her by helping with her sums.

Sherlock stretched his long legs out and put his hands behind his head. 'In our family, it's Mycroft. My parents' hopes are pinned on him.'

'Really?' I found it hard to imagine Sherlock's quick brain as second to anyone's; but I had encountered Mycroft's easy assumption of power, his way of getting to the heart of the matter.

Sherlock's eyes slid towards me. 'You are weighing it up, Nell,' he remarked.

'Oh, no, not at all—' I stammered, then caught the twinkle in his eye. 'I suppose I was thinking it over,' I admitted, reaching out to smooth a lock of hair which fell over his forehead.

'So you should.' Sherlock shifted to face me. 'It amuses me sometimes. Mycroft and I are similar in our intelligence – though he is quicker than me – but while he applies it officially and bureaucratically, I prefer more exciting applications.'

'Indeed.' I smiled, recalling our various expeditions through the streets of London.

'It takes the pressure off me, too,' mused Sherlock. 'My parents would have preferred me to go into a profession.

My mother hinted at the Church until I told her it was quite impossible – stop laughing, Nell, that's very rude.'

'You, a vicar!' I hooted. 'The Church would fall.'

'I know. It didn't stop her trying, though.' Sherlock was silent for a moment. 'As a younger son, my current position is at least tenable.'

'Your current position?' I asked, recovering myself.

'Yes. A hopeless dabbler, a dreamer, a dilettante. Mycroft would never be allowed to get away with it.'

'But what about the cases you've solved? The crimes you've prevented?' I was utterly mystified.

The sidelong look again. 'I don't mention it at home. It suits me better.' Sherlock got up and offered me a hand. 'We should probably follow Dr Watson's example.'

I was silent as we climbed the stairs, wondering what a family gathering at Sherlock's parents' house would be like, and how Sherlock and Mycroft would behave in that environment.

'Are you working tomorrow, Nell?' Sherlock's voice broke into my thoughts, and I started guiltily.

'In the afternoon, yes.'

'Then would you accompany me in the morning? I have a fancy to go back to Wandsworth Prison, and Watson is in surgery.'

So you'll have to do, I added to myself. I debated inventing a prior engagement, an urgent errand of some kind… But I would be cutting off my own nose to spite my face. I desperately wanted to know what was going on.

'I should be able to,' I replied, as noncommittally as I could.

We reached the landing. 'What will you do about Mycroft?'

Sherlock pulled me to him and kissed the top of my head. 'The best I can, Nell. The best I can.'

***

The cab rattled through the spacious streets of Marylebone at such a pace that I had to hold on to the leather strap to avoid being pitched onto the floor. Then we drove alongside Hyde Park.

Sherlock's eyes were fixed on the view. He had not told me where we were going; all I knew was that it was not in the direction of Wandsworth Prison.

The carriage turned into Portland Road, and immediately began to slow. I knew of no-one who lived in this area. Sherlock banged on the roof with his cane. 'This will do.'

When I got out I was none the wiser. Sherlock paid the cabman and told him to wait. 'We shall not be more than fifteen minutes.' The cabman touched his cap. 'Take my arm, Nell,' said Sherlock. 'You will feel safer that way.'

I pulled away and looked up at him. 'Safer?'

He nodded. 'You have nothing to fear, I promise.' He smiled at my expression. 'Trust me, Nell.'

I could not see any alternative but to wait in the cab; and I did not want to seem timid. I took Sherlock's arm and pulled mine tight against it, steeling myself not to tremble.

We crossed the road and turned down a narrower one; and immediately I saw why Sherlock had felt the need to prepare me.

55

In front of me was a rookery. The houses were crammed together, with barely a window intact, and the light grew dimmer the further we advanced. Men lounged in doorways, hands in pockets, watching us with insolent smiles. *You are trespassing*, they seemed to say. Ragged children played in the gutters, but drew back as we approached, as if we might hurt them. The smell was indescribable.

'Why are we here?' I whispered, clutching Sherlock's arm, my resolve to appear composed entirely gone.

Sherlock turned left. 'Here we are,' he said.

It was the heart of the slum. You could feel its density; the bodies packed together in the rooms, a shivering, quaking mass of poverty. Two men were fighting in the middle of the street, cheered on by a crowd of men, women and children, and more watchers hung out of the windows, yelling encouragement. 'I thought this had been cleared,' I said weakly.

'They tried,' said Sherlock. 'Welcome to Notting Dale, Nell. Excuse me a moment.' He put his fingers in his mouth, and sounded a piercing three-note whistle.

'What are you doing?' I cried, backing away. Several of the crowd stared; but on seeing that we were not the police, they turned back to their sport with no more than a few curses flung our way.

'Here he comes.' And Sherlock raised his hand in greeting to a filthy youth who was elbowing his way through the crowd towards us. One spectator, enraged at the disturbance, clouted the youth on the back of the head as he struggled past; but the youth gave no sign that he had even felt it. He seemed familiar, somehow – but where would I have seen him before?

The youth grinned as he approached us, showing a mouthful of jagged teeth. 'I won't offer to shake yer 'and, Mr 'Olmes.' He winked at me. 'If I'd known you wus bringing a lady, I'd have cleaned up a bit.'

Then it came to me; a stream of ragged children running through the kitchen, shouting for Sherlock, refusing to give way to Billy or to me. That had been in the Jefferson Hope case; the case that Dr Watson was writing up for publication. 'Is it – Wiggins?' I asked.

'It is!' he beamed. 'She remembers me!' He clutched his heart and assumed a lovestruck expression.

'No time for all that, Wiggins,' grinned Sherlock. 'I have work for you.'

Wiggins sobered up immediately. 'Yessir. Usual rate?'

'Usual rate.' Sherlock reached into his pocket and spun half a crown in the air. Wiggins's eyes followed its path. 'A small advance now, and a shilling a day thereafter.'

'For wot?' said Wiggins, holding out his grimy palm.

'A long shot,' said Sherlock, depositing the coin into Wiggins's hand. 'Are you acquainted with Whitehall, Wiggins?'

Wiggins scratched a spot on his head for several seconds. 'I know where it is,' he said, at length. 'I can't say as I've been invited in, though.'

'That will do. Are you acquainted with my brother?'

Wiggins grinned. ''Aven't been formally interduced, but I knows him by sight. Tall, broad feller with a big 'ead.'

'The very man.' Sherlock smiled. 'I want you to follow

my brother, Wiggins. What time he leaves his rooms, whether he goes straight to work, if he leaves work with anyone... He might go to Somerset House, too, but if I know my brother he will want to be where things are happening. Watch him until further notice, Wiggins, and report to me at Baker Street if you observe anything which you think I would find – interesting.'

'Right you are, Mr 'Olmes.' Wiggins touched his non-existent cap in a half-salute. 'I'll do me best.'

'I'm sure you will, Wiggins.' Sherlock consulted his watch, and I saw several eyes drawn to the gleam of gold. 'I must hurry on to another case.'

We picked our way down the alley, but I did not trust myself to speak till we were safely in the cab with the doors bolted. 'Sherlock, why have you—'

'Wandsworth Prison, please, and quickly,' Sherlock shouted up to the box. As we rattled off again he turned to me. 'When I told you to trust me, Nell, this was partly what I meant.'

'But what is the point of—'

Sherlock put a finger to his lips and looked out of the window. 'It is a long ride to Wandsworth,' he observed.

I looked out of the other window.

Sherlock nudged me. 'If I were to call it a hunch, Nell, rather than a pointless exercise or a wild-goose chase – which is what your shoulders are conveying most eloquently as your opinion – would that help?'

I sighed. 'Perhaps.'

Sherlock reached for my hand and stroked it. 'Then let us call it a hunch.'

CHAPTER 9

'Completely against policy,' grumbled the warden under his breath as he led us down the corridor, his ring of keys jingling at his waist. 'Turning up with not so much as a police letter—'

'Were you on duty when the prisoner Stanley was taken?' Holmes asked. There was an edge beneath the careless manner in which the question had been asked.

'I was not,' retorted the warden, his face growing even more thunderous. 'You've got ten minutes, that's yer lot.' He wrenched at his ring of keys, selected one apparently at random, and unlocked a heavy steel door. 'I'll be outside, wasting time while you and your *secretary* mess about.' He waved us in and then slammed the door, though mercifully he stopped short at locking it.

I watched Sherlock move around the cell. I had not been inside a prison before, and the pleasant drive through the countryside south of London had not prepared me for the grim reality of this bare cell. If anything, I was pleased that we would not be allowed to remain long.

Sherlock went to the small window and examined the bars with a magnifying glass. 'No give there...' he said, tugging at them in turn. 'Old, rusted screws which haven't been disturbed...'

'Didn't you look at them when you came before?' I asked.

'Of course,' Sherlock replied, still looking at them. He tore his gaze away and ran his hands up and down the brickwork. 'I feel I am clutching at straws.'

I walked over to the plain iron bed, which had a hard bolster at its head and a rough grey blanket folded in a neat square at the bottom. Underneath it was a chamber pot.

'That isn't the bed Stanley slept in,' said Sherlock. 'They broke that one to pieces, hunting for a key. Although how he'd have got hold of one—' He smacked the wall with the flat of his hand. 'It can't be an inside job! But he can't have got out any other way...'

There was nothing else in the cell but a small square table, on which sat a Bible, and a deal chair. I sat on the chair and tried to imagine what it would be like to be confined in such a place, perhaps for years... What had Emmett Stanley's sentence been?

'This is one of the nicer prisons, you know,' said Sherlock. I shuddered.

'Time's up!' The door opened and the warden jerked a thumb over his shoulder at us.

'That wasn't ten minutes.' It was Sherlock's turn to mutter under his breath, and I saw the warden smirk at Sherlock's back as he passed.

I smiled at the warden, hoping he wouldn't detect my real feelings. 'I'm terribly sorry we've put you to so much trouble, Mr—'

The warden's face registered his surprise. 'Sage. Warden Sage.'

'Mr Sage.' I fell into step beside him. 'It must be very hard work, running a prison.'

His craggy face split into a grin. 'Oh, it's not so bad, providing they does what they're told and toes the line. This one, till he went and vanished, he was a model prisoner. Up when he was told, never threw his food about like some of 'em…' The warden appeared to be turning something over in his mind. 'It's funny. When he arrived, I thought he was going to be trouble. He comes through the door in his flash suit. Shiny shoes, posh necktie, gold jewellery. But when we took it all off him, and put him in a prison uniform, you wouldn't have looked at him twice, and he knew it. Docile, he was. Kept himself to himself.' He nodded in approval.

'What did he look like?' I asked.

Mr Sage considered. 'Nothing special. Middle height, dark hair – bit of grey at the sides. Quite a slight man. Mind, everyone gets thinner in here.' He wheezed with laughter. 'We had him on mat-making, he was too small to have much of a chance on the treadwheel.'

A gasp from behind us. 'My watch!' exclaimed Sherlock. 'I must have left it in the cell!'

The warden sighed. 'And I suppose you want to go back for it?'

Sherlock looked contrite. 'I'm so sorry, Mr Sage. It was

a present from my mother,' he added, as Mr Sage turned to march us back.

Mr Sage huffed, fumbling for his ring of keys. Sherlock was alongside him, watching Mr Sage select the key and insert it into the lock.

'Go on,' snapped the warden. But Sherlock ran to the table and turned it over, kneeling and running his hands across the wood.

'What the—!' Mr Sage charged forward, then stopped at the look of triumph on Sherlock's face.

'I have it,' he said, simply, and beckoned us to the table. He put his finger to a knot-hole in the wood, then slid it in, up to the knuckle. 'Do you see, Mr Sage?'

'It's a hole,' said Mr Sage, too confused to be angry. 'A small knot-hole.'

'A small knot-hole,' repeated Sherlock, getting up and brushing down his trouser-knees. 'A hole large enough to accommodate a slender finger, and also, a key.' He held his forefinger out and Mr Sage, comprehension dawning, held the key to the cell next to it.

Then his face clouded again. 'That's a start,' he cried. 'But how did he get the key, and how did he get out?'

'*He* didn't,' said Sherlock. 'We need to see the governor immediately.'

***

'Tell me your theory, Mr Holmes,' smiled Mr Jonas, the prison governor, with the air of someone granting an indulgence.

'I shall.' Sherlock drew his chair closer to Mr Jonas's desk. 'And I think that when I have finished, you will agree

62

that this is more than a theory.'

The governor sat back in his chair, fingers steepled.

'You run a tight ship, Mr Jonas. I took the liberty of discussing the prison routine with Mr Sage, and I am full of admiration.'

Mr Jonas inclined his head.

'Exercise in the yard for an hour, supper at half past five, two hours' work, an hour for reading and writing, and then bed. Wonderful.'

Mr Jonas nodded, but his brow showed the beginnings of a furrow.

'Emmett Stanley went into the yard at half past four for exercise. The yard is dark as the sun is setting, but that doesn't matter, because of the high wall. He walks by himself, as he always does, and he is silent, as per the regulations. Someone runs up to him and hisses in his ear to come and see, perhaps taking him by the arm. He is guided to a spot away from the building, knocked out, probably, for quiet's sake, and left in the dark while the prisoners are called in.'

'But we count them in!' exclaimed Mr Jonas.

'Yes, and you have the right number; a slight dark man in prison garb is in the line. He knows the routine; he knows that Emmett Stanley gives no trouble, and will be passed over. He gets his gruel and bread, eats alone, and falls into line with the others to be marched back to work. As Stanley is a model prisoner he has the privilege of working in his own cell, rather than being put to the more physical, communal labour of the treadwheel. How much work he does I cannot say; any warder who slid open the observation window of Stanley's cell would see a slight dark man, his back turned, apparently engaged in mat-making. He then reads his Bible until lights out at nine, lays in bed, and waits. When he is sure that no warder is near, he rises, takes the key from its hiding place in the table – he has secreted it there previously, stuck with the wax I felt under my fingernail – and lets himself out.'

'I think we would notice a prisoner sauntering about after lights out,' said Mr Jonas, a forced smile on his face.

'You would,' said Sherlock, his eyes on the governor's face. 'Prison uniform is not a snug fit. A warden's uniform could be concealed beneath. Who pays any attention to a patrolling warden, in a dimly-lit corridor, when the prisoners are quiet?'

The governor's Adam's apple bobbed once, and the motion seemed to hurt him.

'Check your list of wardens for those who match Emmett Stanley's description,' Sherlock said, rising. 'I expect you will find a patch of flattened grass in a far corner of the yard. The warder may have tried to disguise the drag marks from when his accomplices removed Mr Stanley in the night; but if he lay unconscious for several hours, the imprint may still be there.' Sherlock pulled his watch from a trouser pocket and glanced at it, winking at Mr Sage as he did so. 'I'll see myself out; we have an urgent appointment to keep.' I rose and picked up my bag.

'But – but – where is Mr Stanley?' stammered Mr Jonas. 'Is he alive, or dead?'

'I wish I knew,' said Sherlock, opening the office door. 'I wish I knew.'

CHAPTER 10

On returning to Baker Street I had barely five minutes to don a wig and catch up pince-nez and a hat before running back out to the waiting cab. Lunch was out of the question; but I did not care about lunch. My mind was full of the morning's events; the meeting with Wiggins, and Sherlock's deduction at Wandsworth Prison. I would have walked straight past Evie if she hadn't waved at me.

'That's not much different from your real hair, is it?' she said. Her expression was neutral, but she sounded disappointed.

'I didn't have time to do much today,' I said, 'I've been – busy this morning.'

Evie beamed, her faith in me restored. 'I'll look after you,' she said. 'Those flowers in your hat are out of season, you know.'

'Are they?' I touched the pink roses with my fingertip.

'It's all camellias now.' Evie pointed at the multicoloured display of silk flowers nearby, and I could see that she was right. 'You go on to the washroom, and I'll join you in a minute.'

'I wish I could hire you as a maid, Evie,' I joked as she ministered to me, taking advantage of her mouthful of hairpins. 'I'd be the best-dressed woman in London.'

Evie didn't speak until she had finished my hair and settled my newly-trimmed hat to her satisfaction. 'I don't know what your husband would say though, *Mrs Hudson*,' she smiled. 'I'd probably lead you into all sorts of extravagances.'

'Maybe you can help with my trousseau,' I said without thinking, and as if that wasn't bad enough, I then clapped a hand to my mouth.

Evie looked at me in the mirror, and then walked round to face me. 'So you're not married?' Her eyes were wide. 'You *seem* married.'

My face was on fire. 'It's, well, it's…' I didn't want to lie to my friend, but how could I explain? 'It's complicated,' I said lamely.

Evie whistled, softly. 'You are a dark horse,' she grinned. 'Whatever next.' And she twitched the pince-nez off my nose. 'You can look *through* them as much as you like, but don't keep them on. It isn't fashionable.' I thanked her and went to make my report to Mr Turner, in the certain knowledge that Evie had let me off lightly.

As I patrolled the store, poking my pince-nez into this and that, a parallel image of the warden patrolling at Wandsworth flashed into my mind. I marvelled at his nerve, his confidence. To lure a prisoner into a trap, take his place, and then switch again and escape, under the

66

noses of the other wardens… I wondered if the man who had done it was still at large, or whether they had tracked him down yet.

I roamed the store, watching the shoppers at play. There were a few women, usually in pairs for moral support, who were plainly-dressed and clearly here for a treat. That was the category I would have placed myself in, particularly given our current financial situation. Most of the women, though, were elegant, drifting through the shop as if they were walking through the rooms of their own house. One of them, nose in the air, was trying on paste jewellery: a string of pearls, a brooch, a pair of pearl drop earrings. She took the earrings off. 'Pearl studs would be better, really,' she remarked offhandedly to the assistant, who nodded eagerly, and turned to pull another tray of earrings from the shelf. She was probably hoping for a tip; even a thrupenny bit would make a big difference to her day. The woman, a bored expression on her face, fiddled with her scarf. *You don't care about the earrings*, I thought, taking in her velvet dress, her fur muff, her embroidered bag. *They aren't expensive enough for you.*

'Why do you do it?' I asked. It had been easy to intercept her as she strolled away; she was in no hurry.

She stopped and looked at me through half-closed eyes. 'Do what?' she said, eventually.

I let my eyes settle on her scarf. 'You know what.'

Her laugh tinkled like the glass drops on a chandelier. 'How embarrassing.' She stayed where she was, eyebrows raised, daring me to take action.

She wasn't blushing; I was. 'Give me the brooch, and

tell me why you do it, and I'll say nothing.' My hand trembled as I held it out.

She held my gaze with that same amused stare as she unpinned the brooch and laid it in my palm. I looked down at it; a gaudy toy of rhinestones and gold-coloured metal, something a child would love. The woman leaned forward, and her musky perfume enveloped me. 'It's fun,' she whispered, with that same smile in her voice.

I closed my hand over the brooch. 'What if you get caught?'

'I would probably be in the papers, and have to go for a rest cure.' She did not seem displeased as she rearranged her scarf. Then she rummaged in her dainty bag. 'Here, give this to the girl,' she said, handing me half a crown. She strolled to the exit, leaving me looking after her, the brooch clutched in my hand. She turned and waved before she disappeared into the street.

***

Mr Turner was all smiles at the end of the afternoon. I had spotted a stout, matronly woman heading for the door at a fast waddle, who turned out, when taken to a back room, to have several yards of dress fabric stuffed into her capacious drawers. Alf was sent for a constable, and the woman, now somewhat slimmer, was led away. As she was hustled from the store she turned, and her eyes found mine. She did not look angry. She looked hurt, as if I had betrayed her.

When I went to Mr Turner's office the fabric was in a heap on the floor, the folds of blue sateen pooling like a small lake. 'You can have that,' he said, waving a casual hand.

I stared at the rippling material and tried to calculate its price. Evie would have known immediately. 'Can't it be washed and pressed?'

'It isn't worth it,' said Mr Turner. 'We'll write it off as wastage. Yours if you want it.'

My eyes were still on the material. The colour would suit me; but I would see the hurt in that woman's eyes every time I opened my wardrobe. 'It would suit Miss Blanchard,' I said, eventually.

Mr Turner snorted. 'It's your loss.'

I found Evie on the glove counter, serving a young woman with a child in tow. When I explained she stared at me, mouth open.

I put my hand on hers. 'I – I hope you're not offended.'

'Offended?' Her voice rang out and drew warning looks from Gladys on the next counter down. She squeezed my hand. 'I'm – we're – saving to get married. There's no money for a new dress, but now…' Evie sniffed, and blinked rapidly. 'Oh I'm going to cry. I can't cry, my face will be a mess!' She wiped her eyes carefully with her two forefingers.

'It will need washing…' I cautioned.

'As if I care for a little thing like that!' Evie stepped round the counter and embraced me, taking care not to crush my dress or endanger my hair.

'I had better go,' I said, patting her arm. 'I have things to see to at home. And no, I can't say any more than that,' I said to Evie's mischievous expression.

I hurried along the busy street. I should have been

thinking about whether Sherlock would be at home; whether he might have been called back out to Wandsworth; what this morning's events could mean. But my mind was full of women's faces; the amusement of the society woman I had caught with the brooch, and the hurt of the woman who had taken the dress material. I had let the rich woman go without censure, while the struggling woman had been arrested, and would probably go to prison. I rubbed my forehead to try and rub her away, but she wouldn't go. Because I had caught her, Evie would have a wedding dress. *Well, that's a good thing,* I thought, as I turned into Baker Street.

And when will you have a wedding dress? I quickened my steps to drown out the spiteful little voice, glancing in shop windows and people-watching to distract myself. It was a lively scene. The street-lamps were lit, the shop-fronts blazed with light to entice people in, and on the street people were laughing and chatting, going home, or stepping out for the evening. Perhaps I could persuade Sherlock to go to a concert—

A cab bowled past me and jerked to a halt. I was nearing home now, and slowed my pace to see if we had a visitor. It was a slim chance; Sherlock had not mentioned any callers, and this part of the street was densely packed with townhouses like our own. Could it be Mr Poskitt, with more information?

The door of the cab was flung open and a tall figure, too tall for Mr Poskitt, jumped down and strode across the street, his open coat streaming behind him. He ran up the steps of 221B, raised his cane, and banged on the door. He kept banging until the door was opened, and pushed his way inside.

What on earth is going on? I hurried past the waiting cab and climbed the steps.

The door had been left open. 'Where is he? Where is he?' The man left the drawing room, slamming the door, and made for the dining room.

'I'm up here.' Sherlock was leaning on the banister of the first-floor landing, his face utterly calm.

The man turned his face up. 'What the hell do you think you're doing, Sherlock?' he shouted. And I knew him. I should have known him before, but I had never seen him anything but calm.

Standing in our hallway, his face scarlet and contorted with utter fury, was Mycroft Holmes.

CHAPTER 11

'I ought to wring your neck!' Mycroft bellowed, shaking his fist. 'How dare you spy on me!'

'I don't know what you mean,' said Sherlock. But I could see a muscle in his neck twitching, and I suspected Mycroft could too.

'Yes you do, you liar! A liar and a spy! I've seen your little toerag hanging about at lunchtime, watching me down the street, waiting for me when I left Whitehall. Do you think I'm stupid?' Mycroft shook off Billy's hand.

'Not at all, Mycroft.' Sherlock's face was as pale as his brother's was red.

'Who hired you, eh?' Mycroft snarled. 'Who was it? Was it Chambers, or Jones? My God, I'll—'

'It was neither of those,' said Sherlock. 'I can't say more than that.'

'What is going on?' Dr Watson's voice was followed by the thump of footsteps and he appeared on the landing beside Sherlock, who took no notice of him.

'Oh yes you can, if I have to beat it out of you!' Mycroft started up the stairs.

Sherlock held up a thick walking stick. 'I have taken precautions. Try it, and I'll knock you down the stairs.' His eyes flashed silver. He meant every word.

I started forward. 'Sherlock, don't—'

'Stay out of this, Nell,' he rapped out.

Mycroft stopped, halfway up the stairs, and when he spoke, his tone had an edge of amusement, a satisfaction, that frightened me more than his fury. 'So like you, Sherlock, to resort to the physical. I expect that, because you can't outsmart me, can you?' His lip curled in a sneer. 'I didn't expect my own brother to be a turncoat, though. You really have outdone yourself this time. But two can play at that game. You can tell your *employer* that I won't play ball. I'll work the way I always have.' Mycroft's knuckles were white on the banister. He turned abruptly and descended the stairs, and I moved aside to let him through.

'One more thing!' Mycroft shouted, raising his stick so suddenly that I gasped and drew back. 'Call your tramp off. If I see him, or even suspect that I'm being followed, I'll make sure Scotland Yard never knock on your door again.' He wrenched the front door open and strode across the road, almost colliding with a man on a bicycle, before climbing into his cab. The door slammed, and the cab drove off.

The soft click as Billy closed the door was the only sound for some time. The silence was broken by muffled sobbing from downstairs. Martha must have heard everything.

Sherlock moved away from the banister and a door closed, smartly. From the direction of Dr Watson's gaze, it was the consulting room.

Billy reached up, almost timidly, slid the bolts home, and turned the key in the lock. 'I'll – I'll see about dinner,' he stammered, and fled down the kitchen steps.

When I looked up to the landing, Dr Watson had vanished.

***

No one ate much at dinner. Sherlock had remained in the consulting room the whole time, and came down fifteen minutes late. He eyed the plate, pushed it away, and went upstairs.

I had spent the time before dinner in the bathroom; it was the only place I could think of where I could be alone. I lifted off the brown wig and began to unpin my hair, and suddenly tears were streaming down my face. My throat hurt from the effort not to cry out loud. I remembered Evie's careful tears – *my face will be a mess* – and that made it worse. When the dinner bell rang I washed my face and twisted up my hair, not bothering to look in the mirror. I knew that my eyes were red and my face was blotchy, and I did not care.

Dr Watson ate in his usual steady manner, the clatter of his knife and fork loud in the silence, until we heard Sherlock's quick, light steps descending. He paused, fork in the air, not even chewing, while the door bolts snicked and the key rattled. The front door closed, and Dr Watson laid down his knife and fork on the half-full plate. 'I have had enough,' he said, pushing his chair back. 'I shall go and read in my room. Good night, Mrs Hudson.'

The house felt like a tomb. Seconds were measured out by the drip of the clock. I wished I could turn back time, could reverse what had happened – no, reverse Sherlock's plan to set Wiggins to follow his brother. But it was too late.

The chime of the clock striking eight made my heart jump in my chest, and I thought of Sherlock, out there, alone. Why had he left the house? My mind raced through the possibilities. He might have gone to warn Wiggins off – but what if he had decided to go after Mycroft, or worse, shadow him himself? He had gone out without speaking to anyone. He could be anywhere, dressed as anyone. I knew Sherlock's stubbornness. But if Mycroft saw him—

I ran upstairs to the consulting room, which had the best view over the street, and drew the heavy velvet curtain aside. I didn't know what I expected to see as I surveyed the lamplit street, but Sherlock was not in the buttoned-up figures hurrying by, or the strolling couples.

My mouth twisted as I recalled a day when I had looked out for Sherlock, not a year ago, before I had even known who he was or what he would mean to me. I saw a young man striding along, full of possibilities. And here I was again, my heart in my mouth, waiting to see if he would come home safe.

My watching would not bring him home. It would achieve nothing. I closed the curtains and went to the bedroom.

I could not sleep, of course. My brain flipped through the events of the day like a never-ending catalogue of cards. The visit to the rookery. Sherlock's triumph at the prison. The lady with the brooch. Evie's tears. The woman's hurt eyes as she was bundled off. Mycroft's rage. Doors slammed over and over in my head and I found myself shaking, shaking and weeping, hiding under the bedsheets, trying not to disturb the silent house.

A creak startled me awake and I screamed, then struggled as a hand clamped down on my mouth. 'For God's sake, Nell!' Sherlock hissed. 'What's wrong with you?'

I shoved his arm away. Sherlock stood above me, illuminated by the gas-light I had left turned low. He appeared unharmed. 'Where have you been?' I whispered.

'I went to pull Wiggins off the case.' He sat on the bed and pulled off his tie, throwing it over the back of a chair.

I pulled myself to a sitting position. 'I was worried.'

'Nell, it isn't ten o'clock. I'd have been quicker, but I decided to walk back.'

'I thought you might have—'

'Might have what?' He twisted to face me, his eyes searching my face.

I couldn't hold his gaze. I looked down at my hands twisting in my lap. 'I don't know.'

'Did you think I would go after Mycroft?' He snorted. 'I'm not stupid.' He unhooked his braces and stood up. 'You know what, Nell? You should stop thinking, if this is the result.'

'When I want your opinion, I'll ask,' I snapped, turning

away and flinging my head on the pillow. As a response, it was much milder than my thoughts.

I waited for an apology, for an acknowledgement that I had been right to worry.

The connecting door to the consulting room clicked.

***

I was woken by a gentle tap at the door. 'Morning tea,' Martha called, with a question in her voice.

'Leave it outside, please.' I looked over my shoulder at Sherlock, still wearing his shirt, curled in a ball on the edge of the mattress. When had he come to bed? Fingers of light were creeping round the sides of the curtain. The servants must have left us to sleep late. How much had they heard?

I shook my head to clear it. Today would be better. I would have a cup of tea, dress, go downstairs, and lose myself in household tasks before getting ready for work. I would instruct Evie to make me especially chic today. That would cheer me up.

I fetched the tea tray and looked about me. There was nowhere to set it down; the dressing table and the nightstands were cluttered. The door to the consulting room was ajar, though. I nudged it open and set the tray on a side table.

The room was in a state of disarray. Books pulled from the shelves lay on the floor, some still open, next to a pile of cushions. The tobacco jar was on the floor too, next to a small morocco case I didn't recognise. I picked it up and pressed the catch.

A hypodermic syringe.

I closed the case and set it down as if it were red hot. Then I stood up and peered round the door. Sherlock seemed to be asleep still. I cleared a space on the dressing table, fetched the tea tray, and pushed the connecting door to. I sat down and poured myself a cup of tea; and as I sipped, I looked in the mirror at myself and at Sherlock, curled up in his shirt.

Inside, though, I was screaming.

CHAPTER 12

I selected a dress at random, concerned less for appearance than speed. I wanted to be out of that room, away from Sherlock. I wanted to busy myself with mundanities.

'That's a nice dress, ma'am,' Martha said as I entered the kitchen.

'Is it?' I looked down at myself. Of all the dresses I had, I had chosen the lilac one. *That dress.*

'Would you like breakfast?' Martha gestured to the oven. 'Dr Watson's had his long since, but I kept the dishes warm for you. Bacon, sausages. I could fry you an egg?'

I fought back queasiness. 'Just a piece of toast, thank you. I'll eat it here.'

'Mr Holmes not stirring yet?' Martha asked, as I sat down at the kitchen table.

I shook my head.

'Ma'am...' Martha pulled out a chair and sat opposite me. 'It isn't my place to ask, but are you quite all right? I heard – noises in the night.'

I almost laughed as I thought of Mycroft's visit, Sherlock's return, and the hypodermic syringe lurking upstairs. 'No, I'm not "all right". Given what happened yesterday evening, it's hardly surprising. A good set of household chores will take my mind from it all, I'm sure.'

'Oh.' Martha got up, speared a piece of bread on a toasting fork, and held it to the fire. 'Everything's done, really. You did the meal plans, ma'am, remember, and Billy's just gone to sort out the butcher's order.'

How typical that when I wanted domestic diversion, none was available. 'I shall go for a walk, then.' Wednesday was usually my day to visit Lottie, but I did not trust myself to get through even a routine call without weeping.

'That's a good idea, ma'am.' Martha turned the bread on the fork. I remembered the sobs coming from the kitchen yesterday evening, and wondered what she and Billy had said to each other in the privacy of their sitting room. I did not like to think what they might have discussed.

I was finishing my toast when footsteps sounded on the kitchen stairs. 'I am going out,' Sherlock said, as he appeared in the doorway. 'Oh—' He looked at me, eyebrows raised. 'I did not expect to find you here.' He was smartly dressed, but there were shadows under his eyes.

'Where are you going?' I asked, putting down the remains of my toast.

'Back to Wandsworth, first. I am likely to be out all day.'

'But your breakfast, sir!' Martha gestured helplessly at

the oven.

'I'm not hungry.' He came round the table and gave me a peck on the cheek. 'Have fun at work, Nell.' And he was gone.

I went upstairs for a hat and shawl. The consulting room was still a mess, but the morocco case had disappeared. I wondered if it might be hidden in the room somewhere, but I would not stoop so low as to rummage through Sherlock's equipment.

I left the house and walked briskly to the park. Regent's Park always put me in a good humour. The people, the ducks, the changing seasons… Today, though, it did not work. As I paced the paths, I was preoccupied by a morocco case that I had seen not two hours before. I needed to *know*. And Dr Watson flashed into my mind. He was at work now, at Barts Hospital, an hour's walk away; but a short trip by omnibus. I almost ran to the stop and, by good fortune, squeezed onto a packed 'bus a few minutes later.

The omnibus creaked and swayed down the long, straight road, but I was not lulled by the rhythmic motion. I saw nothing of the buildings or the people; I lived entirely inside my head until the cry of 'Smithfield and St Bart's' rang out. I got up from my seat and hurried after the women disembarking with their shopping baskets. It was only when I looked up at the imposing stone building that I realised I had not a clue how I would find Dr Watson.

The hospital vestibule was a mass of motion. Doctors, nurses and orderlies buzzed to and fro purposefully, weaving round the slow peregrinations of – were they visitors, or patients?

'Yes, ma'am?' A clerk hailed me from a high desk.

I walked slowly towards him, racking my brains for how to begin. 'I need to see Dr Watson, please.'

The clerk looked me up and down. 'Is it about a patient?' he asked, briskly, pen poised.

'In a manner of speaking...' Then it dawned on me, the thing that I knew would fetch him. 'I have an urgent message from Mr Sherlock Holmes.'

'Oh!' The clerk beckoned an underling, then muttered into his ear. The underling stared at me and hurried off, flinging the words 'Follow me, ma'am' over his shoulder. I did as I was told and we passed across the vestibule, through a small lobby and a room full of more clerks with ledgers, to a room with *Committee* on the door plaque. The underling held the door open for me. 'Do take a seat, ma'am, I shall find Dr Watson and tell him you are here.'

He closed the door reverently and I took in the leather-topped table, the high-backed chairs upholstered to match, the tall mahogany bookshelves filled with bound volumes of the *Hospital Gazette*. The windows gave on to a small chapel. It was not what I had expected.

A few minutes later I heard footsteps and a low conference of voices, and Dr Watson pushed open the door. He was wearing a white hospital coat and frowning, and the frown deepened as he registered my presence. 'That will be all, Hoskins,' he said, and closed the door with finality. 'I did not expect you, Mrs Hudson. Am I needed?' He did not sit down.

'Yes,' I bit my lip. 'I – found something in Mr Holmes's

consulting room.'

'You *found* something? Mrs Hudson, I am a busy man. I do not have time for—'

'I found a hypodermic syringe.'

'Oh.' A look of almost-helplessness wiped the frown from Dr Watson's face. He pulled out a chair and sat down heavily. 'I see.' His eyes measured me. 'You didn't know...'

'I take it you did, then.' I ran my hand over the smooth table top.

Dr Watson bowed his head. 'He hadn't touched it for some time. I hoped he had broken the habit,' he muttered, almost to himself.

Fear gripped my heart. 'The habit? What habit?'

Dr Watson sighed. 'Occasionally morphine. More frequently, cocaine.'

'Oh my God.' I felt nauseous. 'He *injects* it?'

'I am afraid so.' Dr Watson shot me a furtive glance. 'He doesn't know you found the syringe, does he?'

I shook my head. 'I put it back where I found it. I haven't said anything.'

'Good. If he thought... He is a proud man. He tried to hide it from me, too.' It was the most frank, the most open Dr Watson had ever been with me. 'But it doesn't make sense...'

'What do you mean?'

He smiled wanly. 'As you know, it is hard to live with a detective and not catch the habit. Addiction is not my study, but until now Holmes has only used cocaine as an escape from boredom. A stimulant for those quiet times

83

between cases; but he's busy with the Stanley case. This is completely out of character. When did you find the syringe?' The question was almost stern.

'This morning. He was still asleep. It was in a case, next to some books on the consulting-room floor. I only opened the case because I did not know what it was.' Even now, I hated the thought that Dr Watson might think I had pried. 'And when I went upstairs later, the case had disappeared.'

'So, last night then…' Dr Watson passed a hand over his brow. 'Oh dear.'

'What is it?' I implored.

Dr Watson pinched the bridge of his nose, and when his eyes met mine they were full of woe. 'It must have been after the scene with Mycroft. It's the only explanation.' I waited for the blow to fall. 'He wasn't using cocaine as a stimulus. He was using it to escape from reality.' He shook his head. 'I can talk to him, try to reason with him, but—' He looked down at the table for a moment. 'I'm so sorry.'

CHAPTER 13

'Are you sure you can manage from here?'

Dr Watson had escorted me back to the vestibule. I had told myself that I would not cry. I did not; but my throat was a hard knot of pain. I nodded to give myself time before I must speak. 'Yes,' I said, and my voice didn't sound like me.

'On a case today, doctor?' called the clerk who had dealt with me, grinning.

'No. No case,' said Dr Watson, sadly. He took my hand. 'You will let me know, won't you.' I nodded again – speaking was impossible – and watched him walk away as if he had the weight of the world on his shoulders—

No. The weight of Sherlock. We both did.

I caught the return omnibus without difficulty, and arrived back at Baker Street with plenty of time to eat a light meal and dress for work. The thought of food made me feel sick, and the last thing in the world I wanted to do was dress myself up and play detective; but it had to be done. I choked down half a ham sandwich and spent some time in arranging my now dark-brown hair. It was not for vanity's sake; it was to avoid a session with Evie.

I might have saved myself the trouble. Evie was waiting for me; she caught my eye the minute I entered the shop, and hurried over as soon as she could decently rid herself of the customer she was serving.

'Oh that material, Nell, it's simply beautiful!' She took my arm and marched me through the shop. 'It's brand new – there's nothing a launder and a press won't mend, anyway. I have such plans for it!' She continued, sketching frills and shaping and drapery in the air, and she might have been speaking a foreign language for all I knew or cared. Suddenly we jerked to a stop, and I had a distinct feeling that I was supposed to have said something. I had not even noticed our arrival at the cloakroom door.

'*Do* you think a train is too much?' Evie looked concerned. 'You do, don't you, and you're too polite to say.'

I shook my head. 'It's your wedding, Evie. You have what you want.' But the words came out flat and dull. 'I think my hair will do as it is, you know,' I gabbled, and the disappointment on Evie's face deepened.

'I didn't mean—' I put my hands over my face, as much to get away from Evie's expression as to keep in the sobs fighting to rise to the surface. 'I'm sorry.' I breathed deeply and slowly, determined not to cry.

Evie silently stroked my back, and that was it. Up came the anger, the frustration, the resentment, the disappointment, the self-pity. Every mean emotion I could feel was out in the open, running down my face.

I am not sure how long I cried for, but it felt like hours. Evie did not speak until I had cried myself down to the occasional hiccup. 'Shall I tell Mr Turner you've gone home poorly?' she murmured.

'I need to work.' My voice cracked as I said it, but it was true. I needed something to distract me from the real world.

'I'll do my best,' said Evie, with a sigh.

Ten minutes later I was presentable, if not quite restored to normal. 'Is it...' Evie hesitated. 'Is it man trouble?'

'In a manner of speaking.' I tried to smile, but I could tell from Evie's expression that my attempt had been unsuccessful. I shook my head to indicate that I wished to say no more. 'We had better get to work, before Mr Turner comes looking for us.'

'Yes.' But I felt Evie watching me as we returned to the shop floor. She caught my hand as I reached for the door to the main shop. 'Nell, you would say if it was anything . . . *you* know?' Her eyes searched my face for clues.

'Of course I would,' I lied, and pushed the door open.

Where would I even begin, I thought, as I trailed round the store, comparing skeins of wool, nodding to the assistants, examining the trimming on a hat. How could I explain to Evie the complicated mess of my life? I surveyed the neat compartmentalised world of the store, every department its own little kingdom, arranged and governed by the will of its despot. The detail of my strange existence would probably impress Evie far less than my vague hints of a secret identity and an unorthodox relationship. Going into particulars would rub the shine right off. I caught sight of myself in a cheval glass and hastily adjusted my expression to a more neutral one before moving on.

And why are you so upset? I could walk into any pharmacist's shop in London and buy a tonic containing cocaine, but that was different. That was not going to the consulting room, drawing the syringe and bottle from its hiding-place, rolling up a shirt-sleeve, finding a vein, inserting the needle – *ugh.* I shuddered and looked around quickly in case anyone had seen me.

That was it. The secrecy.

Sherlock had kept a secret from me.

And if he could keep one secret, he could keep others.

Could I trust him?

I hurried to another department, then another. I could not keep still. One *what if* after another was chasing through my brain. But as I walked, the path I must take became clearer.

I must tell Sherlock that I knew. And I must look after myself.

I shrank from it at first. I tried to find another way, a way without confrontation, but the truth screamed at me.

If you pretend that you don't know, that you haven't seen, you are lying to him.

He is a proud man, Dr Watson had said. But I was a proud woman, too. I was not prepared to turn a blind eye, to avoid the consulting room in case I stumbled across something I wasn't meant to see. That would feel as if I was allowing it to happen—

Whatever *it* was. I had no idea of the effects of cocaine. I would have to look it up. I smiled at the idea of visiting the library and asking Mr Rogers to recommend a book on the effects of drug use, but there was no need. The library at home would have all the information I needed.

The decision made, my heart felt lighter with every step I took. I pushed away any doubts. Yes, it might be an uncomfortable discussion. I corrected myself; it *would* be an uncomfortable discussion. Perhaps Sherlock would be angry. But at least I would not have to lie, or pretend. Given the constant duplicity of my life – my false identity, my hidden husband, my concealed relationship with Sherlock – I needed one thing that was true.

I caught no shoplifters that afternoon. I doubt I would have noticed if an enterprising thief had unpinned my own shawl and made off with it. I entered Mr Turner's office with some apprehension; but fortunately he chose to see the bright side. 'Word's getting around, Mrs Hudson!' He rubbed his hands. 'They're thick as thieves.' He chortled at his joke. 'They'll have spread the word that we've got a lady detective – no, more than one! A red-haired one, and a dark-haired one – you can never spot her – and that what makes her dangerous. It's the best idea I ever had,' he said, swinging in his chair.

As I walked home, my own brief brush with addiction came into my head. It had happened after Jack had vanished. A doctor prescribed laudanum to relieve the horror of my situation, but it brought a new horror, a new shame. I remembered myself at my worst – wheedling, scheming, desperate for my next dose. Only Billy's care had weaned me from it; and if he had not helped me, I would probably have died.

Sherlock's case seemed nothing like mine. He had seemed perfectly normal when he came downstairs the next morning. Perhaps I was over-reacting and Sherlock's use of the drug was nothing to worry about. But then I thought of Dr Watson's face when I had confronted him with my discovery.

I arrived home with no sense of how I had got there. 'I'm back,' I called down the kitchen steps.

Billy appeared at the kitchen door, looking relieved. 'Mr Holmes has been asking for you for the last hour, ma'am.'

'Why?' I glanced at the hall clock. 'I am not late.'

'He said he needed your help.'

'Nell, is that you?' I turned in the direction of the voice. Sherlock was on the landing, holding a batch of papers.

'I'm just coming up,' I said, taking off my hat.

'Good. Don't bother getting changed, I need you now.' He disappeared from view.

Billy and I exchanged glances. 'Shall I hold dinner, ma'am?'

'It might be as well.' Billy went back into the kitchen and I heard the hum of voices.

I climbed the stairs slowly, uncertain of what I would find at the top. I only knew that with every step a little more of my resolve drained away, and as I tapped on the consulting-room door, my heart felt like a clenched fist.

CHAPTER 14

'Come in, Nell.' The note of irritation in Sherlock's tone scraped on my nerves. I bit my lip and pushed open the door. The consulting room was even untidier than it had been before. I gazed at the wreck for the small morocco case, but it was not there. That, at least, was a relief.

Sherlock stood, papers in both hands, frowning. 'I had it a moment ago…' he muttered.

'I am here, Sherlock,' I said, picking my way through the jumble and taking a seat in the armchair. 'What would you like me to do?'

He looked not at me, but through me. 'I have a set of pen portraits of the warders at Wandsworth. I need you to make a list of any who are a close physical match for Emmett Stanley – when I can find the papers I had a moment ago.' He threw down the papers he was holding, and they fluttered to the floor.

'Is that all you want me to do?' It seemed a ridiculously simple task.

'Yes,' Sherlock snapped. 'I began it, but my brain keeps darting off onto other matters, God knows why.'

I knew why. 'I shall go and change, then—'

'I want you to do it *now*!' Sherlock loomed over me, and his finger quivered as he pointed at the mess.

I stood up, trying not to tremble myself. 'I'll go and change, or I won't do it at all.' I had to pass close to him, close enough to touch. *Please don't grab me,* I begged silently. But Sherlock's arms had fallen to his sides, and now he looked not angry, but frightened. I had never seen him afraid before, and it chilled me to the heart.

'I shall only be a few minutes,' I promised, and opened the connecting door to the bedroom.

On one hand I wanted to take my time; on the other I did not want to risk Sherlock's anger. I snatched the wig from my head with no care for its arrangement, and tossed it on the bed. Then I pulled the pins from my hair, brushed it, and twisted it up. 'I'm just going to wash,' I called, and ran up to the bathroom. The cool water soothed me a little. Having left various smears on the towel in my haste, I made sure that I was at least clean, and hurried back down. At least now, whatever I had to say, I would be saying it as myself.

'I am ready,' I said, as I came into the room, and Sherlock whipped round from the bookcase, hurriedly pushing something back into place.

I walked over to him and put my hand on his arm. 'Show me.'

He shook his head, fear in his eyes.

'Show me.'

He watched as, standing on tiptoe, I pulled out first one book, then another, until the small morocco case was revealed. 'Put it back,' he said as I pulled it forward, but his tone betrayed that he had no hope I would obey him. 'Don't look,' he said, as I opened the case. There it was, muzzled with a sheath.

'I have already seen it,' I said. I closed the case again and put it on the shelf. Sherlock was standing behind me, his breath coming in quick gasps. I took his hand, which was cold and clammy, and with my other hand I drew up his crumpled sleeve. He did not resist.

There were two pieces of sticking plaster on the inside of his forearm, one edged with a purple bruise.

I looked up at Sherlock, but his eyes were closed. I released his hand and returned to the bookshelf.

'Leave it!' cried Sherlock, as I swept the rest of the books to the floor. The treacherous little bottle was behind them. I seized it, read the label, and dashed it to pieces on the hearth.

'When did you take it?' I shouted, my fears of disturbing the house entirely forgotten.

Sherlock passed a hand over his brow. 'This afternoon, when I returned from Wandsworth . . . I don't remember exactly when.'

That was the worst thing. I could endure Sherlock's anger, I could forgive a lapse, but the thought of a worthless drug taking him away from me, blunting the edge of his brilliant mind, twisting his uniqueness into fear and deceit . . . that I could not forgive.

I led him to the sofa and sat beside him. 'You have to

stop.'

He picked at the edge of the older sticking plaster. 'I had stopped.' He half-smiled. 'Watson lectured me on the subject so many times that it seemed the best course of action.' He pushed his hair back and sighed, looking almost like himself. 'I do know it isn't good for me. I'm not stupid. But when the urge is there, the hunger—' He broke off. 'I'm sorry, Nell.' His mouth twitched. 'Not exactly romantic, is it?'

I stroked his hand. 'I think we're both a little past that.'

He put his hand over mine. 'Perhaps we should try harder.'

I looked up at him, but I couldn't read his expression. His grey eyes were opaque.

'Perhaps we should,' I said, remembering the hateful emotions which had oozed out of me at the department store. But now I was with Sherlock, I felt different. I felt stronger, more capable. I wanted to help, not wallow in my own self-pity. I raised my face to his, put my hand on his shoulder, then ran it gently round to the back of his collar —

'No.' Sherlock reached round and took my hand, not ungently, and held it in both his own.

'No?' I asked, discomfited.

'Not like this.' His mouth twitched. 'There wouldn't be much point – I mean, in any of it. When the high ends, it's the worst thing in the world. You feel numb, and then worse than numb. It's as if you've been cast into a pit you can never climb out of.'

I shuddered. 'Why do you do it?' I whispered. I wanted

to never let him go, never let him out of my sight, never let him do it again.

Sherlock bent his head to mine, and kissed me on the lips. It was the chastest kiss he had ever given me. 'Because when you're on a high, it's worth it. You feel invincible, euphoric, as if you could span oceans with a stride. And when you've felt that just once, all you want to do is get back there. Whatever it takes.' He smiled, sadly. 'I know it's an illusion. My rational brain knows it only too well. But once you're up there, you don't care if it's a lie or not. It's the only truth worth knowing.'

My eyes followed his to the shards of glass and spilt liquid on the hearth. 'It doesn't look much like a truth to me,' I said, drawing back a little.

'It doesn't, does it,' Sherlock mused. Suddenly he pulled me to him and kissed the top of my head. 'Thank you, Nell,' he murmured into my hair.

'For what?'

'For trying.' He released me. 'You must be hungry.'

My stomach growled as if it were an actor taking his cue. 'Shall I go and tell Billy to serve dinner?'

'Ask him to put a tray outside for me.' He shook his head at my inquiring expression. 'I am not fit company for man or beast. I—' He paused, searching for words in a way that he would never usually need to. 'I feel like a violin.' His mouth quirked at my furrowed brow. 'A violin which a master craftsman has taken, and sanded away a layer, and tuned so that every note, every touch, makes me shriek.'

'Oh God, Sherlock—' I bit my lip to try and stop myself from crying.

'I shall stay in here tonight.' The words rushed out as if they were trying to push my reaction back. 'If I begin to feel better, I'll come through.' I nodded. I had no words left.

I went downstairs and gave my orders, and when dinner was served I ate it without tasting a thing. After dinner I sat in the drawing room and turned the pages of a novel, while Dr Watson turned the pages of a newspaper at me, and at ten o'clock, unable to be in company any longer, I said goodnight.

The tray outside the consulting-room door had not been touched. I moved it away and set my hand to the cool brass knob. The gas lamps were turned low, but I could see Sherlock, in his dressing gown, huddled against the foot of the sofa, arms wrapped around himself. Every so often he shuddered slightly. I couldn't even tell if he were awake or asleep.

I closed the door and got ready for bed, but before I drew back the covers and climbed in I did something I had not done for many years. I knelt beside the bed and prayed to God – to anyone who would listen – to help Sherlock. I whispered into my clasped hands for what seemed an eternity, until I had poured it all out to an invisible, silent ear. When I at last rose my limbs were chilled stiff, and I grimaced as I lifted myself into the high bed. I lay for several minutes, wide awake, changing position to try and get warmth into my cold bones. It was no use. I tossed and turned for several minutes more, then rolled to Sherlock's side of the bed. It smelt of him. I wrapped my arms around the pillow and held it close, inhaling his scent, wishing he were there with me.

When I awoke the birds were singing outside, and a beam of light sliced the bed in two. I had overslept. I tried to roll over, to get out of bed, but I could not. Sherlock's long, sinewy arm was slung across me, and his body cupped mine. I savoured the slow, regular rise and fall of his chest against my back, and gave thanks. And yet my joy and relief was tempered. The crisis was over – for now.

CHAPTER 15

I startled awake at a tap on the door. 'Ma'am?' Martha called softly. 'It's a quarter to nine. I've brought you a fresh pot of tea.'

'Thank you,' I called.

Sherlock's arm twitched, and he stirred. 'Did I hear a quarter to nine?' he murmured.

'I am afraid so.' I tensed myself for a whirlwind of bathing, dressing, striding round the room.

'Hmmm.' Sherlock's hand explored my hip.

***

'Do you still want me to look at those papers?' I asked.

Sherlock drank the rest of his cooling cup of tea. 'Could we do it together? My head is much clearer, but—' He glanced at me, and I cursed the little wrinkle of doubt between his brows.

'Of course,' I said, throwing the covers aside. 'We had better get breakfast first though, before Martha gives up on us.'

Dr Watson had already left for the day, and we breakfasted together at a corner of the large dining table. I felt like a child playing at being a grown-up, and wished we could shut the world out for a day. But work was looming, and soon we were upstairs in the consulting room, the fire beginning to warm it. Sherlock pulled a long, low table up to the two armchairs, and collected handfuls of papers from around the room.

I eyed the bundle he set down on the table. 'Is that all of it?'

'Were you hoping for more, Nell?' Sherlock divided the bundle roughly in two. 'Here we have pen portraits of the seventy warders employed at Wandsworth Prison. The task in hand is to narrow this bunch down to anyone who would have been physically able to impersonate Emmett Stanley, and if possible, to pick out the most likely candidates.'

I curled up in the armchair, and began to read. It did not take me long to dismiss the first candidate; at over six feet tall, with fair hair, he could never have been the slight, dark-haired Emmett Stanley. I dropped the paper on the floor and studied the next. *Philip Granger. Five feet seven, well-built, short brown hair, blue eyes, clean-shaven. No distinguishing marks—* He was a possibility. And then I recalled when I had done something similar. We had been holed up in Somerset House, in Mycroft Holmes's office, searching the passenger lists of the *Valiant* for another missing man – except that then, Sherlock had been working on my behalf.

I glanced over to see his eyes already on me. 'Are you —?' he asked.

I nodded. 'I am quite all right. But – it brings it back.'

The fire crackled as a log shifted in the grate. I watched the sparks drift upwards for a moment. Then I read on.

It took perhaps fifteen minutes to dismiss half of the wardens in my pile. I lifted up the papers I had consigned to the floor, squared off their edges, and placed them on the table. 'These are my rejects. Would you check them?'

We swapped our piles, and each glanced through the other's papers. 'I agree,' said Sherlock at length, tossing them back to the floor.

'So do I.' I dropped mine on top of his.

'Now for the shortlist.' I pulled my chair closer, and we put our heads together, scanning the pages. *Samuel Cross . . . five feet nine inches tall, black hair, clean-shaven . . . fifteen years a warder...* My finger underlined the words. 'I can't imagine that someone who'd worked there so long would do a thing like this.'

'I agree. Too much at stake.' We riffled through the pile, removing those with ten or more years' service. Sherlock walked his fingers through the remaining papers. 'Fourteen left.' He looked at me. 'Tell me, Nell, what sort of crime does this feel like to you?'

I mused for a moment, gazing into the flames. 'A risky crime, a confident one. At any stage – hiding the key, knocking Stanley out, taking his place, leaving the cell – something could happen to expose him. The reward must have been high. It feels like a young man's crime.'

'Yes,' Sherlock said quietly. 'I see a young man, not in the service long, dissatisfied, perhaps passed over for an opportunity, and easily influenced. Oh, and without the steadying influence of a wife.' He grinned at me.

'Very amusing.' I reached across and gave his hand a light smack. 'Let's get back to the papers.'

My eyes raced down the pages, pausing at certain words, running on.

'No. Wife and young family.'

'No. Recently promoted. He wouldn't risk that.'

'No. Lay chaplain.'

'*Yes.*'

There were three papers left. Sherlock swept the other papers away and laid them side by side on the table. 'Thomas Palmer, William Coates, Simeon Davies.' His eyes sought mine. 'Agreed?'

I looked at the papers. Three from seventy. 'Agreed.'

Sherlock puffed out a sigh. 'Good. Excellent.' He knelt to gather the papers from the floor. 'I shall send a wire. But first—' He leaned on the arm of my chair and kissed me. 'Thank you for your help.'

I smiled through the second kiss. 'I think you could have managed without me,' I murmured, my lips brushing his.

'Managing is not the point.' He drew back a little to look at me. 'You bring something that Watson, for all his virtues, never could.'

I giggled. 'Well, I didn't imagine that you two—'

Sherlock's eyes widened for a moment, and then he laughed in a way I had rarely heard him do before; a short bark of a laugh which popped out of him like a cork from a bottle. 'What I was talking about, you rude woman, was companionship,' he grinned.

I raised my eyebrows at him.

'No, really. Watson accompanies me on my cases more often than not, but he is an observer, a recorder, a scribe. He doesn't affect the outcome. Whereas you are right in there with me. It's a different feeling entirely.' He held my gaze for a moment, lights dancing in his grey eyes. 'And speaking of different . . . don't you need to go to work?'

I twisted round to see the clock. 'Heavens!' I sprang up and ran to the dressing room.

'I like you as a redhead,' Sherlock called.

'Ha! Even if I had asked your opinion, there isn't time!' I pulled down the nearest box, hunting for the styled wig I had worn the previous day, until I remembered it was still in the bedroom. I ran back through the consulting room and shook the bedclothes, then peered under the bed—

'Looking for something?' Sherlock stood in the doorway, one hand behind his back. He held the wig above his head for a moment, before relenting and putting it into my hand.

The wig was weeping hairpins. 'I'll have to take these out and start again.'

'No. Sit down and put your hair up, and I'll fetch you another wig. You can get a cab for once.' He disappeared for a few moments and returned waving the auburn wig like a battle trophy. 'Surprise!'

I took it from him and fitted it over my own hair. 'I hope you don't expect me to dye my hair red,' I said, as I reached for more pins.

'I wouldn't dream of it,' he said, watching me in the mirror. 'I'll go and hold a cab for you.'

Hastily disguised, I ran downstairs to find Billy holding the door open for me and Sherlock at the door of a waiting cab. 'Thank you,' I said, as he helped me in. 'Debenham and Freebody, please!' I called to the driver.

'He knows,' said Sherlock, leaning in to kiss me. But even as I kissed him back, a little voice whispered in my head. *You're leaving him alone, with every druggist in London at his disposal...*

'You won't, will you?' I said.

'Won't what?' he murmured. I saw his face change as he realised what I meant, and wished I had not spoken, not put the idea into his head. He stepped back from the carriage. 'No, I won't,' he said quietly.

I reached out a hand to him, but the cabman was already whipping up the horse, and I could only look as we sped away. We had had a busy morning together, a – what had he said? – A *companionable* morning, such as we had not had for a long time, and my question had taken the shine from it. Yet it was not my fault, I told myself. Surely any wife would have the same concern – but I was not Sherlock's wife, as nearly as I felt myself to be on occasion. And as the cab rattled through the streets I wondered whether I would ever be able to leave him alone without worrying.

CHAPTER 16

I was watching a woman edge closer to a display of scarves when a 'Found you!' in my ear made me squeal.

'What are you doing here?' I hissed at Sherlock, who was grinning at my outraged expression.

'I've come to fetch you. Gregson's summoned me, and I am summoning you.'

'What about Dr Watson?'

'Dr Watson won't do. Come on, Nell, I have a cab waiting.'

Sherlock strode off, but I stood firm. 'What about my job?'

'I had a word.' Sure enough, Mr Turner stood beaming near the door, waiting to bow us out. *What on earth had Sherlock told him?*

'Where are we going?' I asked as Sherlock handed me into the cab. I had caught sight of myself in a mirror as we left the shop, having completely forgotten that I was disguised. 'Do I need to change?'

'Probably not.' He took a seat beside me, slammed the door, and the cab shot forward.

'Don't you know?'

The cab had made two turns before Sherlock replied. 'We're going to the Stanley house in Ealing. Gregson wired telling me to come at once. That's all he said.'

The Stanley house.

Effie Stanley.

I cast my mind back to the last – the only time we had met. It had been my first assignment for Sherlock. In the course of shadowing Mrs Stanley I had taken the table next to hers, made small talk, and offered to post the letter which contained plans to rob the Bank of England.

I had helped to put Emmett Stanley in prison. Perhaps that had made him easier to abduct.

If ever I had wanted to pass unrecognised, today was the day. I pulled a pocket mirror from my bag, heart racing. *What had I worn that day?*

'You had chestnut hair and pince-nez,' Sherlock's eyes met mine over the top of the mirror. He put a hand on my arm. 'You looked quite different.'

'What if she…?'

'She won't.' Sherlock took my hand. 'Nell, Gregson doesn't summon me for nothing. Effie Stanley will have much more to think about than whether the detective's assistant bears a slight resemblance to a lady she once chatted with over a cup of tea.' I felt the warmth of his hand through my thin glove. 'In fact, it could be useful if she still doesn't know what you look like…'

I sighed. 'It's never straightforward, is it?'

He grinned. 'Straightforward is dull.'

The journey to Ealing took less than an hour, even with London traffic. I looked out as Sherlock told me we were getting close, but I could not have been prepared for journey's end. The cab leaned right, rattling down a long curve of gravel drive. I could not see the house until we had passed a small copse of trees, when a square red-brick manor house glided towards us, and the woodland gave way to manicured lawns and formal flower beds.

'She seemed so *normal*,' I murmured, trying not to stare.

'This is normal, for some people,' Sherlock observed, drily.

The cab slowed almost to walking pace, as if it didn't want to disturb anyone. We drove past a gardener standing on the top of a small ladder, snipping at a topiary squirrel. He watched us by, then returned to his trimming.

'I knew she had a footman,' I said weakly, as the carriage rolled to a stop.

Sherlock turned to me. 'Nell, they're people, just like we are.'

'I know, but—' I looked down at myself, and the clothes which were perfectly respectable in a London department store now seemed cheap and tawdry. 'Perhaps I should wait in the carriage.'

'Don't be ridiculous!' Sherlock opened the door and reached for my hand. 'You are my assistant, not a fashion plate. I wouldn't care if you wore a flour sack.'

I smiled in spite of myself. '*I* would.'

I kept close to Sherlock as we climbed the white stone

steps to the entrance. Before we could ring or knock the door swung open, and a footman took our coats. I lifted my hat carefully from my head, feeling as if I was unmasking myself.

'You are expected.' The voice startled me. I had not heard the butler approach. 'Please wait here, and I shall fetch Inspector Gregson.' He departed as silently as he had come, walking down the length of the hallway and vanishing through a door.

I shivered as I looked around me. The hall was imposing, beautiful. Its duck-egg-blue walls were ornamented with white plaster, and in each ornate plaster frame was set an oil painting. The floor was tiled in black and white marble. From the centre of the room rose a mahogany staircase with a runner of bright Turkey carpet. But the hush, the stillness, made it feel like a tomb. I glanced at Sherlock. He seemed completely at home, unfazed, walking from picture to picture as if he were in an art gallery. His words in the carriage echoed in my head. *This is normal, for some people.* What was *his* normal? I thought of Mycroft Holmes's luxuriously-appointed surroundings. Where had Sherlock grown up? For the first time I realised that since we had met, we had been occupied with untangling the mystery of my past, then building a present together. I had never considered Sherlock's background, or his past. He had never spoken of it, except in one conversation about his family.

My reverie was interrupted by a creak overhead. Inspector Gregson was hurrying downstairs. 'Thank God you're here, Holmes.' He advanced, hand outstretched. 'No

Watson today?'

Sherlock shook the proffered hand. 'Mrs Hudson is assisting me today,' he said smoothly, nodding in my direction.

The inspector's face fell slightly. 'Ah. Good afternoon, Mrs—' As he turned to greet me, his bland expression was overlaid by confusion.

'I have come from the department store,' I explained, gesturing towards my auburn wig.

'Oh, of course, of course. All going well at the shop, I take it? Keeping the thieves out of the haberdashery, eh?' He chuckled.

'I do my best,' I said, rather stiffly.

'Capital.' He turned back to Sherlock. 'Well it can't be helped, but Watson would have been very useful today. I assumed— Anyway, we had better go up.'

'What has happened?' I asked.

The inspector stared at me. 'Emmett Stanley has been found.'

'*What?*' Sherlock and I spoke with one voice.

'I was as surprised as you. The telegram came while I was out on another case, and they had to come and find me. I only paused to wire you.' He sighed heavily. 'Stanley was found dumped under a bush in his own garden, gagged and bound. He was covered in fallen leaves.'

'Alive?'

The inspector nodded. 'But—'

'What, is he injured?' Sherlock asked, moving towards the stairs. Inspector Gregson put a hand on his arm.

'Apart from rope burns, there isn't a mark on him that I

can see. But he won't talk. I don't think he *can* talk. He looks as if he's stared death in the face. Any sudden noise, and—' The snap of his fingers rang like a gunshot in the cavernous hall. 'I reckon he'd be gone.' He lowered his voice. 'Mrs Stanley found him when she was cutting roses, and she fainted dead away.' Shaking his head, he mounted the first steps. 'Watson would have known if he's shamming, but my instinct is that it's real. See for yourself.'

The landing was as grand as the hall had been, but our only interest was in the door which stood ajar at the top of the stairs. Inspector Gregson held it for Sherlock and me to pass in.

The bedroom was dark. A miscellany of pictures covered dark green walls and mahogany half-panelling, and the curtains were closed, though a fresh breeze came from behind them. A nurse sat in the corner, knitting. By the bed sat Mrs Stanley – but it was not the Mrs Stanley I knew. Her forehead rested on her clasped hands, one of which grasped a rosary, and she was muttering. I caught the words 'Holy Mary, Mother of God…' and wondered how long she had been praying for. She sounded as if she would never stop, and with the rhythmic clack of needles from the corner, the effect was of a relentlessly moving machine of care.

And at last my eyes reached the four-poster bed near the window. The top of a head was visible; all else was a heap of bedclothes. It was too dark to see more.

'The doctor said dim light and quiet might help him.' Gregson's voice, though not loud, seemed obscenely so in this place. 'Any change, Mrs Stanley?'

The muttering stopped, and Effie Stanley looked up from her clasped hands. Wisps of her dark hair had escaped from her bun, and her face was already drawn from grief. She shook her head mutely, and pressed it down onto her clasped knuckles as if she might lose her place. Gregson raised his eyebrows at the nurse, who said apologetically, 'No change, sir,' and waited a decent interval before resuming her knitting.

Gregson approached the bed and gently moved the cover back. There was no resistance from the body beneath. Emmett Stanley lay curled in a ball, his hands clasping his knees, his head on his chest. His breathing was quick; it rasped out of him as if it were being dragged.

'Mr Stanley,' Gregson said quietly.

The man did not respond.

'*Stanley*,' he repeated, a little louder.

The head lifted slightly, but Stanley gave no other sign.

Sherlock stepped forward and gently laid two fingers on the man's neck. 'The pulse is quick, but steady.' He touched his forehead. 'He is very warm – partly through being bundled up in bed, but I suspect a fever. What was he wearing when he was found?'

'A shirt and trousers. No shoes. You can see them downstairs,' said Gregson. 'He's been put in one of his old nightshirts for now.'

Sherlock leaned closer and peered at the man's hands. 'I see no marks of ill-usage, apart from the rope burns on his wrists. Does he have any injuries?' he asked, turning to Gregson.

The inspector shook his head.

'I would like a closer look, though… Nell, would you mind drawing the curtain for me?'

I moved round the foot of the bed to the window. The tapestry curtain was thick and stiff in my hand. I drew it back a fraction, and raised my eyebrows at Sherlock, who was bending close to Stanley. 'A bit more,' he mouthed.

I moved further up the room, towards the bed, as I drew the curtain, and—

The scream almost made me pull the curtain from its pole. It was unearthly, eldritch, heart-rending. Emmett Stanley, his back arched and his eyes wide, was staring at me, and screaming.

I let the curtain fall and Inspector Gregson took my arm. 'I don't understand,' I said, as he pulled me away. 'I've never—' Mrs Stanley was staring at me too, and her eyes were full of hatred.

'Stay on the landing,' the inspector muttered, between clenched teeth. 'Nurse,' he called into the room. 'Come here, please.'

I waited outside, half-watched by the nurse, for several minutes. Mr Stanley's screams had subsided, but I could hear a low, animal wail in its place. I also heard lowered, angry voices within the room, but I did not dare move closer. Eventually the door opened and Sherlock strode out. 'We have to leave,' he snapped.

'What happened?' I had to half-run to keep up.

Sherlock turned so suddenly that I almost cannoned into him. 'You tell me, Nell. Right now, I'm the only thing standing between you and a prison cell.'

111

CHAPTER 17

A cab was procured, and we began the drive back to Baker Street in silence. I stared out of the window, but saw nothing of the outside world. I was in a dark room, bewildered and upset. I had never seen Emmett Stanley in my life, and yet—

'I don't understand,' I murmured. I looked across at Sherlock, who was frowning at me, but in a thoughtful way.

'You're sure you've never met Stanley?' he asked.

'Quite sure.'

'In that case—' He banged on the roof. 'Turn around please,' he cried. The cab stopped, and after some manoeuvring, we sped back towards Ealing. 'If there's something about this that neither of us can understand, it is almost certainly something worth knowing.' Now that he had a hypothesis, Sherlock was transformed. His shoulders were straight, his head up, and his eyes gleamed at the prospect of a good fight.

The Stanleys' house was just as imposing the second time, but knowing the horror inside, I would not have swapped even the little Clerkenwell flat where I had begun married life for all its grandeur. Sherlock jumped down and helped me out. 'I am sorry I was angry before,' he whispered, as we mounted the steps. 'To be thrown out just when things were getting interesting…'

The door opened. The butler looked down at us, and while on the surface his expression was as impassive as it had been on our previous reception, I sensed the emotions below.

'Please could you ask Inspector Gregson to come down?' Sherlock handed his hat and coat to the butler with an air of finality which stunned me.

The butler merely bowed, and set off for the back stairs. 'I am itching to get into that room again,' said Sherlock, gazing at the grand staircase. 'I had better behave by the book, I suppose.'

Inspector Gregson strode downstairs faster than I had ever seen him move. 'What is it now, Holmes?' he growled. 'I've spent the last quarter of an hour working with the nurse to soothe Mrs Stanley out of her hysterics.' He flung an angry glance at me. 'Mrs Hudson, whatever Holmes has in mind, you will stay well out of it. Another scene like that—'

'On the contrary,' said Sherlock. 'I believe that Stanley's reaction to my assistant is a clue.'

The inspector's glare intensified. 'If I find out that you have been mixed up in this business—'

'How could I be mixed up in it?' I cried. 'I have barely

left Baker Street lately, except to undertake the work which you assigned me!'

Inspector Gregson backed away, lifting his hands as if to ward me off. 'All right all right, Mrs Hudson. One hysterical woman is enough, thank you.' If looks could kill, he would have lain dead at my feet in an instant. 'Holmes, what exactly *do* you want?'

'I propose an experiment.' Sherlock took the inspector by the arm and drew him aside. I could see his strategy – make the inspector feel that they were men together, rational, sensible men who would get the job done. I turned away to hide my annoyance. 'If we assume that Mrs Hudson is not involved in this business – and I do not see how she could be – then it is something about her which has triggered Mr Stanley's reaction. I suggest that we clear the bedroom, and see if we can identify the trigger.'

'Hmm.' Inspector Gregson nodded in a wise manner. 'I see what you are getting at.' He rubbed his jaw, considering me. 'I shall suggest to Mrs Stanley that she goes to another room for a break. The poor woman is exhausted. Wait here.'

'What do you think the trigger might be?' I whispered to Sherlock, watching the inspector's broad back ascend the stairs.

'I have no idea,' he whispered back.

A few minutes later the inspector appeared at the top of the stairs and beckoned us up. I could feel myself trembling as I climbed.

'Are you all right, Nell?' Sherlock took my arm.

'I – it's rather nerve-racking.'

'Of course,' said Sherlock, after a pause. 'I'll try to be quick.'

We stopped outside the bedroom door. 'How do we begin?' asked the inspector.

'You and I go in first and get settled by the bed,' said Sherlock. 'Mrs Hudson, will you then come in, go to the window, and draw back the curtain, just as you did earlier?'

'I shall do my best,' I said, though the thought filled me with dread.

'Good.' Sherlock followed Inspector Gregson into the bedroom.

I gave them a couple of minutes to arrange themselves, and then entered. Mr Stanley was curled up as he had been before. I approached the foot of the bed and walked slowly to the window, my eyes on Emmett Stanley the whole time. His eyes shifted towards me and even in the low light I saw his terror. I backed away.

'Take off your wig,' mouthed Sherlock. I lifted it off and set it on the dressing table, then approached the window. Emmett Stanley became agitated the moment I came near. I retreated, shaking my head.

'Try going to the other side of the bed.' The inspector was studying me, and I couldn't read his expression. Did he seriously think I was mixed up in this? Would I find myself under arrest? I bit my lip and walked forward, and Emmett Stanley's eyes, wide and distraught, found me.

I stood against the wall. 'I don't think I can do this,' I whispered, blinking hard.

Sherlock got up and came to me, taking my hand.

'There is something, there is something… The moment you come near his muscles tense, then he looks for you—Ha! He is afraid *before* he sees you. What is it, what is it?' He stepped back a few paces, closed his eyes, and advanced slowly towards me. His eyes snapped open. 'I believe I have it. Nell, when you were at the department store this afternoon, did you put on a new perfume?'

My mouth dropped open. 'I did!' I smelt my wrist. 'I was watching someone on the next counter, and I asked the assistant if I could try one, just to give me a reason for loitering.' I held my wrists out to Sherlock, who bent and sniffed. 'Jasmine,' he muttered.

Inspector Gregson sprang up and came round the foot of the bed to us. 'Did you say jasmine?' he asked, his superior manner wiped away.

Sherlock nodded.

'Is there a way we can test it?' His tone was almost deferential.

'It depends…' Sherlock led me to the dressing table, the top of which was crowded with scent bottles and preparations. 'You probably know more about this than I, Nell. Is there anything here which approximates to the perfume you are wearing?'

I felt like a trespasser as I ranged among Mrs Stanley's things. 'This one,' I said finally, holding out the stopper for Sherlock to smell. 'This is the closest match.'

'Stay where you are.' Sherlock took the bottle, replaced the stopper and advanced to the bed. Emmett Stanley seemed to be asleep. Sherlock lifted the stopper and held it towards Stanley.

The effect was electric. Emmett Stanley clawed the air, looking wildly around, and screaming. Sherlock had moved away as soon as the reaction began, and stood watching, a peculiar expression on his face. After a minute, Stanley began to quieten, his movements becoming less frenetic, until he lay quiet again.

'Well!' The inspector stepped forward, rubbing his hands. 'It appears you are right, Mr Holmes. Most interesting, most interesting. Especially when coupled with — Wait a moment, and I will show you.' He disappeared from the room, returning with the nurse a few moments later. 'There. Come downstairs. I meant you to see it earlier, but, well—' Our unceremonious departure hung in the air.

We left the nurse to her knitting and went down to the cold hall. Inspector Gregson had a word with the butler, who raised his eyebrows, but led us through the sunny morning room and unlocked the French windows leading to the garden.

'This way.' The inspector took us along a winding path, through an arch planted with clematis, to an informal garden. He waved at the rose garden beyond. 'Mrs Stanley was coming back from there when she saw him.' He took a few more steps forward, then doubled back and approached a large bush starred with yellow flowers. 'He was under there.'

I shivered. It seemed incongruous that such a cheerful plant could play a role in this affair. 'May we?' I mimed approaching the bush.

'Of course,' said the inspector. 'We have a drawing of

the footprints leading to and from the bush. Much good it'll do us; half the household had been over the ground before we arrived.'

Sherlock and I went together. I bent and lifted a canary-yellow bloom to my face. 'I don't understand,' I said, bewildered. 'I can't smell anything.'

'You won't,' said Sherlock. 'This is *Jasminum nudiflorum.* Winter jasmine. Attractive, prolific, hardy, but almost entirely scentless.'

He looked at the inspector, who nodded. 'I'm a gardening man. I knew it the moment I set eyes on it.'

I wrapped my arms around myself. The day was drawing in, and the sky had that curious shadowy quality it acquires just before dusk, when everything seems not quite real. 'The jasmine-scented notepaper,' I said.

'Yes.' Inspector Gregson counted on his fingers. 'Jasmine on the notepaper, Stanley terrified by the scent of it, and he was dumped under a jasmine bush. By God, I wish I understood.'

Sherlock rubbed his face with his palms. 'We are dealing with a twisted mind. They have tortured a man, and cast him aside knowing that he cannot – will not – betray them. I suspect that, however much care he receives, Emmett Stanley is utterly broken.'

'What should we do next?' asked Inspector Gregson.

Sherlock shrugged. 'What we can. Question the warders we identified as possible suspects. Speak to Mrs Stanley, when she is recovered. Examine the area round the bush, when we have enough light.' He began to walk back to the house, but his usual decisive stride was shorter, more

118

tentative, and he seemed to be casting around for clues.

'I'm much obliged to you both,' said Inspector Gregson, when we had reached the comparative warmth of the hall. 'Let me know what you want to do tomorrow. Bring Watson, if you can. And you must come too, of course, Mrs Hudson.' He smiled at me, and the smile I returned was not without a twist of irony.

'I shall speak to Mr Turner,' I said.

'Oh, don't worry about that,' said the inspector, winking. 'I'll wire him. This is far more important than ladies' fal-lals.'

Ladies fal-lals have been paying the bills, I thought; but I sensed now was not the time to say it.

We were treated to the Stanleys' own carriage to convey us home. 'What do you think?' I asked Sherlock. It seemed such a simple question; but Sherlock's thought was bound to be complicated, wide-ranging, utterly strange and at the same time completely logical.

Sherlock looked out of the window for some time before he answered, though there was little to see but darkening fields and the dying light in the sky. 'Honestly, Nell?'

'Of course honestly.'

Again he paused. 'I think we are dealing with a monster.'

CHAPTER 18

'Nell . . . Nell...'

I was being shaken gently. Yet I was not in my bed. It took some time for me to come to full consciousness. I was sitting up, and my head was pillowed on something bony, which turned out to be Sherlock's shoulder. 'Where are we?' I blinked, but we were still in darkness.

Sherlock drew up a shade and gaslight illuminated a London street. 'We are at Baker Street. You fell asleep about ten minutes after we set off.'

'Oh.'

'All those hairpins are very uncomfortable, you know.'

I put my hand to my head, where my hair was pinned severely down. Where was my hat? What had I—? And then I remembered the auburn wig, and the scent of jasmine. I could still smell it on myself. I shuddered as Emmett Stanley's screams rang in my head.

Martha answered the door. 'You look all in, begging my pardon. Both of you.'

'We are, rather.' Sherlock handed me over the threshold. 'Anything we need to know?'

'Not that I know of, sir,' said Martha, closing and bolting the door. 'Where have you been? I thought ma'am was at the shop today?'

'I was,' I said, taking off my jacket. 'I was poached.'

'We couldn't have managed without her,' said Sherlock, taking my jacket and hanging it up. 'Is dinner underway?'

'Of course, sir.' Martha raised her eyebrows. 'It will be ready for seven o'clock as usual. If that is what is required.'

'Good, good.' Sherlock rubbed his hands. 'Nell, go and run yourself a bath, and I shall have a word with Dr Watson. I assume he is in?'

Martha nodded. 'He is reading in the drawing room, sir.'

I climbed the stairs with a distinct feeling of dismissal. Perhaps I was tired, but I felt as if I were being over-ruled. First I had been taken from my workplace, then Inspector Gregson had snubbed me, before Sherlock had saved me from arrest. Having provided a key clue, I was to be pulled from my work again tomorrow; but in the meantime I was packed off to my bath while the men consulted.

I took my injured feelings out on my hair, pulling out the pins and brushing until my head tingled, then skewering it up for my bath. I changed into my dressing-gown and slippers and climbed the stairs to the chilly bathroom.

The wonder of running hot water still amazed and delighted me. I put my hand under the tap and let the water cascade over it, forming a miniature waterfall. I remembered lugging cans of hot water up the stairs just a few months ago. My life had changed in so many ways. *Perhaps I should be thankful.* I poured in some bath salts and inhaled the scent of roses. *Anything but jasmine.*

There was a tap at the door as I was preparing to get into the bath. 'Who is it?' I called.

'Me,' said Sherlock. 'May I come in?'

'On one condition,' I replied. 'You have to scrub my back.' I unbolted the door and Sherlock inserted himself through the gap, grinning. I turned my back on him as I slipped off my dressing gown and stepped carefully into the bath. 'Is this a social call?' I asked. 'And have you bolted the door?'

'Of course.'

'Good.' I began to wash myself but Sherlock's direct gaze made me blush and fumble with the sponge. 'Why don't you join me?'

'I hoped you'd ask.'

I repaid Sherlock's compliment by leaning my elbows on the edge of the bath and watching him undress, to which he, too, turned his back. 'Touché,' he said lightly. I giggled and moved forward as he got into the bath behind me. 'You're all slippery,' he murmured in my ear.

'I prefer elusive,' I said, handing the sponge over my shoulder.

'Mm.' He squeezed water down my back. 'It's been quite a day, hasn't it?'

'You could say that.' I wiggled my shoulders. 'Did you talk to Dr Watson?'

'I did,' Sherlock ran the sponge down my back again. 'It's not as much fun as talking to you.'

'And?' I persisted.

'He'll visit Emmett Stanley tomorrow.'

'What shall we be doing?'

'I haven't decided yet.'

'Do you definitely need me?'

The sponge stopped. 'What, would you rather be apprehending ribbon thieves?'

'That isn't the point,' I said, glad Sherlock couldn't see my face. 'I would prefer to be consulted, that's all.'

'I would like you to come, Nell,' Sherlock said, at length. 'I think you'll be useful.'

'Then I shall come,' I said.

I stiffened at another tap on the door. 'Ma'am?'

'Yes, Martha?'

'I'm sorry to disturb you, but Mr Poskitt is here.'

'Can you tell him I'll be down in a few minutes?'

'Of course.' A pause. 'Do you know where Mr Holmes is?'

'I'll let him know,' I called. Sherlock shook with silent laughter.

'Yes, ma'am,' said Martha, crisply.

We waited until her footsteps had receded downstairs before emerging from the bath. 'I wonder what he has come for,' Sherlock mused, towelling himself vigorously. 'A progress report, perhaps.'

I wrapped myself in my dressing gown. 'I hope it's not —' Our eyes met. 'More bad news.'

Sherlock flung his clothes on. 'I'll go down. Join us

when you're ready.' We left the bathroom together, Sherlock bounding down the stairs to the drawing room, while I hurried to the bedroom and put myself back into the dress I had been wearing.

I heard voices as I approached the drawing room, which ceased when I knocked. 'Come in, Nell,' called Sherlock.

I pushed the door open and my smile faded at the grave expressions before me. 'You were right,' said Sherlock, glancing at Mr Poskitt.

'I was just telling Mr Holmes and Dr Watson.' Even in crisis, Mr Poskitt was as formal as ever. 'Mr Holmes has been suspended from his duties. On full pay, but nevertheless, suspended.' He looked ready to weep.

'I am so sorry.' I sat next to Sherlock on the settee. 'Why, Mr Poskitt? What has happened?'

'More secrets,' Mr Poskitt said miserably. 'More betrayal.' His hands gripped his stick so hard that his knuckles were white. 'An ambush at Port Said this time, with many casualties. We are doing our best to keep it out of the newspapers, but word will spread eventually. No doubt the mole will make sure it does. Our tame ambassador tipped us off again.'

'But why has Mycroft been suspended?' Sherlock was on the edge of his seat, brow furrowed.

'He tried to get into a meeting.' Mr Poskitt passed a hand over his forehead. 'He hadn't been invited, and he bluffed his way in. When Sir William Chambers, the Secretary for War, ejected him, Mr Holmes was, apparently, very rude.'

'That doesn't sound like Mycroft,' I said, softly.

'You haven't lived with him,' said Sherlock. 'So that's why he's suspended? For being rude?'

'Partly,' sighed Mr Poskitt. 'I have been listening to the whispers in the corners, and the view is that your brother is a loose cannon. I know it is wrong; but Mr Holmes's, ah, impulsive behaviour towards Sir William has lent the theory some weight, and given the circumstances…'

'I see,' said Sherlock. 'Oh God, he'll be beside himself —' He ran his fingers through his hair. 'Mycroft without an occupation . . . it doesn't bear thinking about. He'll turn himself inside out. He'll eat himself alive. I had better go and see him.' He sprang up, but Mr Poskitt shook his head.

'Not yet, Mr Holmes. He is still angry, and he has said harsh words about you, too.'

'Then what can I do?' Sherlock began to pace.

'We must find the mole,' said Mr Poskitt, simply.

'Fine, fine,' snapped Sherlock. 'Who are the suspects?'

'Not suspects,' Mr Poskitt said, with a look of distaste. 'Possibilities.'

Sherlock wheeled round. 'Who are they?'

Mr Poskitt chewed the question over. 'By naming people, I do not mean to suggest that they are likely to have leaked state secrets,' he said slowly. 'It is merely that they have access to them.'

'That is understood,' said Sherlock.

'Very well. Mr Holmes is the only person privy to these matters who is not part of the Ministry of Defence. Apart from the Prime Minister, of course. I think we may rule him out,' Mr Poskitt said, with a dry little smile.

'And secrets at this level?'

Mr Poskitt sighed. 'The Foreign Secretary, the Secretary for War, and the Under-Secretary for War. Plus their secretaries. Men who have served the nation for years. Men of the utmost discretion, with impeccable records.'

'I see.' Sherlock flung himself back onto the settee. 'So Mycroft makes an easy scapegoat.'

'I am afraid so,' said Mr Poskitt, studying the rug.

Sherlock stared at the fire. 'I had one of my Baker Street Irregulars tail Mycroft, you know. Mycroft spotted him immediately.' He got up and poked the coals, sending sparks up the chimney. 'I imagine the men you speak of will be no different.'

'Could you shadow one of them?' pleaded Mr Poskitt.

Sherlock shrugged. 'I could. But if they spot me, and it comes out that I am Mycroft's brother, I doubt that will work in his favour.' He pushed his hair back. 'I met Sir William and his deputy at an event last year.'

Mr Poskitt's shoulders drooped. 'There must be something…'

Sherlock sighed. 'Get me everything you can about the three of them. Friends, clubs, families, the lot.' He stood and held out a hand. 'I can do no more for now.'

Mr Poskitt rose too, and shook the proffered hand. 'I understand,' he said. 'I know you will do what you can.' He left the room as if he had been handed a death sentence.

'Damn Mycroft!' Sherlock exclaimed as soon as the front door had closed. 'What business does he have getting into this sort of scrape?'

'Now, Holmes, I don't think he meant to,' said Dr Watson, laying a restraining hand on his arm.

'That's all very well,' said Sherlock, shaking him off and beginning to pace again. 'I'm not my brother's keeper —'

A tap at the door. 'Shall I bring dinner in?' called Martha.

'You may as well,' Sherlock replied, pulling the door open and almost upsetting Martha as he strode by.

'Sorry, Martha,' said Dr Watson, steadying her. 'Mr Holmes has had some bad news.'

'So I see,' she remarked, straightening her cap.

Sherlock pushed the excellent food around his plate, before throwing his napkin into the middle of it. 'I'm going upstairs to think,' he said, pushing back his chair. The door banged behind him.

I looked at Dr Watson. 'You don't think he's…'

The doctor chewed, considering, then swallowed. 'I don't know.'

'He knows I know,' I blurted. 'I caught him, and smashed the cocaine bottle.'

'In that case I doubt Holmes has had time to procure another supply.' He forced a smile.

'You don't seem particularly concerned, Dr Watson.' I put my knife and fork together on the plate.

'My concern is neither here nor there,' the doctor retorted. 'Holmes is a law unto himself. I doubt that you or I could stop him from doing anything. Excuse me.' His heavy tread proceeded upstairs.

I tapped at the consulting-room door before entering. Sherlock was folded into an armchair, arms round knees, and appeared almost to be in a trance. 'Trust Mycroft to get himself into a mess,' he remarked.

'Are you all right?' I asked.

He snorted. 'If you mean have I taken cocaine, then no, I haven't; tempted as I am. My mind is in a maze – running, doubling, finding dead end after dead end.'

'Perhaps you should wait for Mr Poskitt's dossiers.' I sat on the arm of the chair and stroked his hair. 'They may help.'

'I doubt it,' said Sherlock. But he rose, and followed me downstairs.

CHAPTER 19

I stirred and reached out for Sherlock, but my hand met with a cool sheet. I opened my eyes. It was starting to get light. I strained my ears, and heard kitchen noises downstairs.

Sherlock came in. 'You're early,' I said.

'Did I wake you? I'm sorry.' He leaned over and kissed me, bringing a faint whiff of shaving soap and tooth powder with him.

'I was waking up anyway. What time is it?'

'A quarter past seven, or so.' He sat beside me and buttoned his shirt to the neck. 'I had to do something. I've sent Billy to wire the inspector, asking him to meet us at Wandsworth Prison. I've wired the governor to expect us. Oh, and I've knocked Watson up.'

'I imagine he was delighted.'

'There's work to be done. Come on, lazybones.' He extended a hand to me.

I swatted it away. 'How many times have I left you

sleeping, Sherlock?'

Sherlock frowned. 'I see I shall have to use additional persuasion.' He waved his long fingers in the air before lifting the sheet and tickling me.

'All right, I'm getting up!' I shrieked, swinging my legs down and running to unhook my dressing gown as protection.

Martha served up bacon and eggs. 'You'll need a proper breakfast, going out at this hour,' she scolded. Dr Watson hunched blearily over his plate, ruminating.

'Any thoughts on the patient, Watson?' Sherlock asked between bites of toast.

Dr Watson shook his head. 'I shall reserve judgement until I have seen him, Holmes. *Patient* is the key word, you know.'

'Dr Watson, I am not sure that yesterday would be quick enough for Mr Holmes.' I reached for the salt and pepper, considering my egg before seasoning it.

'You're a pair of slow-coaches,' said Sherlock; but he was smiling as he said it.

After breakfast we repaired to the consulting room, where Sherlock pulled three volumes from the bookcase, piling them on the table. 'Here are volumes I-J and V-W of my index, and Edmund's *Toxicology*. Jasmine or winter jasmine.' He picked up the top volume, and Dr Watson and I took the others.

'Anything?' Sherlock asked two minutes later, putting his book back on the table.

'Not much,' said Dr Watson. 'The worst thing I have discovered about jasmine is that it may cause skin irritation. From what you have told me of Mr Stanley, I imagine that is the least of his problems.'

'It's used in perfumes and can be made into tea,' I said, closing my book. 'Oh, and some countries use it in celebrations and rituals.'

'I can contribute nothing better,' said Sherlock. 'Another dead end. Let us hope that the rest of our day is more fruitful.'

Our cab drew up outside Wandsworth Prison at a quarter past nine. 'The day will be well along here,' said Sherlock, handing me out. We walked to the gatehouse arm in arm. 'Mr Sherlock Holmes and Mrs Hudson,' said Sherlock to the guard.

'You're expected,' he replied, touching his cap and waving us through.

The looming building still had the power to chill me. I tried to shake the feeling off as we approached the great studded door, but it only grew stronger.

We were shown to the governor's office. 'You are betimes,' he said, rising and waving us to the chairs set in front of his desk. 'Inspector Gregson has not yet arrived.' He raised an inquiring eyebrow. 'I believe you have identified three persons you wish to speak to.'

'Yes, three of your warders. We think one of them might have been instrumental in kidnapping Emmett Stanley.' Sherlock stretched his legs.

'Names?' The governor reached for his pipe.

Sherlock reached into his inner pocket and pulled out the pen portraits we had pored over the day before. 'Thomas Palmer, William Coates, and Simeon Davies,' he said, handing the sheets to the governor.

The governor pressed a bell on his desk. Two minutes later a dark, well-dressed young man entered.

'Lawrence, get Palmer, Coates and Davies brought to the warders' recreation room. If any man is not on duty, send someone to bring him in.'

'Sir.' The young man half-bowed, and closed the door gently behind him.

'My secretary,' said the governor. 'Very good man, Lawrence. He'll be back in a few minutes, see if he isn't.'

Mr Lawrence proved the governor right by returning two minutes later. 'Coates and Davies are on their way, sir, and Sage is fetching Palmer. He lives two streets away, so if he is at home it is a matter of minutes.'

'At this rate he will be here before the inspector,' chuckled the governor. 'Thank you, Lawrence.'

Mr Lawrence bowed, and withdrew.

'He's an Oxbridge man, you know,' said the governor, indicating the door Mr Lawrence had passed through. 'Son of a friend. I was hesitant about taking him on, but now I wouldn't be without him.'

'Good staff are hard to find,' said Sherlock.

'Quite so, quite so.' The governor flicked through the pen portraits Sherlock had handed him. 'Hmm, yes.'

A tap at the door, and Lawrence entered again. 'Inspector Gregson is here, sir.'

'Wonderful. Show him in, and bring another chair.'

The inspector sat down and looked at us expectantly. 'Are the men ready?'

'Two are, the other is being fetched,' said Sherlock.

'Excellent.' The inspector rubbed his hands. 'We'll deal with the first two, then.'

'Now, don't overdo it,' said the governor. 'Innocent till proven guilty, Inspector Gregson. I have trouble keeping a full roster as it is.'

Mr Lawrence led us down the corridor which, as he turned the corner, transformed from a wide, carpeted, well-lit space to a narrow, bare run. 'Here we are,' he said, opening a blue wooden door marked *Recreation*. 'I would suggest that you interview in this room, since it has a table and chairs, and put the other man in the anteroom.'

'Thank you so much,' said Sherlock. 'Inspector, will you take the lead?'

'I generally do,' said Inspector Gregson, striding in. Sherlock held the door open for me, then followed.

The two men were sitting on the long side of the table, heads together. They jumped apart at the inspector's entrance, their eyes darting between the three of us.

'Gentlemen,' said the inspector. 'I'll take you one at a time, if I may. You first.' He pointed at the man sitting on the left. 'You, wait in the anteroom, please.' The second man got up and walked to another blue door set into the back wall, glancing at us again before he left.

Inspector Gregson sat heavily in the middle chair, pulling out a notebook and pen. 'Name?'

'Simeon Davies,' replied the remaining man, a slight fellow with thinning brown hair, though his features suggested he could be no more than thirty.

Sherlock and I hurried to sit down. The inspector continued, confirming age, address, and length of service.

'Do you know why you are here, Davies?'

Davies shook his head. 'Mr Lawrence just said I was to come.'

'Did he.' The inspector sat back and tapped his teeth with the pen. 'It concerns the abduction of Emmett Stanley.'

'Who is Emmett Stanley?' Davies's expression was innocent and blank as a freshly-laundered sheet.

'One of the prisoners. A now former inmate. He was in E wing, and he was taken last week.'

'Oh!' Davies' mouth formed a perfect O. 'How did that happen? I don't know E wing at all. I'm new, you see.'

Sherlock and I exchanged glances behind the inspector's back. Either Davies was innocent, or he ought to have been on the London stage.

Inspector Gregson established quickly that at the time of Emmett Stanley's disappearance, while the prisoners had been in the exercise yard, Davies had been with another warder, first restraining a prisoner who had collapsed in a fit, then accompanying him to the dispensary. 'He struggled something awful, sir, you wouldn't believe. It was all Trevor and I could do to stop him swallowing his tongue.'

'All right, all right.' The inspector made a note. 'Which wing do you work on?'

'A wing, sir, right over the other side.'

'What did you do when you went off duty?'

'I went down to the billiard hall, sir, and played a couple of matches. My friends will vouch for it.'

Davies was sent back to work, and Coates summoned in

134

his place. He was a pale sickly man, who coughed as he took his seat.

'You don't seem well,' observed the inspector.

'No,' Coates coughed again. 'I have only just been signed fit to return to work. Bad bout of pneumonia. I've always had a weak chest.'

'Were you at work on the sixteenth?'

Coates shook his head. 'I was laid up at home. My neighbour was so worried that he called the doctor out.'

'And your doctor is…?'

'Dr Delaney. He has a surgery in Garratt Lane.'

The inspector made a note. He asked a few more questions about length of service and knowledge of the prisoner, but I could see that his heart wasn't in it, and he had dismissed Coates out of hand. He sent Coates to cough his way back to work. 'Where's this Palmer fellow, I wonder? Surely he hasn't flown the coop.'

We made small talk for some minutes, until the sound of quick footsteps made us look to the door. It sprang open, and Mr Lawrence came in, leaving it ajar. 'Sage and the governor are behind me.' He pulled out a chair and sat down without ceremony.

'What has happened?' asked the inspector.

'The governor will be here directly,' said Mr Lawrence.

A few seconds later the governor appeared, out of breath and flustered, and behind him trailed the wheezing form of Sage. 'What a carry on,' he said, clutching the door frame and catching his breath before ambling into the room.

'What is it?' asked Sherlock.

The governor sat next to Mr Lawrence. 'Not good news, I am afraid. Sage here has just got back from Palmer's rooms. There was no answer to his knock, and no-one had seen him, so at first Sage thought Palmer had fled. But there was a smell—'

'A bad one,' Sage interjected. 'So I looked through the keyhole, and—'

'Yes, yes,' the governor said, motioning Sage to be quiet. 'Mr Sage broke in, and he found Palmer hanged from a hook in the ceiling.'

'An' from the smell,' added Sage, ''e's been there some days.'

CHAPTER 20

We made but a sorry procession to the rooming house where Thomas Palmer had ended his life. The landlady, weeping, was waiting for us in the doorway. 'I never thought – I mean, he was quiet, he was always quiet. No trouble… I just thought he'd gone away for a few days.' Our eyes followed hers to a brisk, stout, tweed-suited figure coming up the path. 'Here is Dr Meredith. Oh, thank God.'

'Good morning, Mrs Harmsworth,' said the doctor. 'I understand there's been a death.'

The woman shrank back. 'I shall lose all my paying guests!'

'Nonsense,' said the doctor. 'You don't have to tell 'em how the man died. Anyway, let's get down to business.' He led the way in. 'Where can we find him?'

'Second floor back,' she gulped, looking up the stairwell as if she expected a thunderbolt to descend.

The doctor went up the steep, rickety stairs, followed by

Mr Lawrence, then Sherlock, then Inspector Gregson. The governor had stayed at Wandsworth. 'I can be far more use here than there,' he had said. 'Lawrence will look after you, and he can identify the body too, if necessary.' I brought up the rear, hoping that I would not be required to enter the room and see the body. It would only be the second corpse I had seen; but the second within a year.

The smell, a mixture of rotting flesh and mustiness, grew stronger the further we ascended the staircase. 'I can't believe it's taken this long to work out he's dead,' said the doctor, testily. 'Anyone with a nose could tell that something was up.' He pulled out a large cotton handkerchief and placed it over his nose and mouth, tying the corners at the back of his head. 'I strongly recommend that you follow my example.'

The men did so; my handkerchief was too small to suffice, though. 'I shall wait on the landing,' I said, thankfully.

'You could always borrow one of ours, ma'am,' chuckled the doctor. 'If you're really interested, that is.'

'I am sure you will be able to tell me everything I should know,' I said, backing away.

'Brace yourselves, gentlemen,' said Dr Meredith, and flung open the door.

I had retreated to the furthest part of the landing, but an evil impulse made me look. I saw the dangling body turn slowly before I ran downstairs, bile rising in my throat.

The landlady was below. 'It's horrible, isn't it, dearie,' she said. 'Come and sit down, the parlour's free. My tenants are all at work during the day.' I allowed myself to be led into a room stuffed with cheap furniture, and seated on a hard sofa whose horsehair was escaping from the seams.

'Would you like a cup of tea? It settles the stomach something wonderful.'

'That would be very kind.'

'I'll put the kettle on.' She bustled away, glad to be doing a domestic, mundane task.

I looked about me, but little was to be gleaned from the room, whose only ornament was a collection of broken china shepherdesses on the mantel and a print of a stag at bay hung above. How long would the men be up there? What would they need to do?

'He used to sit in here most evenings.' The landlady's voice made me jump. 'I would open this room up to all my gentlemen, since most of them didn't have room for more than one chair.' She set down her tray, and while pouring, serving and drinking tea she kept up a litany of when Mr Palmer had left for work, when he had returned to his room, and a succession of remembered titbits of things that he had once said, leading on to speculation about his family. 'He was a close man, you see; friendly enough, but he didn't invite questions, if you know what I mean.'

'Did he ever invite people back to his room, or to sit in the parlour?'

She thought for a moment, stirring sugar into her tea. 'I don't recall anyone in particular. Certainly no women. It's a house rule, but you'd be surprised how many of my gentleman have tried to sneak someone past my door.'

'Had he had any visitors in the last month or so?'

'Noooo. But there was an odd thing, though I thought nothing of it at the time. You never do, do you, until something happens and everyone's all over you with questions. Not that I mean to suggest—'

'No, not at all,' I said. 'What was the unusual thing?'

'It's probably nothing.' The landlady added another spoonful of sugar to her tea. 'It was just that he came home in his warder's uniform late one night. "That isn't like you," I said to him, as he went upstairs. And it wasn't. He always said that he spent enough time in the uniform, and he was glad to take it off at the end of his shift. He didn't want people to know he worked at the prison. I think he was worried one of the former inmates might recognise him and come after him.'

'Did Mr Palmer say why he hadn't got changed?'

'Not really. He raised a hand and said "I'm tired." And sometimes he *was* tired when he got back, especially if the prisoners had been naughty—'

'Right!' Dr Meredith came in, followed by the others, and sat down heavily opposite me. They had pulled down their handkerchiefs, which remained tied around their necks. 'It appears to be a clear case of suicide by hanging. A length of rope round the hook, a chair kicked away, and a note in his hand saying "I AM SORRY". And as far as anyone can tell, given the state of him, the man hanging upstairs is Thomas Palmer.' The doctor thrust a reeking paper under the nose of the landlady, who recoiled. 'Is that his writing?'

She uncovered her face and peered at it. 'I couldn't say, I'm sure,' she said, finally. 'I mean, that's printing.'

'Could I see?' The doctor shrugged and held it out to me. The cheap white paper and block letters looked horribly familiar.

'Sherlock…' His eyes met mine, and he nodded. I turned to the landlady. 'Mrs Harmsworth, can you recall which evening it was that you saw Mr Palmer going upstairs in his uniform?'

'Well!' She puffed out her cheeks with the effort of recall. 'It can't have been Monday, because I went to bed early myself, and I was writing letters in my room almost all Tuesday evening. And it was definitely more than two days ago, so…'

'Remind me on which morning Emmett Stanley's cell was found empty?' said Sherlock quietly.

'The sixteenth,' said Lawrence and the inspector, in unison.

'When you saw Mr Palmer that day, Mrs Harmsworth,' I asked, 'did he turn round when he spoke to you?'

Her eyes widened. 'Why, no. Like I said, he raised a hand, said he was tired, and carried on up the stairs.'

'I am sorry, Dr Meredith,' Sherlock said, twitching the note from his hand. 'I do not think this is a clear case of suicide. I believe it is murder. The man who assisted in the abduction of Emmett Stanley then went on to murder Thomas Palmer. Once he was in Stanley's cell, he stripped off his prison garb to reveal a warder's suit. He then let himself out, made his escape from the prison, and walked to Palmer's rooms. We shall need to check if Palmer was working, and if so which shift; but the man you saw, Mrs Harmsworth, was almost certainly the murderer.'

'Yes!' I interrupted. 'Mrs Harmsworth said that Mr Palmer never wore his uniform home. Mr Palmer bore a reasonable likeness to Emmett Stanley – and, logically, so did the murderer. The uniform would be enough to convince a casual viewer that he was Palmer.'

'Oh my!' Mrs Harmsworth clutched at her heart. 'I have had a murderer in my house!'

'I am afraid it looks like it, Mrs Harmsworth,' said the inspector. 'We shall be conducting further investigations, of course, and I have to warn you that—'

'But why would anyone kill Mr Palmer?' she cried. 'He wouldn't hurt a fly!'

'Perhaps that was why,' said Sherlock. 'He was in the right place at the right time, and they thought they could pin the abduction on him.'

'They?' Inspector Gregson wheeled round.

'Haven't you smelt this note, Inspector?' Sherlock held it out to him. 'The cheap white paper, the printed capitals, and, under the stench of a dead body, the scent of jasmine.'

CHAPTER 21

'Can you at least open the window to air the room?' Mrs Harmsworth called through the door.

'We are quite busy at the moment,' Sherlock shouted back.

Mrs Harmsworth wrung her hands. 'I shall never get the room right again!'

I touched her arm and she jumped. 'We should go downstairs. They could take hours.' She allowed me to lead her away, and for the next hour I listened to her complaints about the many lodgers who had damaged her furniture, run off without paying, or committed numerous other crimes. Every so often we would hear movement in the otherwise silent house; once there was a ghastly *thud*.

'What was that?' whispered Mrs Harmsworth, her eyes raised to the ceiling.

'I think they have cut him down,' I said.

Shortly afterwards footsteps came down the stairs and the front door closed. Mrs Harmsworth got up and peeped through the curtains. 'The young man is leaving!'

'Perhaps he has to get back to work. Or maybe he is taking a message to the prison governor.'

'Mm.' She did not seem satisfied with this explanation.

Shortly afterwards there was a rap at the door, immediately followed by Sherlock. 'Is there somewhere I can wash my hands, please?'

'The kitchen and scullery are at the back of the house,' Mrs Harmsworth said, faintly.

'Thank you.' He disappeared, returning a few minutes later and taking the nearest chair. 'I need a break. God, it's disgusting.'

Mrs Harmsworth yelped, and I shot Sherlock a warning glance.

'I'm sorry,' he said. 'Mrs Harmsworth, Lawrence has gone to wire Scotland Yard, to get a doctor sent out. They will take the body. We are almost finished in the room, and then you can have it back. I apologise for the inconvenience, but it is procedure.'

'That's quite all right, sir,' she hiccuped. 'If you don't mind, sir, I have rooms to dust.' She stumbled from the parlour, muttering to herself.

'Have you found anything?' I asked.

'Not much. We've gone through his things and all is as you would expect; a book or two, a jar of coins, a bundle of letters from his mother and sister, a Sunday suit... A small, cramped life.'

'Do you have any idea how it was done?'

'Nothing definitive. I suspect an injection of some kind, perhaps a tranquilliser or a muscle relaxant. A struggle would have been heard. When the doctor comes from the Yard I shall suggest an analysis of Palmer's blood, to detect any undispersed drugs. Given that it has been a few days, though, that is a very long shot. They might not be able to squeeze a drop out of him. I could be entirely wrong; and yet, if I am right…'

'What, Sherlock?'

'If I am right,' he said, slowly, 'the probability is that Thomas Palmer was killed by someone who knew him. The killer could not assume that Palmer would be in bed asleep, with the door unlocked. Therefore he must have been someone Palmer would admit to his room on sight, even at a late hour.'

I moved closer. 'Have you shared this theory with the inspector?' I whispered.

'I have not. We can get no further until the body has been examined and the analysis is complete. Besides—' he leaned across and whispered in my ear, 'I have a suspect in mind.'

I cupped my hand round Sherlock's ear, and whispered a name, and he nodded. 'Say nothing, for there is not a shred of proof. We shall let him continue, perhaps with observation from an Irregular, and hope that he makes a slip. An accusation now would make me a laughing-stock.'

A sudden bang at the door startled us both. Mrs Harmsworth scurried down the hall, and a loud voice barked 'Where's the inspector?'

I followed Sherlock from the drawing room. Standing in the hall was a well-dressed man with a military bearing, holding a doctor's bag. 'Ah, Mr Holmes.' The man offered a hand.

'Dr Carter,' said Sherlock, stepping forward. 'How did you get here so quickly?'

'Luck, boy, luck. I was due at the Wandsworth and Clapham this morning, and Scotland Yard, knowing I had an appointment there, re-sent the wire over to me. Wonderful stuff, technology.' The doctor rubbed his hands. 'Now, where will I find the body?'

'It's on the second floor; I'll take you up. I fancy there might be a toxicology report in it, too.'

'Excellent, I'll go and get a receptacle. For our patient, I mean,' he said, seeing my eyes stray to his leather Gladstone. 'I shall need a hand down the stairs, too.'

A few minutes later, after much stamping, banging, and shouted direction, a canvas bundle proceeded down the stairs, with Sherlock at one end and Inspector Gregson at the other. It seemed far too small to contain a man. 'That's it,' called Dr Carter. 'Jolly good. The carriage is outside. Mind the step.' He watched the inspector struggle to open the carriage door and retain hold of his burden. 'Between you and me, my dear,' he said behind his hand, 'it wouldn't matter if he did drop him. The body's already decomposing.'

Inspector Gregson slammed the door of the carriage. 'We're about done here,' he said. 'Mrs Harmsworth, I'm afraid that one of your sheets is in with him. Five shillings should cover it.' He fumbled in his pocket and poured a small heap of change into the landlady's hand.

Mrs Harmsworth looked outraged. 'That was one of my best sheets!'

'Madam, if that was one of your best sheets I would hate to see what your less-favoured guests are sleeping on,' chuckled the doctor. 'I'll pass on any news as soon as I can, but you'll need to sleep on it. These things take time.' He tipped his hat to the scowling landlady, and walked to the waiting carriage.

'Could I see the room, do you think?' I asked the inspector.

'Not much to see, Mrs Hudson, but of course you can.' I followed the inspector back into the house and up the stairs. 'Cover your nose and mouth,' he cautioned before opening the door. 'We've opened the window, but it's still pretty bad.'

Inspector Gregson did not exaggerate. The room was a hell-hole. The shafts of light which managed to pierce the grimy window illuminated a space both bare and cramped. An iron bed, a tallboy, a small table and chair, and a threadbare rug at the bedside. The half-filled drawers of the tallboy stood open, and a couple of cheap novels stood on top. But my eyes kept avoiding, and then returning to the scrap of rope dangling from a hook in the ceiling.

'We've got his letters, just in case there's anything to them, but I doubt there will be.' The inspector shook his head sadly. 'A bad business. Not even a shirt-button or a fingernail paring for a clue.'

'Do you see anything more here, Sherlock?' I asked.

'I wish I did,' said Sherlock slowly. 'I am trying to visualise how the scene played out, and it is difficult. But I do not think we need to be in this room any longer.'

Mrs Harmsworth clearly agreed, for she was hovering

outside the door, peeping in every so often, and muttering to herself. 'Could one of you gentleman take off that piece of rope?' she asked.

Sherlock reached up, but even with his height and long arms, his fingers could only just touch the hook. He stood on tiptoe and worked the rope off, then stood turning it over in his hands. 'This could have come from any hardware shop or chandler's.'

The inspector tutted. 'Come on, we are wasting time.' He led the way downstairs. 'Thank you, Mrs Harmsworth, for bearing with us.'

'That's all right,' she said, abstractedly. 'I daresay you gentlemen can see yourselves out.'

'Of course,' said the inspector, raising his eyebrows. 'Good day to you, madam.' As we walked to the door, the landlady went into the parlour.

I looked back when we had crossed the road. The net curtain at the ground-floor window twitched into place, and I noticed that the front part of the hand-lettered sign, which had previously said '*No* Vacancies', had been removed. I imagined the clank of the bucket, the slop of the mop, and the removal of Thomas Palmer's few worldly effects to await a claimant, as Mrs Harmsworth made the second-floor back ready to welcome another paying guest.

CHAPTER 22

'You've got an idea, haven't you,' Inspector Gregson said as we walked back to Wandsworth Prison. He framed it as a statement, not a question.

'I have,' said Sherlock. 'But no proof, yet.'

'And I don't suppose you'll let me in on it till you have.' The inspector shook his head in the manner of an uncle over his favourite wayward nephew.

'I'd like to see the staff roll.' Sherlock remarked, and said no more until the building loomed before us.

This time Mr Lawrence came to collect us from the gatehouse. 'I do apologise for leaving you alone back there,' he said, hurrying us along. 'The guvnor was keen to know what had happened, and then there were orders to be signed, and the wage bill to pay—'

'Ah, how fortunate,' said Sherlock. 'I need to see a list of everyone employed in the prison, and the pay-bill would serve admirably.'

Mr Lawrence stopped, an expression of gentle

puzzlement on his face. 'The pay-bill, sir?'

'It gives the most accurate indication of who is currently working here, and you obviously have it to hand,' Sherlock said smoothly.

'Of course,' said Mr Lawrence, his brow clearing. 'It is rather irregular, though.'

'You see,' Sherlock lowered his voice conspiratorially, 'I wonder if one of the *other* staff might be involved. Someone in the kitchen, or the stores. Perhaps we made a mistake in focusing solely on the warders. Is there anyone that you would have in mind, Mr Lawrence?'

'Ah, I see what you mean,' said Mr Lawrence, nodding sagely. 'Now that I think of it, there are a couple of men in the kitchens who, shall we say, have experience on the *other side...*' He tapped his nose. 'I can let you have their names, and I daresay a glance at the pay-bill, for thoroughness, will not be out of the question.'

Mr Lawrence instructed us to wait when we arrived at the well-appointed area outside the governor's office. He hurried to the door, tapped a little pattern, waited a second, and we heard Mr Jonas's voice, with a smile in it, say 'Come!'

He came out a few minutes later, beaming, and opened a small, plain door which I had not noticed before, painted to match the wall. 'This is my domain.'

Mr Lawrence's office was small but comfortable, with a leather-topped desk, a padded chair, and rows of filing cabinets. It was decorated with a selection of watercolours. 'The Lake District?' queried Sherlock.

'That's right,' said Mr Lawrence. 'We spent our

summers up there, and my sisters are addicted to painting.'

'Ah, are you one of the Cumbria Lawrences, then, near Penrith?'

'We are!' beamed Mr Lawrence. The inspector and I stepped back and exchanged glances as Mr Lawrence and Sherlock talked of fell-climbing and the ascent of something called Scafell Pike, which sounded both difficult and dangerous, but which apparently both men had accomplished.

'I suppose we had better get to the pay-bill,' Sherlock said regretfully.

'Indeed we should.' Mr Lawrence chuckled. 'I shall let you read it first, and then I will show you the men I have my suspicions about.'

Inspector Gregson stepped forward. 'Might I see the list too?' I wished he could have managed to make his voice a little less plaintive.

'Of course you can, Inspector!' Mr Lawrence said brightly, as if granting a special indulgence. He pulled a ledger from the top drawer of his desk and riffled through the pages of beautiful copperplate. 'Here we are!'

There did not seem much point in joining the party. Three heads were already bent over the ledger, and there was no room for me. I walked to the wall and examined the watercolours instead. 'View over Buttermere, June 1879', 'Wrynose Pass, August 1880.' These were signed *TL*, in black ink with a fine flourish. I was no judge, but to my eye they looked accomplished. What must it be like to have a summer home to go to, and to have accomplishments? I wondered whether TL was married now, perhaps with

151

children, and whether she had the time and inclination to wander off and paint landscapes. I grew meaner and more tawdry to myself as I gazed at the expansive, generous landscapes that TL had painted. *If you and Sherlock do marry,* said that small, mean voice, *will he suggest a honeymoon scrambling over rocks and gazing at scenery?*

I shook my head impatiently to get rid of it, and listened instead to Mr Lawrence. 'These are the two I had in mind – here.'

'Ah,' said Sherlock. 'What makes you suspect them?'

'There is a certain amount of history…' Mr Lawrence's voice dropped, as if the words were unfit for my ears. After a few seconds, both Sherlock and the inspector laughed. I felt my face growing warm, and wished I were anywhere but here – patrolling the department store, or gossiping with Lottie, or even planning menus at Baker Street. I heard pages turning behind me. I walked further away, and studied 'Coniston Old Man,' this time by *AL.*

'Something puzzles me,' said Sherlock. 'In fact, it seems positively criminal.' His voice was light, playful. I tried to relax my shoulders, to seem as if everything was normal; but my ears were straining. 'Lawrence, your salary is positively negligible! What are you thinking of, old man!'

Lawrence's answering laugh was full-bodied, unrestrained. 'Holmes, you forget that I am a stripling learning my trade. I have been in my current post less than a year, and I am scarcely twenty-two years old.'

'Perhaps,' Sherlock's voice was considering, elder-brotherly. 'But a Cambridge man, surviving on such meagre wages? How on earth do you do it?'

'Oh, it is not as bad as all that,' Mr Lawrence purred. 'I have an allowance, you know, and that sees me through. But between you and me, I am looking about for a private secretary post.'

'Of course you are!' I heard a *thump* which could only be a clap on the back. 'I would expect nothing less from a man such as yourself! Now, show me those two rogues again and I'll take their names down. I feel another round of interviews coming on.'

'Might I sit in?' Mr Lawrence's voice was eager.

'Nothing easier!' Sherlock exclaimed. 'I have more than one case on the go, though, so I can't say when it will be. I should be somewhere else this very minute, really.'

'The detective in demand,' smiled Mr Lawrence. 'I must ask you – how did you know I was a Cambridge man?'

'Oh, that was simple,' Sherlock said airily. 'It's the set of your pocket-handkerchief. I'd know it anywhere.'

'Oh, are you Cambridge too?' Mr Lawrence sounded genuinely delighted.

'Peterhouse,' said Sherlock, carelessly. 'I left before the Tripos nonsense, though. Waste of time, in my opinion.'

'Mmm.' Mr Lawrence nodded agreement.

'I suppose you took yours?' Sherlock inquired, solicitously.

'Lower Second,' admitted Mr Lawrence.

'Capital!' exclaimed Sherlock. 'A fine mind, but not a slave to work. The best degree there is. I take it you didn't work?' he muttered confidentially.

'Oh good Lord, no,' Mr Lawrence assured his new friend.

'Thank heaven for that,' said Sherlock grandly. 'Here's my card. Look me up at my rooms if you're ever in the area.'

'I shall,' said Mr Lawrence, putting it in the inside pocket of his jacket. 'Thank you, Holmes. I would return the favour, but my own rooms are not in an area or a state where I can encourage visitors.'

'I quite understand,' said Sherlock, inclining his head gravely. 'We've all been there.'

I waited until we had bade Inspector Gregson farewell and hailed a cab before speaking further. 'Was all that peacocking really necessary?'

He chuckled. 'I think so. I am sorry that you and the inspector had to endure it, but I was testing young Lawrence. He is susceptible to flattery, impressed by status and wealth, and I suspect he has been placed as the governor's secretary with the promise of much more to come. I imagine he saw the abduction of Emmett Stanley, followed by the murder and framing of Thomas Palmer, as little more than an elaborate initiation ritual. A way, heaven help us, to prove that he has the "guts" for further responsibilities.'

I shuddered. 'All right. What happens next?'

'Lawrence will set all manner of red herrings before me. Perhaps I shall let the inspector have them. Meanwhile, I shall put a watch on his rooms.'

'But you don't know—'

'Oh, I do.' Sherlock pulled out a small black notebook

and wrote rapidly. *Third Floor, Laurel Mansions, Water Street, Wandsworth*. 'All the addresses were on the pay-bill. I shall also be making inquiries about his time at Cambridge, and his acquaintance there.'

'Sherlock . . . did you really know Lawrence was a Cambridge man because of his pocket-handkerchief?'

'Oh, that!' he grinned. 'An abominable piece of showmanship, I am afraid. No, the pale blue pennant on the wall was the giveaway, but no-one would have been impressed with that. I want Lawrence to feel he is in safe hands – protected even, until the moment comes.'

'Did you really leave Cambridge before taking your exams?'

Sherlock snorted. 'I was never there.' He drew the blind up and gazed out of the window, and was quickly lost in thought.

I had plenty to think over, too. Sherlock's easy assumption of the privileged 'old boy' manner had shaken me. What on earth would his family think of me; a girl from Clerkenwell, a policeman's wife, a former school-teacher? I recalled what Sherlock had said of their treatment of him and Mycroft. Perhaps if Mycroft were the favoured one, Sherlock's choice of wife would not matter; but what if it did? On impulse I took off my glove and reached for Sherlock's hand.

He turned back to me, smiling. 'I was in a world of my own, Nell.'

'What were you thinking?'

His smile broadened. 'I was considering the various drugs which Lawrence might have used to paralyse

155

Thomas Palmer.'

I smiled back. 'Of course you were.'

'I shall have to wait for Carter's report, of course, but I have three substances in mind, all of which are controlled and difficult to obtain. A possible route to the centre of the spider's web.' Sherlock squeezed my hand, enveloping it in his long, slim fingers.

It was already mid-afternoon when we arrived back at Baker Street, and the day was beginning to fade. *Another day lost at the shop*, I thought, wondering if I should ever get back there.

The door opened almost before the cab had stopped. 'There you are!' Billy exclaimed. 'I've a telegram for you, the boy said it was urgent.'

'An urgent telegram, eh?' said Sherlock, jumping down. 'I'd better see it then.'

'Oh no, sir, it isn't for you,' said Billy, looking a trifle embarrassed. 'It's for Mrs Hudson.'

CHAPTER 23

Please visit me S House Attic 4 this pm STOP Opportunity STOP Tell no one P

I crumpled the telegram in my hand. 'I need to collect something, and then I shall go out again. Billy, could you possibly make me a sandwich?'

'Of course, ma'am.' Billy vanished into the house.

'What is it?' Sherlock looked half-amused, half-concerned.

'I'll tell you later, if I can.' I went into the house and ran upstairs. Where had I last seen the key to Attic Four? It was not in the consulting-room bureau, where I had expected to find it, but lying in the small glass tray on the dressing table, mixed up with stray cufflinks, ticket stubs, and other odds and ends.

Billy knocked. 'Your sandwich, ma'am.'

'Thank you, Billy.' I ate half the sandwich in a few bites, then took the other half downstairs with me.

Sherlock was in the hall. 'I kept the cab for you,' he said, his expression neutral.

'Thank you.' I stood on tiptoe to kiss him.

'Good luck. Whatever it is.'

I opened the door as Sherlock went through to the drawing room. I knew he would watch me go.

'Charing Cross Station, please,' I said to the cab driver. Somerset House was a short walk, and anyone overhearing my destination could make little of it.

I spent the journey in puzzled speculation. *What does Mr Poskitt want with me? And what is so secret that I can confide in nobody?* By the time the cab drew up outside the station I was no wiser.

'Pleasure trip is it, ma'am?' the cabman said as I paid my fare.

'That's right,' I smiled. 'Just a short one.'

'Hope you enjoy it.' He touched his hat. I walked into the station, out of a different exit, and cut down Craven Street to the Embankment. As I strolled along I felt the little key in my palm.

The Embankment was quiet at this time of day, but I looked around before slipping into the shadows. The key turned easily and I whisked in, closing and re-locking the door. A short corridor separated me from the main hall, and it was empty.

I knew the way to Attic 4 from the back stairs; but I did not know how to get to the back stairs save by walking through the main hall. Would I be stopped, and asked for identification? I put my eye to the keyhole and peered. Men and women were criss-crossing the hall, some

158

carrying documents, all with a sense of purpose. I was plainly dressed, in a style similar to the women I was observing, except that they were bareheaded. I would have to take the risk, and if I were stopped, rely on Mr Poskitt to get me out of trouble. I removed my hat and shawl and stuffed them into my bag, took a deep breath, and opened the door.

I was in luck. Near the door was an alcove, in which stood a trolley full of post. I flicked through the items and pulled out a large buff envelope addressed to *Miss C Jamieson, Room 209A*. Clutching it to my chest, I hurried across the great hall, looking neither left nor right. No footsteps followed me. No outcry was made. I gained the corridor which I knew led to the back stairs, and turned left. Only when I was safely on the back stairs did I allow myself a sigh of relief.

Up I went, flight after flight, to the top of the building, to an uncarpeted, unlit, narrow corridor. It was so dark that when I came to Attic Four I felt the number on the door to check the scanty evidence my eyes presented me with.

Satisfied I was in the right place, my hand found the doorknob, but I hesitated. Could it be a trap? I cursed my lack of forethought. Sherlock would have considered the possibility immediately. Then I heard the funny, nervous little sound of Mr Poskitt clearing his throat. I would have known it anywhere. I smiled at my doubts, and opened the door.

Mr Poskitt rose as soon as the door opened. He had been perched on an upturned box. Another box was set opposite, with a cushion for me. 'You came!' he cried.

'Didn't you think I would?' I answered. We shook hands and I took my seat on the box.

'And no-one knows you're here?' he asked, his eyes darting to the door. He got up suddenly and locked it, leaving the key in the lock.

'I have told no-one, and no-one has seen the telegram. I have it with me. I took a cab to Charing Cross Station, cut through, and walked here. I was not followed.'

'Good, good. Well, I suppose I had better get on to the reason for my invitation. Although now that you are here, I am worried that you will think me impertinent, and it is not meant in that way—'

'Mr Poskitt, please . . . do tell me why you wanted to see me.'

He sighed. 'Or even, perhaps, downright rude...'

'Mr Poskitt, I promise I won't, if you will tell me the reason for your summons!'

'Sir William Chambers' parlourmaid has given notice,' said Mr Poskitt, his eyes on me.

'Excuse me?'

'The Secretary for War needs a new parlourmaid,' Mr Poskitt said patiently, 'and you are the only person I can think of.'

'*What?*' I stared at him.

'I know it is rather a tall order,' said Mr Poskitt. 'For security reasons, senior Whitehall staff use an approved agency for their domestics, and Lady Chambers is coming up to town tomorrow to interview a selection of parlourmaids. So we don't have long.'

My head was in a whirl. 'Mr Poskitt, let me get this

straight. You are asking me to go undercover as a maid in a Cabinet minister's house?'

'That's exactly it,' beamed Mr Poskitt. 'We have to find the source of this leak somehow, and there will be no better opportunity to get a spy – for want of a better word – into Sir William's private residence.'

'How long would this – engagement – last?'

Mr Poskitt sucked in air as he considered. 'It's hard to say, Mrs Hudson. I mean, it could be weeks, or...' He caught sight of my expression. 'Of course you could give notice at any time you wished. And the remuneration would be handsome.'

'How handsome?' I asked, suspiciously.

'Well, there is no-one else I could possibly ask, so... A pound a day, with bonuses for any information you manage to secure?'

I was brought up short. Seven pounds a week was a ridiculously high wage; more money than I had ever dreamed of making. 'If you had mentioned that part first, Mr Poskitt...' I smiled. 'I am inclined to accept your offer.' I imagined Sherlock's face when I told him. He would help me get ready, pack my box, kiss me goodbye...

'Excellent! There is just one more thing. No-one must know where you are or what you are doing, save me.' Mr Poskitt's face was suddenly grave. 'If young Mr Holmes knows, he will almost certainly try to communicate with you; and as Mr Holmes's brother, that is very dangerous indeed.'

'I understand,' I said; but my head was spinning.

'So you will do it?' The relief on Mr Poskitt's face was

tremendous.

'I – I need time to think,' I stammered. Mr Poskitt sat composedly on his box.

My emotions were fighting each other.

I will have my own undercover assignment . . . but what about Sherlock?

Sherlock is busy, and happy, and engaged in a case. A case where my skills are incidental.

I thought of the times when the inspector had patronised me; when I had been pulled from my job at the store to be Sherlock's assistant; when I had had to argue with Mr Turner for my eight shillings a week...

Dr Watson will look after him while I am away. As much as anyone can.

'It will be a hard, menial job,' said Mr Poskitt, warningly, 'and of course there is no promise of success. There may be nothing to find.'

But it will be a case, and a job, of my own. No-one will be able to take it from me.

'I shall do it,' I said.

'Wonderful.' Mr Poskitt gripped my hand in both of his. 'You will need to be at the Regent Hotel in Mayfair by noon tomorrow, dressed appropriately. Miss Dainton, my contact at the agency, tells me that Lady Chambers prefers plainly-dressed maids. All Miss Dainton will know about you is that I have my own reasons for recommending you for the post.' He squeezed my hand. 'I can't tell you how grateful I am that you have agreed.'

'I may not be chosen,' I reminded him gently.

'Miss Dainton will make sure that you are,' said Mr

Poskitt. 'Sir William takes *The Times*. Watch the personals column; any messages from *Mercury* will be for you. If you have anything for me, put it in a letter to this address, and sign it *Mercury*.' He scribbled in a leaf in his pocket-notebook, tore it out, and handed it to me. *Mr T.L. Jones, c/o Westminster Post Office, to be left till called for*, I read.

He stood. 'I had better return to my office.'

I stood too. 'I had better go and make ready.' The enormity of it all had still not sunk in. I was to leave everything familiar, everything known, to be a servant. Not just a servant; a spy. 'Goodbye, Mr Poskitt.'

'Goodbye, Mrs Hudson, I hope to see you again soon.' Mr Poskitt smiled warmly at me as he let himself out; and he was gone.

I gave him two minutes' grace, then retraced my steps down the stairs, across the hall, and out of the little door, depositing poor Miss Jamieson's undelivered envelope back into the trolley. I put several yards' distance between myself and Somerset House before daring to slow my pace. Then I returned to Charing Cross, cut through the station, and got a cab from the rank. My head buzzed with things to do all the way home; but underneath a little voice whispered *How will you leave Sherlock?*, and another murmured *A case of your own...*

CHAPTER 24

Billy was loitering in the hall when I arrived home. 'Did it go well, ma'am?' he asked, eagerly.

'It's hard to say.' I glanced up the stairs. Would Sherlock expect information?

'Mr Holmes has gone out, ma'am. He said he was off to see Wiggins. He'll be back for dinner, though.'

'I am sure he will.' I took off my hat and shawl and went upstairs. I had my own research to do. I found the battered, worn copy of Mrs Beeton's *Household Management* stuffed into the bookcase, and began to read. *Duties of the butler . . . duties of the lady's maid . . . duties of the housemaid . . .* it all blurred into one. I tried to recall the parlourmaids I had seen when accompanying Sherlock on a case. A black dress, a white apron and cap, quick and deft in movement, never looking directly at you. And so silent you forgot they were there. I sighed. Well, I could be silent, certainly for a pound a day.

I slipped the book back and went to the dressing-room.

I was not sure why, but I had never thrown away my mourning outfit. It was all neatly folded in drawers. I had had a niggling feeling that perhaps it might be useful one day. However, today was not that day. The black dresses were too stiff, too fine for a maid. What else did parlourmaids wear? I longed to ring and ask Martha, but I might as well take out an advertisement for my intentions…

Evie! I grinned as inspiration struck me. Evie, with her obsessive interest in clothes, would know what parlourmaids wore. She might have friends in service. I would go to the department store early tomorrow, hand my notice in to Mr Turner, and spend some time with Evie. Perhaps I could even take her shopping…

My pleasant reverie was interrupted by the bang of the front door. Dr Watson never banged the door. I opened the wardrobe and took out my dark purple silk. Tonight I would dress for dinner, since it might be the last time I would be able to do so for weeks.

Sherlock's light footsteps ran upstairs. 'Nell! Where are you?'

'In the bedroom,' I called, unhooking my dress. 'But I am not fit to be seen.'

'Even better.' Within seconds he was grinning at me in the connecting doorway. 'What, do we have company?'

'No.' I smiled. 'I just felt like dressing up, for once.'

'Then I shall match you.' He shrugged off his jacket and waistcoat, undid his tie, and began to unbutton his shirt. 'Watson will wonder what on earth is going on.' He pulled the shirt over his head. 'So, do you have anything to

165

tell me?'

I smoothed my skirts into place before I answered. 'I'm afraid not. It was a summons from a friend which turned out to be no more than a gossip session.'

'Ah.' I watched him reach into the wardrobe for a fresh shirt: a dress shirt. 'These cloak-and-dagger affairs often fizzle into nothing. It's always the unpromising ones which yield gold. Now, where are my studs?'

'Dressing-table tray, where you left them last.' I had already replaced the key, mixing it back into the jumble. Sherlock swirled a finger through the mass, picking out his collar studs. 'Did you get hold of Wiggins?'

'I did. He'll shadow Lawrence for me at the usual rate, but I shall be taking a hand myself too. Lawrence is too valuable a fish to let go, and I suspect he will lead us to the source of the trouble.'

'I hope so.' I sat down at the dressing table and unpinned my hair. Then I took up my brush. *One . . . two...* I doubted I would have time to brush to a hundred every night in my new occupation.

'Are you all right, Nell?'

I froze. Sherlock was watching me in the mirror. 'Yes, of course. Why do you ask?'

'You're frowning.'

'Oh!' I stuck a smile on my face and continued to brush. 'I was thinking about the butcher's order.'

'Well stop it, or you will be late to dinner.' Sherlock removed his tail suit from the wardrobe. 'When I've dressed up for you, too.'

I began to coax my hair into a chignon. If I was going to

dress up, I might as well go all out. Evie would have done a much better job, but eventually the last pin was in, and my hair was up. I added a gold necklace and earrings, and reached for the perfume bottle.

'I'll do it.' Sherlock was behind me, fully dressed. He reached round me for the bottle, unstoppered it, and kissed my neck before stroking the cold glass on the place where he had kissed. 'You look good enough to eat.'

'I think you'll find dinner even nicer,' I replied. My pulse where he had kissed me beat hard and fast. *You are leaving all this...*

Sherlock grinned. 'Stand up, Nell. You can't wear those flat things on your feet, not in that dress.' He went through to the dressing-room, returning with a pair of high-heeled black satin evening slippers dangling from his fingers. 'Come, I shall be Prince Charming and see if they fit.'

I giggled as he knelt at my feet and slipped them on. 'You do realise that I can scarcely walk in these? I shall probably fall downstairs.'

'Then I shall catch you.' He offered his arm. 'Let us make our grand entrance.'

Martha hid a smile as we came downstairs at a stately pace befitting our attire. 'If I had known we were so grand I would have changed the menu. It's cottage pie and spotted dick.'

'Delightful,' Sherlock inclined his head, and we swept into the dining room.

'Ah, there you a—' Dr Watson began, before his mouth fell open and he fairly goggled at us. 'Is there something I should know?'

'Not at all.' Sherlock shook out his napkin and took his seat with a flourish. 'Just a fancy. How did you get on with Emmett Stanley today?'

'It was fascinating.' Dr Watson paused while Martha served us, and waited until the door had closed. 'I believe Emmett Stanley to be in a catatonic state. He is largely motionless, responding to few external stimuli.'

'Yes, but why?' Sherlock leaned forward.

'It is hard to say,' Dr Watson replied composedly, toying with his fork. 'I suspect it is a response to whatever ordeal he has endured. I obtained permission to examine him, and as far as I can tell, apart from the bruise on his head where he was knocked out, and the rope burns from his bindings, there is not a mark on him. You will have to bear in mind, though, that I could not make a full examination. His body is so stiff and twisted that I could not do more than unbutton his shirt and roll up his sleeves and trouser-legs.'

'But you don't think he's shamming?' asked Sherlock, his eyes gleaming.

'I do not.' Dr Watson said emphatically.

I ate my dinner in appropriately genteel small bites and listened to the two men talking shop. I wondered what Effie Stanley was doing at that moment. Perhaps she was dining in a great dining room; perhaps she was eating supper on a tray. But I felt sure that, wherever she was, the chatty, lively Effie I had known was all alone.

'Will he recover, do you think?' I asked.

Dr Watson looked at me with some surprise. 'We cannot say, at this early stage. There are treatments, but I would not risk any of them. Mr Stanley's health is too delicate. I believe it is a case of wait and see.'

After dinner I went to the drawing room and took up my book; but the exploits of Paula Power could not hold my attention. The servants were washing up downstairs, while from above came the animated hum of Sherlock and Dr Watson's voices in the consulting room. The dinner-time talk had shifted from Emmett Stanley to Thomas Palmer, and I suspected they were busy compiling a list of drugs. I sighed. Tomorrow evening, if all went to plan, I would not be here to listen.

CHAPTER 25

Sherlock murmured as I gently moved his arm. 'Whassa —'

'Ssh,' I whispered, kissing his shoulder. 'I am going to the bathroom.'

I could not see what time it was, but from the movements downstairs, and the grey light through the gap in the curtains, I suspected it must be around seven. So much to do; and I still was not sure how to tackle it. I locked the bathroom door, leaned my forehead on the cool white tiles, and thought. The store opened at nine o'clock; but the shopgirls would be there earlier, titivating themselves and their domains for the public. If I got there for eight o'clock I guessed I would be able to catch Evie.

I would need money for dresses and accessories. Some of my own, simpler, more worn items would do; but my hairbrush, an expensive one, could not come with me. I looked down at the ring on my finger. It was slim, and plain gold; but inside the band was engraved *Nell, from*

Sherlock. A pang shot through me at the thought of leaving it behind. I could not – the message it would send! Perhaps I could entrust it to Evie . . . but no, it was not fair to expect her to keep a secret like that. *I shall think about it later*. I turned the taps on to wash the problem away. *Goodbye, running hot water*. Back to carrying cans up and down stairs, I suspected, although hopefully as I would be a parlourmaid, that task would fall to someone else.

It's a good thing Mother doesn't know. She would laugh herself silly. Mother's opinion of my housekeeping skills was low at best. 'I pity the poor woman who has to depend on *your* service,' she would have said, an amused gleam in her eye. *I must write and tell her* – what? Perhaps that I was going away for a while and would not be able to write or visit. I could ask her to tell people I was visiting Clara, on the south coast – *no*. I did not want people to lie for me.

But I would write letters. Once my appointment was confirmed, I would write and post letters. That would take care of it all.

Sherlock was dressing when I returned to the bedroom. 'I want to return to Ealing and have a proper look at the garden,' he said, attaching his braces. 'Will you come, Nell?'

'I have a few domestic things to do,' I said.

'Oh, domestic things…' Sherlock sounded deflated. 'I wish you would leave that to the servants.'

'Someone has to run the place,' I said mildly, walking over to kiss him. 'Will you be out all day?'

'Probably. Tell Martha I shan't want lunch.' He kissed me on the mouth, a kiss without thought, and left the

171

room.

I touched where his lips had been. I wanted to remember it. I did not know how long it would have to last me. *If you only knew*, I whispered, and shook myself. Sentimentality would do no-one any good.

I chose a plain grey dress, one I would not be sorry to lose, and when I was ready went down to the kitchen. 'I shall be in trouble,' I said lightly, taking down the housekeeping jar and extracting a ten-shilling note. 'I have just remembered it is my mother's birthday.'

'Will you visit her today?' said Martha.

'I shall, and take a present – I do not know what, yet.' I took another note from the jar. 'Perhaps a poinsettia. She likes flowers.' I filched a piece of toast from the rack on the kitchen table.

'Aren't you having a proper breakfast, ma'am?'

'I don't think I have time,' I said. 'There is the present to buy, and the visit, and my library book is due, and I shall be at work later…' I bit into my toast and stood up. 'I shall take this up while I finish getting ready.'

Five minutes later I was hatted, shawled, and walking out of the front door. Fifteen minutes later still, having taken a roundabout route, I was in Wigmore Street.

The shopgirls would use the back entrance. I loitered in an alley nearby, checking my watch – another luxury I would have to surrender. The more I thought about what I planned to do, the more unwise it seemed.

At last I was rewarded by the sight of Evie, tall, slim and elegant, strolling down the alleyway whistling.

'I didn't think ladies did that sort of thing,' I grinned,

stepping out.

Evie clutched at her chest. 'Nell! I nearly had a fit!' She leaned against the wall, surveying me head to foot. 'What are you doing here at this hour?'

'Never mind that.' I beckoned her over. 'I need your help,' I whispered, 'and you mustn't tell a soul.'

Two minutes later Evie had secured Gladys, whispered a stream of words into her ear, and sent her in. 'She'll cover for me,' Evie said, winking. 'Come on, let's get a cab.' She led me down the alleyway and whistled for one. 'Petticoat Lane, please.'

Evie took the lead, pushing and shoving through a scrum of humanity to examine heaps of shabby dresses. 'I need to be presentable,' I said hastily. 'If plain.'

'Don't worry,' said Evie. 'Well-worn but respectable is what I'm thinking. My older sister's a lady's maid, you know. It wouldn't suit me, but it takes all sorts.'

A few minutes of snatching, comparing, and bargaining later, Evie had secured a black dress and a print one ('for day', she said), a flannel corset, a rusty black hat with a drooping artificial rose, and a straw hat with a blue ribbon ('summer wear on your days off').

'I don't plan on doing this next summer,' I said.

'It's as well to be prepared,' said Evie, picking up a pair of flat black boots. 'What do you think of these?'

I examined them. 'Won't they be too big for me?'

Evie looked down at my feet. 'Perhaps a bit, but you'll have thick wool stockings, remember. Anyway, my sister says that if there's one thing mistresses don't like, it's an attractive maid. Too much temptation for the men.'

173

I grimaced. 'I can see I'm going to enjoy myself.' I inspected a battered black suitcase.

Our purchases packed, we hailed another cab. 'I'd take you back to my house,' said Evie, 'but my mother's there, and she's nosy. I'll smuggle you into work, and you can sneak out the back way when we're finished.'

'You won't be able to do much anyway, Evie. I mean, I can't wear anything that could be discovered. No wigs, no rouge…'

Evie heaved a sigh. 'You do make life difficult, Nell.'

I tried not to tremble as Evie sat me down in the ladies' cloakroom. 'Don't do anything too terrible, will you?'

'Just keep still.'

I sighed, and submitted. Evie took the pins from my hair, considered, and set to work. I noted that she had placed my chair so that I could not see a mirror. I closed my eyes so that I could not see her; but I felt her put something on my hair, and comb it back. 'Pomade,' she said. 'I'll plait and coil it, so it's easy to keep neat.' She worked for a few minutes. 'There. What will you say when they ask you about yourself?'

I had been thinking this over. 'I'll tell them I worked as a maid till I got married; and then since my husband died I've been mending and taking in washing for a few years, but I've decided to go back into service.'

'That will cover any mistakes you make, but your hands will give you away.' Evie took my hand, then took her scissors and cut my nails down to the quick. 'Now, scrub your hands hard while I finish your hair.'

I took the wet nailbrush and did as I was told, until my

174

hands stung. Evie sorted through our purchases. 'Here, put this one on, with the stockings and boots.'

I went into a stall and did as I was told. I exchanged my corset for the flannel one, which did nothing for my figure, and put on the itchy woollen stockings. The dress was a reasonable fit, but too short in the arm, so that my wrists protruded, and my hands seemed redder than ever. The boots, as predicted, were a size too big, so that I clumped when I walked. My heart sank to the very bottom of them.

But Evie wasn't finished. 'Sit down and close your eyes.'

'Don't you think you've done enough?' I snapped. 'I'm pretty sure I won't pose a risk to any eligible men.'

'That's as may be,' said Evie, 'but I can still see it's you. I promise I won't take too much off.'

'Off what?'

'Just hold still.' Evie put her hand to my forehead, and I felt a little tweak at my eyebrow. 'It will grow back.' I didn't dare move after that, though I winced as each hair was pulled out.

'You can look now.' Evie's voice was flat. She laid a hand on my shoulder. 'I'm sorry, Nell. It's not the sort of help I would have liked to give, but I think you'll pass.'

I opened my eyes. My hands were sore and red, but they were still mine. I stood up, and caught a glimpse in the long glass—

I closed my eyes and opened them again. This, now, was me. A thick-waisted, big-footed woman, red hands dangling, hair scraped back from her small head. I was out of proportion. I put a hand to my hair, and felt grease.

175

I took a step towards the mirror, and another. Evie had plucked off the ends of my eyebrows, and changed their shape so that I wore a perpetual frown. I could see the lines of the comb in my greased-down hair, which appeared to be dark brown. The lack of sleep showed under my eyes, and unsurprisingly my cheeks had lost their colour. I would have put myself at about forty.

'I – I—'

'Don't say anything,' pleaded Evie.

I smiled at myself in the mirror, but it looked wrong. Even my smile wasn't my own any more.

'You've done an excellent job, Evie.' I tried to keep my voice steady. 'I had better go.' I reached for the rusty black hat and jammed it on my head.

'Please don't hate me—'

'You should probably go back to work,' I said. 'Gladys will be anxious for you. Remember, don't tell anyone what you have been doing.'

'I'll see you out first.' Evie swallowed.

I folded up my grey dress, my elegant boots, my little black hat, and packed them under the other things. 'I am ready,' I said, picking up my new case.

'You will come back and see me, won't you?' Evie looked distraught.

'Of course I shall,' I said.

Evie led me to a back door which led out onto a narrow alley piled with rubbish. 'Good luck, Nell,' she whispered. 'I'll be thinking of you.'

'Not a word to anyone,' I said, and walked away.

I avoided shop windows all the way to Paddington

station, where the clock said that it was almost ten-thirty. I took a ticket for the left-luggage office and deposited my suitcase. I would return for it later, and find somewhere to dump the clothes from my former life.

I bought myself a cup of tea and a bun at the station tearoom, dividing the bun into small pieces, as if to make it last. The real reason was that I was worried I would be sick. I had never thought of myself as a vain woman; but the strength of my reaction to the miserable specimen I now was frightened me. *This is temporary, Nell*, I told myself. In six months, it will be forgotten and everything will be back to normal.

I touched my eyebrow, felt the absence of hairs, and sighed.

I put another piece of dry bun into my mouth and chewed slowly. There was no point in feeling sorry for myself. I had to take this job. There was absolutely no way that I could return to Baker Street as I was. I had no fear now that anyone would recognise me. I barely recognised myself.

CHAPTER 26

The Regent Hotel was a grand, gilded establishment, tall and white as a wedding-cake. I would have been a little overawed by it in my own person. Dressed as I was, I was not even certain that they would admit me. The doorman, however, let me pass in. I wondered how many other aspiring parlourmaids he had waved through already that day.

I scanned the foyer for someone who might be Miss Dainton. An angular, long-necked woman was sitting at a table alone, with a sheet of paper in front of her. She was reading a novel. I began to walk towards her.

'Excuse me!' A man in striped trousers came hurrying over and I stopped, blushing. 'Do you have business here?'

I drew myself up as tall as I could in my flat boots. 'I have an appointment with a Miss Dainton.'

He subsided at once, like a pricked balloon. 'Oh very good, very good. Follow me.' He led me towards the long-necked woman. 'Miss Dainton, I have a charge for you.'

Miss Dainton looked up from her book, and her eyes flicked over me. 'Come and sit, dear,' she said, without a smile. I took a seat opposite her and folded my hands in my lap. 'That will be all, thank you,' she said to the hovering man.

'Excellent, excellent,' he said, and scurried back to his desk.

Miss Dainton watched him go, and then turned to me. 'Now then, am I to understand that you are Mr Poskitt's protégée?' She consulted her list. 'Mrs Martha Platt?'

I took in my new name, and nodded.

'I assume you have experience of waiting on, and working in a big house?'

I thought of the numerous meals I had cooked and served at Baker Street, the cans of hot water I had carried, the mantelpieces I had dusted. 'Yes, ma'am.'

'Good.' She appeared relieved. 'The last thing I wish is to recommend you and then find myself a laughing-stock. Some of Mr Poskitt's recommendations have not – worked out.'

'I will do my best, ma'am.'

'I am glad to hear it. This is a good place, if you can keep it.' Miss Dainton leaned forward and lowered her voice. 'The work is light, comparatively speaking, but the mistress of the house is inclined to be . . . difficult.'

'Difficult?'

'Perhaps exacting is a better word.' Miss Dainton sat back as if she had already said too much. 'Now, Lady Chambers is coming at half past twelve and we shall call you in at a quarter to one, so you are not required until

179

then.' I rose, dismissed.

I could think of nothing else to do but walk around the block. My left boot was rubbing at the back of my heel, and I stopped to tighten the lace. No doubt I would have a blister to add to my other woes by the end of the day. I wondered what questions I would be asked, and racked my brains to remember the passages of Mrs Beeton which seemed to have floated away. A carriage drew up outside the hotel. I wanted to approach, to see what Lady Chambers looked like, but I did not dare. I shrank back, and peeped round the corner at the well-veiled lady who emerged from the carriage, followed by a short, round woman in black not too dissimilar to my own.

At twenty minutes to one I re-entered the hotel, and this time the clerk did not scurry over. Within a few minutes Miss Dainton came through a door at the back of the foyer. 'This way, Martha,' she said encouragingly.

The room was bright after the discreetly-lit foyer, and it took my eyes a while to adjust. I blinked, and blinked again. Sitting at her ease, her veil put back, was the woman who had stolen a brooch from the department store. I would have known those half-closed eyes, that amused smile anywhere.

My first instinct was to say that I had made a mistake and flee. But there was no light of recognition in her eyes, no change of expression. *What did I wear that day?*

'This is Mrs, ah, Martha Platt,' said Miss Dainton, waving a hand in my direction. 'Martha, this is Lady Chambers and Mrs Harper, her cook-housekeeper. Don't be nervous, now.'

Remembering what ought to be my manners, I bobbed a little curtsey. 'Pleased to meet you.' My voice came out high and thin.

Lady Chambers whispered to Mrs Harper behind her glove. Then she surveyed me from head to foot, her lip curled slightly as if I smelt unpleasant. I could feel my cheeks reddening as I stood there. '*Do* sit down,' she said, eventually.

'Have you been a parlourmaid before, dear?' asked Mrs Harper, gently.

I nodded. 'Yes, I have, ma'am. I was a parlourmaid before I was married.' I touched the gold band on my finger.

'Has your husband passed, dear?' she asked in the same gentle voice.

I nodded again, and hung my head. 'Three years ag—'

'All right,' Lady Chambers interrupted. 'Does she have references?' she asked Miss Dainton.

'Of course!' Miss Dainton looked indignant. 'Excellent references, if I may say so.'

'Then I suppose we'll take her. Unless you have any better ones?'

Miss Dainton, grateful to have the ordeal over, shook her head.

'At least she doesn't appear pert. I can't stand a pert parlourmaid. Do you think you can make something of her, Cookie?'

'I am sure that she will do very well,' said Mrs Harper, smiling at me.

'I'm not,' said Lady Chambers. 'Still, we can always

181

send her back.' Her careless little smile made me want to slap her. 'So, Bessie, I assume you can start at once?'

'Our parlourmaid is always called Bessie,' Mrs Harper interjected.

'Yes, milady, I just need to pack my things.'

'Good.' She reached into her little bag and passed me a visiting card and a ten-shilling note. 'Take the five-thirty train to Maidenhead Junction this evening, and Tom will be waiting with the trap. You may have the time between now and then to pack and say your goodbyes.' Her expression suggested that she did not think it would take long. 'Miss Dainton, you can deal with the rest of it; I have shopping to do. Come along, Cookie.' She stood up and walked to the door.

Mrs Harper held out a hand to me. 'I shall see you later, Bessie.'

'Thank you, Mrs Harper.' I took her hand and bobbed again.

'Come *on,* Cookie.' Mrs Harper hurried after her mistress's departing back.

Miss Dainton watched them out before fanning herself with her list. 'That went better than it usually does.' She leaned back in her chair. 'Don't worry, milady's bark is worse than her bite. Twenty pounds a year, a day off *every* month, church time on Sundays, and you'll be found in caps and aprons.' Her tone was almost wheedling.

'That sounds very generous.' *A day off every month…* How would I survive?

'And Mrs Harper will look after you,' she added, smiling brightly.

'Miss Dainton, why did the last parlourmaid leave?'

Miss Dainton sighed. 'Milady found her pert, and – said some things which led her to give notice.' She stood up and held out a hand. 'Good luck, Martha.'

'Thank you, Miss Dainton.'

And so my new life was fairly begun. I spent the rest of the afternoon buying a few cheap necessities: a hairbrush, a small Bible, stockings and underthings. I also bought a brass ring, a small photograph of a middle-aged man in a pewter frame to serve as the departed Mr Platt, paper and envelopes, and a package of postage stamps. Then I collected my suitcase from the left-luggage office at Paddington, packed everything inside, and went to a cafe for a simple meal.

It did me no good, though; I pushed the food around my plate, barely able to swallow a mouthful. I had letters to write; but I could not face them yet. I was not sure that I could face this evening, and yet I had said that I would do it. I had said I would to Mr Poskitt, and now to Miss Dainton. No-one had forced me into the decision; and yet I felt as if I had been pushed into it. I knew, though, that I could not go home. What, oh what would Sherlock be thinking? He would think I was thoughtless – heartless – but I was afraid that he might track me down, even from a note, if I sent it too soon. Had it only been this morning that I had moved his sleepy arm from its casual ownership of me? I squeezed my eyelids shut; but it did not stop the tears from flowing.

CHAPTER 27

Dear Mama,

I am writing to let you know that I shall be away for some time – I do not know how long yet – and shall not be able to write or visit. Please do not worry; I am safe and well. If anyone enquires after me, please could you tell them I am very busy at present.

Yours with affection,
Nell

Dear Dr Watson,

I expect you have already noticed my absence from the house. I shall be away for some time, and unable to write or visit. I am safe and well, but engaged on business which I cannot discuss.

Please can you look after Sherlock while I am gone, and dissuade him from trying to find me, if he has a mind to. I shall return as soon as I can. In the meantime, I am sure that Martha and Billy will take care of you both as well as ever.

Yours sincerely,
Nell Hudson

Dearest Sherlock,

I am so sorry that I have not been able to write before now, and sorrier still that I cannot share with you anything of what I am engaged in. I have been called away suddenly, and I shall be unable to write or visit until my business is concluded. Do not try to find me; that will endanger the work I am doing.

I am safe and well, and send all my love to you. I shall return as soon as I can.

Please take care of the enclosed for me; I cannot wear it at present, but I shall return to claim it, rest assured.

I love you,
Nell

The last letter was the hardest to write, and I had spoiled many sheets of paper with blots and tears in the making of it; but it was done. I took off my ring, kissed it, and placed it in the envelope with the letter, sealing it before I could change my mind. The brass ring felt light and unreal in its place.

I had tied up in my shawl the belongings from my former life; my dress, and boots, and silk stockings – oh, how I ached to keep them. If I had thought, I could have posted them back to Baker Street; but I had neither time nor materials. I put the letters into my bag, and took up the bundle. A short walk brought me to a poor district, and it was the work of moments to leave the bundle next to a sleeping beggar-woman. *At least she might get some benefit from it*, I thought, hastening towards the station. Close by was a pillar-box, and as my letters hit the bottom, my stomach lurched.

I bought my ticket and went straight to the platform, though I had twenty minutes to wait. I wanted to be gone. Ridiculous as it was, now that I had posted the letters I imagined Sherlock and Dr Watson hurrying to find me, running along the platform, calling my name. My heart thumped, and I started at every shout, every whistle, as though I were a fugitive.

The train pulled in and I hurried on, packing myself away in a corner of third-class. It would not be a long journey – Maidenhead was only in Berkshire – but I braced myself for a stopping train, and for the curious looks of fellow-travellers getting on and off. I wished I had a magazine I could bury myself in; but it was too late.

I imagined my letters arriving at Baker Street; they would be there that evening, by which time I would be safely in Berkshire, closed into a private house, and engaged in my new life. I wondered what the men would say when my letters arrived. Then I realised that they might not even recognise the letters as coming from me until they opened them. I had never had to write either to Sherlock or to Dr Watson before.

The train jolted me out of my speculations as we moved out of the station, swaying and lurching first through high cuttings, then emerging into fields dotted with houses and cows and sheep. I had not bargained for how quiet the train would be, since most people had already left the capital. Sir William Chambers was probably among them. Would I see much of him? Was this whole enterprise worthless before it even began? *No*, I told myself. *Think of the guineas, Nell.* I comforted myself with dreams of the dresses I would buy, the fine stockings, the silk flowers, the hair tonics. I touched the front of my hair, which was stiff with pomade. Like a protective shell.

The train was bowling along now, pausing briefly at wayside stations, but hurrying to my destination. How many more stops? I was not sure. I felt a sharp tug of homesickness which I was quite unprepared for, as I had never considered I might have to leave London. *You are being ridiculous, Nell*, I told myself. *It is only a short train ride away.*

A village of white cottages whizzed past. *A world away.*

And suddenly the conductor called 'Maidenhead Junction, next stop.' I hurried to get my suitcase from the rack, almost falling over my own feet in their too-big shoes. I straightened my hat and composed myself as the train slowed. Then I opened the heavy door and got myself and my suitcase out onto the platform. I was the sole person leaving the train, and apart from the station official, the only person on the platform. Suddenly I felt very scared, and very alone. I was tempted to cross the platform and wait for the next train back.

'Miss!' The stationmaster strode towards me. 'Your ticket, please.'

'Oh. Oh yes.' I fumbled in my bag and brought out the

little half-torn slip. He glanced at it and waved me through the gate and out into the road. That was it. And I could not go back, for I did not have enough money for a ticket home.

'Hoy!' The call came from a smart little green-painted trap waiting opposite. The man in charge waved at me. He was perhaps thirty, wearing an open-necked shirt and breeches, and his livery coat was slung over the back of his seat. 'You for the hall?'

'Yes, I'm the new parlourmaid.' I held out a hand and he gripped it. His was hard, calloused, probably from years of holding reins.

'Bessie, yes?' I nodded, feeling that giving him my 'real' name was probably not worth the trouble. 'I'm Tom, and I look after the stables and carriages. Here, hold Blaze while I put up your case.' He jumped down and handed me the reins, which I took with trepidation. 'He won't bite!' He laughed, stroking Blaze's nose.

'I've never held a horse before,' I said, a little indignantly.

'I can tell.' Tom swung my case into the trap and took the reins back. 'Let's get going. Blaze and I have been hanging about for ages. Do you need a hand up?'

'I can manage,' I said, holding my skirt out of the way to get my foot to the step. Tom watched, grinning.

'You've never been in a trap before either, have you? London girl?'

'Through and through,' I panted, sitting down with gratitude.

'Make sure you hold on. It isn't far, but there's a few

188

potholes.' He clicked his tongue as the London cabbies did, and Blaze set off so rapidly that I grabbed the first thing that came to hand – the back of Tom's seat – closed my eyes, and clung on.

The trap swayed and lurched like a ship in a gale, not that I had ever been on one, but Tom continued to chat. I heard none of it, preoccupied as I was with keeping my seat. I was more glad than I could have imagined that I had not eaten before boarding the train, for I would surely have lost it.

'Here we are!' Tom sang out, and the trap turned through an imposing wrought-iron gate. I opened my eyes and braced myself, but as the drive curved round, I saw a square house of warm red brick, not unlike a smaller version of the Stanleys' mansion. 'Welcome to Chambers Hall. I say, Bessie, you look a bit green,' he chortled.

'I shall be all right when we stop,' I said. I tried to smile but it must have come out wrong, for Tom halted the trap with a jerk, jumped down, and handed me out.

'Walk with me to the stables,' he said, taking my arm. 'If you go in like that you'll probably be quarantined.'

I waited while Tom put the trap away, took Blaze out, and attended to his needs, bringing him a blanket and hay. The smell of stable and horse, even outside, was as strong as I could bear after that long ride. Tom gave Blaze a final pat. 'Ready to go and meet the team, Bessie?' He picked up my suitcase as though it were empty.

I took a deep breath and wished I hadn't. 'I think so.'

'Come along then. Hey, where are you going?'

I stopped, cursing myself. In my absent-mindedness I

had walked towards the front of the house. 'I just wanted to look,' I faltered.

'Feast your eyes,' laughed Tom. 'You'll see plenty of that door from the inside, for you'll be answering it. One foot on Ada's clean steps, though, and she'll have your guts for garters.' Still chuckling, he offered an arm. I took it, and Tom led me round to the back of the house. 'This is our door,' he said, opening a small wooden door, its black paint cracked and sun-weathered, with a pane of distorted glass set into the top half. Next to it was a bell-pull, and a neat brass plaque: *Tradesman's Entrance*. 'Go on, in you go.' He gave me a gentle nudge.

I stepped over the threshold. The corridor within was whitewashed, with a cheerful, threadbare runner covering the stone floor. Plain wooden doors led off, and I heard voices, and banging, from a room further down.

'Cookie's at work,' said Tom, jerking his head in the direction of the sounds. 'I'll hand you over to her, and she'll show you the ropes. Follow me.' And with every step I took my former life grew more remote. My mission, my life with Sherlock, London – everything I had done before peeled away, piece by piece. I was a servant now, forbidden the front door and the main stairs, at everyone's beck and call. And I was scared to death.

CHAPTER 28

'Cookie!' Tom bellowed, pushing open the kitchen door. 'The new parlourmaid's here!'

The noise was terrific. Pots bubbled on the stove, and I heard clattering from the scullery as the maid washed up. Mrs Harper – Cookie – was no longer a quiet woman in modest black, but a whirling, swooping figure in a striped cotton frock and a bright white apron, singing to herself as she banged and crashed around her empire.

'Cookie!' Tom walked round to face Cookie, who jumped back several feet.

'Oh, Tom, you did give me a fright! You're enough to turn the cream, you are.'

'Sorry, Cookie,' grinned Tom. 'I've brought Bessie for you.' He waved a hand in my direction, then went to the sideboard and carved a hunk of bread for himself. 'Any jam left?'

'You of all people ought to know where the jam is,' Cookie retorted, waving a spoon at him resignedly. 'Leave some for the house, if you don't mind. Now dear,' she said, wiping her hands on her apron. 'Just let me get these vegetables on and I'll give you the tour. The Cook's Tour, heehee!'

'You ought to be on the stage, Cookie,' Tom said, through a mouthful of bread and jam.

'And you ought to be in the circus,' Cookie said mildly. 'We're a friendly house, as you can see. You'll have to speak up to me, though, I'm a trifle deaf.' She slammed the pan down on the stove and marched into the scullery with me following at her heels. 'This is Janey, our scullery maid.' Janey started guiltily and took her hands out of the sink as if she had been caught in a crime. 'Janey, this is Bessie, the new parlourmaid.'

Janey dried her hands on her apron and gave a funny little bob. She looked about twelve, a scrawny girl with lank hair and limbs like a foal. 'Good evening, Bessie.' Her voice was surprisingly soft and sweet.

'Good evening, Janey.' Should I bob back, or curtsey, or shake hands? I nodded to her, and that seemed satisfactory.

'You two will need to cooperate over the use of the sink,' said Cookie. 'Janey washes up our crocks and my pots and pans, but the family china and plate and cutlery is your job. Breakfast, luncheon, dinner, supper, and afternoon tea if milady has a mind, and your polishing day is Tuesday. The family ware is in Mr Craddock's cupboard – Mr Craddock is the butler – and he is *very* particular about it. Any breakages come out of your wages.' Her voice was matter-of-fact. 'The coal store is outside, not that you'll need to know that.' She walked back into the kitchen. 'You'll be waiting on at family meals, including breakfast, doing the downstairs rooms, and answering the door, but otherwise you'll lend a hand in the kitchen. Janey does quite well, but she's young, and Ada is rushed off her feet as it is. Ada's the housemaid,' she said, in response to my look. 'Nanny's got her up and down the stairs constantly with this and that for the children.'

'Oh, are there children?' I exclaimed.

'Miss Millie is five and Master Toby is two,' said Cookie. 'You probably won't see them hardly, they spend all their time in the nursery. You might get a peep at them if they're on a walk, or being driven out.' Her face softened. 'I take it you don't...'

I shook my head. I had been pregnant, once, but had suffered a miscarriage.

'I'm so sorry, dear,' Cookie put a large, warm hand on my arm. 'I didn't mean—'

'No, no, it's quite all right,' I said, hastily. 'It was a long time ago.' It felt like another life, which, in a way, it was.

Cookie's eyes were full of sympathy, and I wondered for a moment where Mr Harper was – if there had ever been a Mr Harper – and whether she had had children of her own. 'Come along, dear, and I'll show you the rest of our quarters.' She opened the door at the far end of the kitchen, which led straight into a large room containing a huge, battered wooden table ringed with chairs, and a few old armchairs before the fire. 'This is the servants' hall, where we have meals and gather. It's directly under two of the reception rooms, though, so we can't be too noisy.'

As if on cue, an elderly man in striped trousers and a cutaway coat, who had been dozing in an armchair, stirred. 'Just a few – oh so sorry milady, so sorry –' he blustered, getting hurriedly to his feet and looking around him.

'It's all right, Mr Craddock, you can go back to sleep. I'm just showing our new Bessie round.'

'Parlourmaid, eh?' Mr Craddock peered at me. 'Are you a good girl, Bessie?'

I blushed. 'I hope I am, sir.'

'Good, good.' He subsided into his chair.

Beyond the servants' hall was a corridor. 'Mr Craddock's room,' said Cookie, jerking her thumb at a closed door. 'Make sure you give him plenty of time when you want anything out of his cupboard. He's a good man, but he takes an age. My room is next door. The boot room is the other side, next to the flower room.' She gestured to a door at the end. 'That's the way to the main house, only for use when summoned. Never mind seen but not heard; it's not seen *and* not heard in this house, unless you're doing your duty. The only exceptions are Nanny and Susan.'

'Who is Susan?'

'Milady's maid.' Cookie's tone had cooled considerably. 'Her territory is milady's boudoir, but milady summons her all over the house, if she has a mind. You'll meet her soon enough. Now—' She bent and peered through the keyhole. 'The family are upstairs. We'll chance it.' She quickly turned the key in the lock, and whisked through the door.

I found myself in a long hallway hung with family

portraits and rich with brocade. 'Lovely, isn't it?' said Cookie, gazing round. 'This is Sir William's family home.'

'How long have you worked here, Cookie?'

'Forever,' said Cookie. 'My mother and father were cook and butler, and I grew up in a cottage on the estate. I always dreamed I'd live here one day.' She smiled contentedly. 'Ada will oil the bolts on the front door for you once a week. It's a heavy old thing, but you'll master it, I'm sure.' Cookie's step had lightened perceptibly now that she was in the family's part of the house. 'So we have the drawing room, the breakfast room, the dining room, the library, and Sir William's study.' She paused as quick footsteps sounded in the room at the back, and a neat young woman popped her head around the door. 'Ah, here's Ada. She'll be glad to see you, Bessie, she's been doing double duty since the last Bessie left.'

Ada came forward, wiped her hand on her apron (I was beginning to note this as a servant trait), and shook mine firmly. 'Pleased to meet you, Bessie.' I would have said she was a few years younger than me, perhaps twenty-five. Her expression was friendly, but there was a hint of wariness in her eyes.

'Pleased to meet you too,' I said, looking into her eyes and returning her firm grip. I had a distinct feeling that Ada, apart from being a useful ally as my approximate equal in the house, would also be able to give me the low-down.

'I'm glad you two have met,' said Cookie. 'I should get back to the kitchen. Ada, will you take Bessie up to your room and show her where to wash? You can finish in there

195

afterwards.'

'Yes, Cookie.' Ada bobbed.

'Good girl.' Cookie steamed away to the connecting door.

'I need to put my dustpan and brush away, and then I'll take you upstairs.' Ada hurried into the study and I followed, curious to see Sir William's sanctuary. It was a haven of dark panelling and green leather, furnished in mahogany, with two large bookshelves flanking a large desk, its top clear except for a banker's lamp, a large blotter, and a pen tray. Ada ran her finger along one of the shelves, and sighed. 'I shouldn't be doing this now, but it's been impossible to fit it all in. If you think this is a dust-trap, you should see the library. Well, I suppose you will, starting tomorrow. I'll carry on with the mucky jobs, but you'll be sweeping, dusting and airing, of course. Oh, and ironing Sir William's newspaper.' She said this with a straight face, which I took to mean that it wasn't a joke. 'Have you got your box with you, or did you send it on?'

'A box?'

'Yes, with your things,' Ada said patiently.

'Oh! Yes, I brought a suitcase with me. Tom left it in the back porch.'

'Can you manage it?'

'Oh yes, it isn't heavy.'

We returned through the connecting door and Ada led me back to the porch. 'Here it is,' I said, picking it up.

'Onwards and upwards, then,' said Ada. We went back down the corridor, skirting the kitchen, and Ada opened a door I had not noticed before, which gave straight onto a narrow, steep staircase with bare wooden treads. 'Mind the third step up, it's a bit loose.'

We went up, turned, and went up again, and again, and again. 'We're in the attics,' said Ada. 'The seniors get the first floor rooms.' She opened a door and waved me in. 'Welcome to your new home.'

My heart clenched tight as I walked forward. Two iron beds, one on either side, with patchwork quilts. A low chest of drawers, with a cracked glass nailed above it and a jug and basin on top. Ada's other dress hung on a nail in the wall, with her hat over it, and her Sunday shoes placed beneath. A small square work table and two wooden chairs. A small pile of books and two photographs on the windowsill.

'Your bed is on the right; I've changed the linen. We get fresh every fortnight. You don't snore, do you?' Ada asked.

'I – I don't think so.' I put my case on the bed. I had never considered the possibility that I would have to share a room. How foolish, how stupid. What else had I not thought of?

'The bottom three drawers are yours, and your nail is there,' Ada said, pointing to it. 'If you want to wash, there's the bowl, or our bathroom is on the next floor down, but you'll have to ask for hot water downstairs.' Her tone suggested this would not be a wise proceeding. 'I'll leave you to put your things away, but you'll need to be downstairs in half an hour, to wait at dinner. Tomorrow's Sunday, so it's a little more relaxed. Sir William breakfasts at nine, but if milady wants a breakfast tray in her room you'll take it. If she comes down for breakfast you'll have a bit longer; but you never can tell what milady wants.' She nodded to me briskly, and soon I heard her light feet on the stairs.

Mechanically I opened the clasps on my case. I set the meaningless photograph on the windowsill, and placed the Bible next to it. I hung my other dress on the nail, and put everything else in the drawers. Then I put my face in my hands, and wept. 'What have I done?' I whispered to myself, tears running through my fingers. A servant, with no free will, space, or privacy, even at night. *What have I done?*

CHAPTER 29

Gradually I slipped into my new life. The thing I found hardest to get used to was the abrupt transition between noise and silence, motion and stillness. It began at five in the morning as the household shook itself awake. Mr Craddock's footsteps would creak along the corridor, punctuated by his hacking, constant cough and a sharp rap on each door. We would hear him harrumph to clear his throat, then 'Time to rise, one and all', followed by groans, complaints and the occasional curse. From that moment until I left the servants' quarters at half past six, I would be surrounded by shouts, bangs, and clatters.

I found it hard to leave my bed on those black mornings, and Ada was usually half-dressed by the time I struggled out, bedraggled and blinking. At least I did not have to think about what to wear. A print frock and a white cap in the morning; a black dress after lunch; a white apron at all times. Even so, Ada would be running to breakfast before I was properly awake, leaving me the dregs of the jug on the washstand. By the time I was dressed I knew that the most I could expect in the servants' hall was the dry heel of the loaf with a scrape of jam, and a mug of lukewarm, stewed tea, while around me chairs squeaked as everyone went about their business, and Janey began the washing up, rattling cutlery and clanking pans as if the din would make them clean.

The tolling of the large mantel clock – two chimes to mark the half hour – signalled the beginning of my solitude. I opened up the downstairs rooms; drawing the curtains, lifting the window sashes to air them, sweeping the floors. I would dust later, when the sun had risen properly, before laying the table for Sir William's breakfast. My flurry of activity would give place to standing, silent, at the side of the room, waiting in anticipation of a butter-dish to be handed, a dropped fork to be replaced, a cup to be filled. I was only noticed if I was not quick enough; a slight frown, a tut. At length Sir William rose, without acknowledgement, and I was left to gather up the dirty plates and smeared cutlery, and make them sparkle in time for the next meal. The house was awake now, but I would be silent and invisible until the kitchen door had closed behind me.

Once every piece of silver and china had been counted into the cupboard under Mr Craddock's watchful eye, my duties varied by the day. Monday was towel-washing day, on Tuesdays I polished the silver; a dirty, hard yet finicking job that made me sweat and sneeze and itch. On Wednesdays I turned out the pantry, clearing and washing the shelves and checking the food for spoilage. Thursday and Friday were my thorough-cleaning days, where I moved furniture to sweep into every cranny, beating rugs and polishing wood to a shine. Often I had to hurry upstairs to make myself presentable before laying the table for lunch. Usually only milady was there, and she would pick at her meal absently, reading a novel or a periodical, then wander away without a glance. The table cleared, the washing-up began again. Only then was I free to take my own lunch. After such hard physical work I ought to have been hungry as a hunter; but strangely I was not. I would often leave half my own plate of food, leading to recriminations from Cookie.

The afternoons were easier. My special treat, provided the family were not in the garden, was to cut flowers to replenish the vases in the downstairs rooms. Once I had changed my print dress for afternoon black I roamed the rose garden and the hothouse, lost in a world of colour and scent and stillness which made my existence seem harder. I lingered over the task of choosing as long as I dared; but even then the pleasure was not finished, for I could then spend time in the flower room, alone, fussing over the flowers as I arranged them in their crystal prisons.

That task done, I proceeded to a different kind of arranging; cutting thin bread and butter, making finger sandwiches and filling the cake stand with Cookie's delicacies, breaking off every few minutes to answer the door to another caller, and show her in to milady. Often I would spend an hour in the drawing room, handing bread and butter, refilling teacups, passing the cake stand, replacing cutlery, and putting used items out of sight of the guests.

Milady was 'not at home' once the clock had struck five. She would murmur 'Thank heavens for that,' and, picking up her embroidery or choosing a book, would drift off to another room, casting a disgusted eye at the stack of used plates and the half-empty cake stand. Everyone would fall on the leftover cakes when I bore them back to the kitchen; everyone except me, for after standing next to the mingled smells of vanilla and jam and cream and chocolate for so long, I usually felt slightly sick, a feeling I cured by retreating to the scullery and washing up.

The household ate late, so we ate early; stews and casseroles, cold meat and pickles, huge fluffy potatoes and vegetables from the garden. *Now* I was hungry, and cleared my plate with relish, so that Mr Craddock nicknamed me 'the trencherwoman,' and declared with a twinkle that I was swelling up before his eyes. Everyone laughed, for fat was the last thing I could have been called. On the rare occasions when I caught sight of myself in a mirror, my cheekbones stuck out. I had to lace my flannel corset tighter to keep it from slipping. When I used the big bathroom I left undressing till the last moment, and got washing over as quickly as possible. Sometimes, though, in bed, in darkness, I would squeeze my arm, feeling the muscle beneath the skin, and wondering at the change. But dinner was a time for jollity, so I joined in with the laughter and told Mr Craddock that I had a mind to eat the plate too.

On weekdays dinner was usually just Sir William and milady, perhaps with a guest or two, but every weekend there was a dinner party. On those days Ada and I bustled to and fro checking the company rooms, giving a final sweep, plumping a cushion, straightening an ornament, and she would help me lay the table till it groaned with every bit of gleaming silver and fine china that we could fit on it. I would load the centrepiece with more fresh flowers, and then rush for a clean cap and apron before the doorbell sounded, over and over and over. There would be pre-dinner drinks, giving us time to help Cookie with the final touches, and then Mr Craddock would turn up his jacket sleeves and cough ceremoniously before sounding the dinner gong. Mr Craddock would wait at table with me, Ada, and Susan, although *she* would only wait on milady and Sir William, leaving the guests' needs to us. I began by straining my ears for every word that was said, while maintaining the blank expression of a model servant, until I realised that stock prices, hats, and Hardy's latest novel were as thrilling as the conversation got. Everyone was far too well-bred to raise a topic which might lead to controversy or excitement.

Eventually the ladies would repair to the drawing room while the gentlemen lingered over port and cigars. I wondered if those conversations were more exciting; but the separation of the party was our cue to clear away and wash up. Little Janey helped as best she could; but she was dead tired by that time, and we kept her to handling things which could not be broken.

Carriages were ordered for midnight, and it was all I could do to stay on my feet, trying not to shiver as I held the door open while guest after guest adjusted their wrappings, or exchanged a final joke with Sir William, or pecked milady on the cheek. But as soon as the front door was locked and bolted my duties for the day were done. I dragged myself up to bed, stumbling on the rickety third stair, and undressed to my chemise before falling into bed and pulling the quilt over my head. I had no energy to do more. We would be allowed an extra half-hour in bed on Sunday, but it was never enough.

Was I unhappy? If I had had time to think, I would probably have said yes; but the truth was that I focused almost entirely on getting through the day, on doing my work to the required standard, on not being shown up as an impostor. We were a small staff; Ada had whispered to me in confidence that milady was 'hard on maids'. My real work for Mr Poskitt rarely entered my head. If I heard voices in the main house, I would listen; if visiting cards, or letters, or a telegram lay on the silver tray in the hall, I would stop and look; if I had the chance I would slip into the study, try the drawers of the desk, and check the pigeonholes. But that was all. My one regular task, which I had grown to perform automatically, was to wait for Sir William's copy of *The Times* every morning, sneak into the drawing room, and peruse the personals column for any news from Mercury. But Mercury never wrote, and, closing the paper carefully, I would take it to the kitchen and heat an iron on the fire. Sometimes I wondered if Mr Poskitt had forgotten about me, but then I would shake myself out of it, and tell myself that perhaps today would be the day that I found a note, or heard a conversation, or – something that I could pass on which might allow me to leave. I would not let myself think further than that. And as for thinking of Sherlock... Our life together seemed so unreal, compared to my present life, that sometimes I wondered if it had happened at all.

CHAPTER 30

It was a strange life, to spend my time in the service of people I rarely saw. At mealtimes I could not watch them; that would have been rude. I might be summoned at any time by the downstairs bells; but that involved spending a moment in the room to learn the person's bidding, and scurrying away to fetch whatever was required.

But one day was different. It was a Wednesday, and I had just begun clearing the pantry shelves when a bell jangled in my ear. It was the bell for milady's boudoir.

'That's strange,' said Cookie. 'I'm sure Susan's there.'

The bell rang again, for longer. 'You'd best go up, Bessie.'

I washed my hands quickly and hurried up the back stairs. Excitement mingled with fear. I had never had reason to venture onto the family's bedroom floor. I had never seen milady's boudoir; what would it be like? I imagined silk wallpaper, delicate furniture, milady reclining on a daybed, perhaps. I opened the connecting door cautiously, and hurried towards the sound of milady's raised, angry voice. She responded to my timid knock with an exasperated 'Come in!'

I entered to find milady tapping her foot and glaring at Susan, who stood by with a sulky expression on her pretty face. 'Bessie,' said milady, still scowling at Susan, 'do you see that vase of flowers on the bureau?'

The bureau stood near the window, and on its top was a small vase. The roses in it were drooping their heads, and a petal or two lay underneath. 'I see it, milady.'

'Are those flowers in a fit state to be in my boudoir?'

I glanced at Susan, whose lower lip was jutting out. 'They are not quite fresh—'

'That isn't what I asked you. Should those flowers be in my room?'

I knew what she wanted. 'No, milady.'

'This is the second time I have found half-dead flowers in here.' Milady's voice was dangerously level. 'Since the flowers downstairs are adequately maintained, you had better add my boudoir to your list, Bessie.' Her voice had an edge which made me feel as if I were being reprimanded.

'Yes, milady.'

'Now take the vase away and deal with it. Every other day, please.'

'Thank you, milady.' My hand shook a little as I reached for the vase. As I made for the door I had to pass Susan, and the venom in her look shocked me so much that I almost dropped the vase. As I crossed the landing milady remarked, casually, 'One more slip like that, Susan, and you'll be on the street.'

'What was it?' asked Cookie, as I hurried through the kitchen.

'Flowers,' I said, not stopping. 'Milady wants me to do them for her boudoir.'

'Do what?' I turned to see Ada at the kitchen door.

'These.' I held the vase up. 'Milady's asked me to do the boudoir flowers from now on.'

Ada whistled softly. 'Susan won't be happy.'

'She isn't,' I said. 'And milady won't be, either, if I don't get these changed.'

I breathed deeply as I entered the garden, but the calm it normally brought me was not there today. I tipped the old flowers onto the compost heap by the shed, found a pair of secateurs, and walked down to the rose garden. It was a cold morning, and the flowers had a thin rime of frost on the edges of their petals. I chose a scented variety and cut three just-opening blush-pink flowers.

I was filling the vase at the scullery tap when Susan walked in. 'Give me those,' she said, holding out her hand. It was the first time she had ever spoken to me directly; our paths only crossed in the servants' hall.

I turned off the tap. 'Milady asked me to take them up.'

'No she didn't. She asked you to change the flowers. Milady's boudoir is my business, not yours.' Susan took a step forward. 'She doesn't want you in there.'

Ada came through the doorway. 'Shut up, Susan, and get out of the way. Bessie's doing her job.'

'Stay out of it, Ada,' Susan said, without moving. Ada moved forward, took Susan by the shoulders, and forced her to the side of the room.

'Get off me!' Susan cried. Red blotches showed on her face and neck.

'Off you go, Bessie,' said Ada. 'Susan, if you promise to behave, and not bother Bessie, *then* I'll let you go.'

I hurried past with my vase of flowers, remembering the rickety third step in time, and tapped on the boudoir door.

'Come!' called milady. I took a deep breath and opened the door.

This time I had a chance to admire the room. The wallpaper was the colour of old gold, with an intricate raised pattern. The furniture was darker and heavier than I had thought, carved with elaborate, exotic designs. With its jewel-coloured carpet, the room could have been a chamber in a foreign palace. At its centre, curled up like a cat in a red leather armchair, was milady, reading a magazine. The heavy furniture and rich colours made her seem more delicate, more fragile, but she suited them exactly.

I went straight to the bureau and put the flowers on top, and glanced at milady as I walked to the door. She gave no sign that she had noticed me. Presumably that meant the flowers had passed muster.

I heard footsteps outside as I opened the door, and found Susan hovering, a pile of snowy linen in her arms. She stood back to let me pass, eyes down, before knocking and entering.

Ada had left the kitchen when I got back downstairs. 'She's doing the grates,' said Cookie, rolling out pastry on

209

the marble slab. 'You must stand up to Susan, Bessie, or she'll walk all over you.'

I continued to clear the pantry, stacking packets and jars on the big table in the centre. The dull, repetitive movement helped to clear some of the twitchiness I felt, the urge to run, to escape this place and these people, but my brain still raced. The thought of standing up to Susan frightened me, though I could not have said why. She seemed somehow exempt from the conventions that the rest of us lived under; helping each other, working together, being pleasant. I set a can of water on the fire to warm and went to fetch the soap and a clean cloth. Scrubbing the shelves would help to work my feelings out.

I had no opportunity to speak to Ada alone until the end of the day, when we were undressing for bed. 'Thank you for helping with Susan,' I said. 'It was kind of you.'

Ada put her boots side by side, sat, and rolled down her stockings. 'That's all right,' she said. When she looked up there was an impish gleam in her eye. 'To be honest, I enjoyed it.'

I fought back a smile. 'I'll try and stand up to her myself next time.'

'You do that.' Ada pulled her nightgown from under her pillow. Her next words were addressed to her bodice buttons as she undid them. 'You're one of us now that Susan's had a go at you.'

Warmth washed over me. 'Really?'

Ada nodded, her head still down. 'The last Bessie, Susan and her were thick as thieves. You'd come across them whispering in a corner, giggling, all sorts of silly talk. I never could get on with her, and I was glad when she went.'

'Why did she go?' I asked, trying to sound innocent. I fetched my own nightgown and started to unpin my plait.

Ada did not speak again until she had slipped her nightgown over her head. 'I think Susan turned her head and she started to give herself airs. She was a pretty girl, not out of her teens. She wasn't with us long.' Ada moved to the mirror and began to take her hair down. 'There was talk, but I don't listen to that sort of thing.' Her mouth was set firm as she picked up her hairbrush, and I guessed I would hear no more from Ada on that subject.

'Would you never want to be a parlourmaid, Ada?'

'Ha!' Ada brushed with vigour. 'Good hard work is what I know, not flowers and needlework and silver and waiting on. I couldn't be doing with that nonsense at meals, it's bad enough at dinner parties.' She peered at her hair in the cracked, spotted mirror, laid her brush down, and plaited it into a tail. 'I thought you might be a bit fa-di-la when you came, what with having lived out, and been married and all. But you pitch in and do your bit.' She nodded decisively. 'Now stop chattering, I'm dog-tired.' Her smile took the sting from her words.

I lay in the dark, thinking. *You're one of us.* The words had pleased me, but why? Was it that I had fooled the servants? No, it was more that I had been accepted as part of their community. I frowned. *Acceptance is part of your job*, a little voice wheedled. But I made a stern memorandum to myself: *Don't forget why you are here. Never forget your real work.*

211

CHAPTER 31

The next morning I tidied and sorted and swept the downstairs rooms just as usual, until the rattle of the letterbox announced the newspaper. Glad of a break, I took it to the drawing room. My fingers were so practised now that more often than not I could open the paper to the right page first time. I walked to the window and scanned the snippets of print.

Mercury leapt out at me. I gripped the paper so hard that I crumpled it.

Queen: Further news imminent. Watch the King. Mercury

I read the line several times, puzzled. It *was* for me, wasn't it? Although if the king was Sir William, I certainly wasn't the queen. I looked up for inspiration. Of course! I was the parlourmaid. *The queen was in the parlour, eating bread and honey.* I smiled at Mr Poskitt's joke, then turned back to the newspaper. *Further news imminent.* Did that mean another leak had happened? And would it be reported in the paper? I resolved to rise earlier in future and get my work done before the paper arrived, so that I could read the headlines too. What had been handed to the enemy this time? It must be very serious, for it sounded as if it could not be hushed up. I scanned the first few pages for clues, but it did not seem to be public knowledge yet.

I closed the paper and smoothed it, but the creases remained. I would have to press it thoroughly to remove the signs of my perusal. I went to the kitchen, put an iron in the fire, and fetched a clean cloth. By the time I was finished, the newspaper was passable. *Be more careful, Nell*, I told myself, folding the warm paper precisely in half. I opened the connecting door and almost cried out as I came face to face with Sir William.

He saw what I was holding, and put out his hand. 'Coffee and toast, please.' He went into the breakfast room, closing the door. Whatever it was, he knew; his face was as grey as his hair, and while that was as well-brushed and his clothes as neat as ever, he had the dishevelled look of an insomniac about him.

I fled to the kitchen. 'Sir William is up, and wants coffee and toast,' I gabbled.

Cookie paused, her teacup halfway to her mouth. 'Sir William is up? At this time?'

I began to cut bread. 'I don't know how he likes his coffee brewed.'

'I'll do it while you toast.' Cookie put her cup down and reached for the biggin pot on the top shelf. 'It'll have to be ready-roasted, I doubt he'll wait for fresh.' She spooned fragments of coffee into the pot. 'Send my

213

apologies, will you, when you take it in.'

I nodded. I disliked making toast, for I always ended up feeling as if I had toasted myself as well, but finally it was done. I cut the toast into triangles, put it into the rack, and laid a tray with all Sir William might want. 'That's me done until the children are up,' remarked Cookie, sitting down and drawing her cup back towards her.

I struggled out of the kitchen with the loaded tray. There was no answer when I tapped on the breakfast-room door, but I heard the crackle of turning pages. I turned the knob, gripped the tray, and entered.

Sir William was in his usual place, the newspaper spread in front of him. His head was down, reading. 'Leave it on the table,' he said.

I put the tray down and began to set out the items.

'Just leave it.' I withdrew, closing the door softly. Then I thought again, and reopened it.

Sir William looked up, a hint of annoyance in his face. 'Excuse me, Sir William,' I said, 'but should I ask Tom to get the trap out?'

'Oh! Yes, that would be useful. And there is a Bradshaw – a train timetable – in the top left-hand drawer of my desk, in the study.' I bobbed and hurried out.

I found Tom sitting on the mounting block in the stable yard, smoking his pipe. 'What brings you out here, Bessie?' he called. 'Come for a riding lesson?'

'Sir William wants the trap, please.'

'Does he, now?' Tom blew a smoke ring.

'Yes, and quickly. I must go in.' My boots slapped on the cobbles. I looked back as I closed the door. Tom had got up and was talking to Blaze, rubbing his nose.

I found the timetable where Sir William had said it would be. I took a second to try the drawers beneath, but they were locked as ever. I tapped on the breakfast-room door and laid the Bradshaw beside Sir William's plate. The newspaper was closed now; folded haphazardly, its pages all anyhow. Half a triangle of toast lay abandoned on the plate; the rest was still in the rack. 'You ought to eat more than that, sir, if you're going all the way to London.' The words were out of my mouth before I had thought of my impropriety. 'I am sorry, sir, I didn't mean—'

'You are right.' Sir William's eyes were on his plate. 'I should. But I find myself without appetite.' He thumbed through the timetable and ran his finger along the page. 'Ah yes, that will do.' He let the book fall closed and pushed back his chair. I opened the door for him, standing back to let him pass. Then I went to the hall-stand and, as I did on most mornings, helped him on with his coat. His hat had a light scattering of dust on the top, which I hastened to brush off. 'I do apologise, sir, I hadn't got to your hat.'

Sir William put it on. 'I have disturbed the routine of the house, I perceive.' He put his gloves on while I drew back the bolts of the front door and levered it open. The trap was waiting with Tom on the box, holding Blaze to a short rein. Blaze was trying to toss his head, impatient to be off.

'Quick as you can, Tom,' Sir William called as he got into the trap. 'I want to catch the seven-thirty.'

'Right you are, sir.' Tom reached for his whip. 'Come on, Blaze!' I raised a hand as the carriage moved off and, to my surprise, Sir William lifted a hand in reply. I waited until the carriage was out of sight before closing the door.

Cookie tutted as I delivered the remains of breakfast back to the kitchen. 'Trouble at work, I'll be bound. That's the only thing that puts Sir William off his food.'

'Do you think?' I asked casually, as I shook crumbs into the slop bin.

'I know,' said Cookie. 'Now don't you have work to do, Bessie?' She looked at me pointedly, and I took the breakfast things to the scullery for washing.

As I scrubbed and rinsed the china I turned the morning over in my mind. It was barely seven, and yet everything seemed different. Mr Poskitt's message had galvanised me. I was a spy, not a servant. I cursed myself for the attention I had paid milady at the expense of Sir William. I cast my mind back to dinner the previous night. Sir William must have known the news then, and I had noticed nothing. That would cease. This morning I had made an effort for Sir William, even forgetting my place in the process, and been rewarded with more speech than I had ever had from him before. I would continue in that path as long as it worked. Any doubts as to my usefulness were gone, for Mr Poskitt had contacted me at last, and his message indicated that the case was not solved. That I was needed. I allowed myself a smile of quiet satisfaction, and stacked the plates in the rack to dry.

CHAPTER 32

I went in to lunch a little late; I wanted to listen, not talk. I had waited on milady at lunchtime, but she seemed the same as always, pecking at her meal while turning the pages of a magazine. She showed no signs of distress or anxiety. I wondered what, if anything, Sir William had told her.

Most of the talk was of the grand fun planned when our wages were given out, which was not far away. 'We'll get jugs of beer from the village, and a bottle of spirits or two, and live like kings for an evening!' crowed Tom.

'Make sure you're fit to work in the morning, that's all,' said Ada, darkly.

'Don't fuss so, Ada,' Tom snapped. 'The family will give us a bit of leeway, they always do.'

'What if you have an early start like today, Tom?' Cookie wagged her spoon at him. 'I don't think Sir William will give you a bit of leeway if you tip him into the ditch.'

'How often is he up and out that early?' Tom argued. 'Once in a blue moon.' I longed to ask questions, but bit my tongue. Whatever had happened must be very serious indeed.

A telegram arrived for milady at half past three, and I took it straight up. Milady took it from the tray, ripped it open, and scanned the contents. 'Tell Cookie it's just me for dinner tonight,' she said, and returned to her letter-writing.

I relayed the message to Cookie, who sighed. 'More leftovers for us, I suppose.' She glanced at the oven. 'Or he can have it cold for supper when he gets back.'

'Is it to do with Sir William's business?' I asked, as innocently as I could.

Cookie laughed. 'Sir William isn't a merchant, you goose! He's an important Government man – a minister!'

'Oh!' I opened my eyes as wide as I could to convey how impressed I was. 'I didn't know.'

'I'd be surprised if you did. Sir William's a modest man, but if you'd seen the people we've had here – the Prime Minister, no less!' Cookie opened the oven door and examined the joint roasting within, then slammed it shut. 'He could be consulting with our Sir William *right now.*' She nodded sagely.

The doorbell rang just after ten o'clock that evening, and I hastened to answer it. Sir William stepped in, handing his hat and coat to me. 'Where is Lady Sophia?'

'She is in her boudoir, sir,' I said.

'Bring me a supper tray in the study, please.' He went upstairs without another word. Oh, how I wished I could be a fly on the wall to hear what he said to milady!

'Was that Sir William?' Cookie asked, as soon as I entered the servants' hall.

I nodded. 'He would like a supper tray.'

'How did he seem?' she asked, her face full of maternal concern, though she was probably the same age as her master, if not younger.

'Much as usual.' My answer was a lie. Sir William had looked as if he desperately needed to talk to someone. But I could not tell the truth without revealing myself as observant.

It did not matter; Cookie was already up and examining the contents of a covered dish. 'It's a little dry, but at least it's warm.' She set the dish on a tray. 'Bessie, get a plate and cutlery, and I'll put some chutney in a bowl. There's plum duff for pudding, too.'

I took the tray to the study. Sir William was not there yet, and I busied myself in putting a mat down to save the fine desk and setting a place for him. He came in as I was setting down the covered dish. 'Ah, very good.'

'There is plum duff for pudding if you wish, sir,' I ventured.

Sir William lifted the cover and sniffed the rising steam. 'I shall see how I get on with this. No need to wait.' I curtsied and withdrew, noting how stiffly he held himself, and how he did not meet my eyes.

He did not ring again that night. Eventually Cookie dismissed me to bed. 'You can't wait for ever, Bessie. It'll have to be cleared in the morning.' I lay awake for some time, wondering what Sir William was thinking, what he might be doing, in his study so late.

Mr Craddock's voice shocked me awake the next morning. As ever, I opened my eyes to blackness. I could hear the rustle of Ada getting ready. I swung my legs to the floor purposefully, ignoring the chill. Today I would be down on time, to give me a chance to read the paper – and perhaps I might find something significant in the study.

I secured a large slice of toast and jam and a steaming mug of tea, and worked through them quickly. 'Hungry are we, Bessie?' Cookie laughed.

'Eats like a horse,' murmured Susan, at the other end of the table. She was dressed to go out for her day off, otherwise she would never have been up so early.

'Works like one too,' I retorted, which brought a few guffaws round the table.

Susan's nose wrinkled. 'That would explain the smell.'

I stared at her until she dropped her eyes to her plate.

'That will do, Susan,' snapped Cookie. 'You know the rule.'

'Be polite to one and all,' Susan recited, pushing back her chair. 'Don't I just.' She left the room without bothering to put her chair in.

I dropped my head and surreptitiously sniffed at myself. I honestly couldn't tell. 'Ada,' I muttered, 'I don't smell, do I?'

'Don't let that cow rattle you,' Ada whispered back. 'You don't smell any more than the rest of us.' And with that I had to be content. I resolved to give myself a thorough scrub in the tub at the next opportunity.

I had actually remembered to put my cap on, which

meant I could start work immediately. I brushed Sir William's coat and hat, then went to the drawing room. I whipped around it, and then the breakfast room, checking that all was neat and clean and laying the cloth. A few flowers were beginning to droop. I nipped them off with my fingers and dropped them into the wastebasket concealed in the sideboard.

A *thud* in the hallway. The newspaper! All thoughts of flowers vanished as I ran to get it. I wanted to open it then and there, but the risk was too great. I would take refuge in the study, read in comfort at Sir William's desk, and try the desk drawers and pigeonholes yet again before removing last night's tray and taking the paper to be ironed. I could hear footsteps and chat through the connecting door nearby. The household was going about its business, and in any case, I intended to make no noise. I smiled to myself as I pushed open the door. The smile faded in an instant as I came face to face with Sir William.

'So sorry, so sorry sir—' I backed away.

'What do you mean, coming in without knocking?' His voice was low, and furious.

'I didn't – you're not usually up at this time, sir, and I thought—'

'What did you think? Why have you got my newspaper? That doesn't belong in here!' His voice was rising, and panic rose in my chest. I could not afford to panic; my position depended on keeping a cool head. 'Answer me!'

'I'm sorry, sir, it will never happen again, I swear it,' I gabbled, casting through my mind for an excuse.

'That isn't an answer.' Sir William's voice had

quietened, but it had an edge to it that made me want to weep. 'Answer me, Bessie.'

I blinked, and felt a tear run down my cheek. 'I'm sorry, sir. I – when no-one's about, and it's quiet, I try to read a bit of the paper, sir.'

'You try to read the newspaper?' Now he sounded puzzled, not angry.

'Yes, sir. I never was good at reading, and I wish to get better.'

Sir William chuckled. 'So you want to read, Bessie?'

I nodded, and bit my lip.

'Give me the paper.' He beckoned me forward, and I put the paper into his hand. He unfolded it and placed it on the desk. 'Read, Bessie.'

I leaned over the paper. Sir William's anger had unnerved me, and I knew I had to give a good performance. I blinked again, and a tear dropped on the paper. 'Don't make me read, sir. I'm – I'm ashamed.'

'Try, for me.'

My finger shook as I put it under the large 'The' of *The Times*. I recalled the hundreds of children I had taught their letters; their stumbles, their mispronunciations. 'Th-eh... The?' I looked at Sir William, who nodded encouragingly. 'The.'

'Try the next word.'

I moved my finger along. 'Tuh . . . tuh-ih-mmm. Tim . . . ee . . . sss. Tim-ee-sss.' I hung my head. 'I don't know it, sir.'

'The word is *Times*, Bessie. It is the name of the newspaper. *The Times*.' Sir William refolded the paper; but he did it calmly.

'I can't read fancy words, sir,' I said in a rush. 'I can read easy words, words you meet every day, like cat and dog, egg and bacon, flour and salt. But I don't know book words. Don't shame me, sir.'

'It isn't your fault, Bessie,' Sir William said, soothingly. He tapped the paper. 'You should try something easier. This is full of – fancy words.' I wiped my eyes with the back of my hand. 'I didn't mean to shout at you, Bessie. I am tired, and my work is a little difficult at the moment.' He smiled. 'You are a good girl, Bessie.'

'Thank you, sir.' He nodded, which I took as dismissal.

I went to the drawing room, as far from everyone else as I could get, and wept out my tension. I had got away with it, for now. I had fooled a cabinet minister into believing that I could scarcely read. *What if he remembers the Bradshaw,* a voice asked as the tears ran through my fingers. *What will you say if he ever catches you reading?* But I was in no state to think of answers. My nerves were shredded by the shock I had received.

I looked up and almost cried out. Sir William was standing in the doorway, watching me. 'Go and wash your face, Bessie, and then bring a simple breakfast. Oh, and tell Craddock I want him.' He closed the door.

I rose, brushing down my skirts, and did as I was told, peering at myself in the piece of mirror over the basin. What I could see was not encouraging. My cheeks were blotchy, and my eyes rimmed with red. The only thing that made me feel better was that my eyebrows were beginning to grow back, and the querulous expression I had worn constantly was fading. I tried a smile, and while pathetic, it looked more like my own than it had for some time. I winked at my reflection, which nearly made me laugh outright, and set off downstairs to place an order for breakfast.

CHAPTER 33

The servants' hall was full of chatter that evening. We were nearing the end of a long day in a long week – indeed, the earliest risers were finished, and enjoying a mug of beer with their fried fish and chipped potatoes. I was still on duty, since I must answer the door, and I would be required to wait at dinner later, though milady would be dining alone. Mr Craddock had told us, very importantly, that Sir William would be away, and returning on Sunday. 'With the Prime Minister in London! He asked me to pack, and…' he lowered his voice, 'to put in his tail-coat.' There were oohs and aahs around the table, and I joined in, but I would have staked a sovereign that the weekend would not be a social affair for Sir William.

A bell jangled, and all eyes looked to see which it was. Milady's boudoir. I glanced automatically towards Susan's place, but there was an empty chair.

'Day off,' said Mr Craddock, to me. 'Up you go.'

'Me?' I faltered. 'But milady—'

'Doesn't matter. You're the parlourmaid, you cover the lady's maid. Besides, you're dressed.' I was pristine in my uniform, while several of my companions were wearing slippers and missing aprons and caps.

The corridor was chilly after the warmth and noise of the servants' hall. I checked that my hair was tidy and my cap on straight. I was halfway up the back stairs when the bell jangled again. I broke into a run, only stopping to collect my breath before tapping on the door.

Milady turned from her dressing table and her face fell. 'Where's Susan?' she demanded. She was wearing a silk kimono, and her black hair cascaded down her back.

'It's her day off, milady.'

She looked me up and down. 'Fish and chips tonight, I take it, from the reek you've brought in with you.'

'I apologise, milady. I didn't think I would be needed until your dinner time.'

'Well, you are needed. I'm going out, and I need you to help me dress. I wanted Susan, but I shall make do with you.' Her emphasis on *make do* made me feel gnat-sized.

'I didn't know you were going out, milady,' I said, to fill the silence.

She snorted. 'I didn't realise I had to report in.' She turned back to the glass. 'Now get on with it. Oh, and ring for the carriage. I leave in half an hour.'

'Are you going somewhere nice, milady?' There had been no mention of a trip out tonight, either by milady herself or in the servants' hall.

'Of course.' I waited for an elaboration. 'Or I wouldn't bother to go.'

I laced milady into her corset, and rolled her stockings on. When I knelt at her feet I could feel her eyes on me. 'You're not as clumsy as I thought you would be.'

I wasn't sure how to respond. In the end I settled for 'Thank you, milady.'

'Can you put my hair up without making me look a fright?' She gazed at my own hair, scraped back under its cap.

'I'll do my best, milady.'

She sighed. 'You know how I usually wear it. Like that, but a bit higher.'

I set to work with hairbrush, rats and pins, feeling as if I needed another pair of hands. Ten minutes later the last hairpin was in, and she patted it critically. 'Not a bad effort. Considering.' She eyed me, a little sneer spoiling the line of her upper lip.

I let the jibe wash over me. 'Which dress would you like, milady?'

'The burgundy satin. But not yet. Perfume first.'

I reached for the cut-glass bottle on the dressing table.

'Not that one.' Milady's voice was sharp as a knife. 'Second drawer on the left.'

The drawer slid open silently. Inside was another, smaller, glass bottle. 'Careful with that. Break it, and you'll be working for free for the rest of the year.'

I set the bottle down and eased out the stopper. The scent of jasmine flowers rose; exotic, heady, powerful—

I almost cried out. I saw myself reflected in the dressing table mirror, eyes wide. I composed myself and dabbed the stopper onto milady's neck and wrists.

'There,' she said, drawing a deep breath and smiling at herself. 'You may fetch my dress now.'

Milady's dress was brought. Milady was helped in, the neckline settled, the ruffles shaken out, the train draped over her arm. Milady's jewel case was fetched, her jewellery selected and put on. Milady's feet were eased into her little satin boots, and the hooks fastened. Milady's fur cape was put on, and adjusted. Milady's hat was placed and replaced on her head till she was satisfied, and her bag put into her waiting hand. But as I dressed her I was somewhere else entirely.

I was looking at a sheet of cheap white notepaper printed with the words *Tell your husband to keep his mouth shut*. Notepaper which, beneath the smell of meat and straw, was scented with jasmine.

I was standing by the winter jasmine bush under which Emmett Stanley had been found.

I was backing away from Emmett Stanley as he screamed and writhed at the perfume I wore.

'Don't stand gawking.' Milady walked to the cheval glass and admired herself. 'Although you have exceeded my expectations.' Her lips curled in a mischievous smile. 'Perhaps I shall tell Susan that I have found a better lady's maid.'

'Oh no, please don't, milady,' I stammered, hoping that my show of reluctance would appeal to her perverse nature. I was desperate to be given free rein in milady's boudoir; to range through her things, read her letters, examine her boots... 'I wouldn't want to cause trouble.'

Her smile broadened. 'No, I don't suppose you would,

228

but I think I'll leave things as they are. Neat-fingered you may be, but I couldn't look at you every day.' She beamed at me, and swept out. 'Tell Nanny not to keep the children up. I'll be late,' she called over her shoulder.

I moved around the room, closing the drawers of the jewel case and replacing it on the tallboy, shutting the wardrobe doors, doing everything expected of a careful, efficient lady's maid, in case milady came back. I plumped the cushions, I dusted the mantelpiece with my handkerchief, listening for a step, a creak—

All was quiet. Then from outside, the slow crunch of wheels turning on gravel, and Tom's voice, 'Hup!' He would know where milady was going. How could I get him to tell me?

I shook myself. She was gone. I picked up the small, delicately-worked perfume bottle and sniffed the stopper again. Exquisite, but deadly.

I had perhaps two minutes. I opened the dressing-table drawers, gently lifting cosmetic boxes and moving gloves aside, but nothing unusual came to light. I opened her letter case, which held nothing but notepaper and envelopes of thick cream stock. *No cheap white paper for milady,* I thought, and looked for a sample of her writing. The blotter on her bureau showed in reverse a firm, flowing hand, nothing like the block printing of the note I had seen. But her pen tray held a Cross stylographic pen, and a bottle of Stephens' black ink stood next to it. It was not absolute proof; but it was enough to make me sit down abruptly. I must get a message to Mr Poskitt. But first I must go downstairs before anyone had a chance to miss

229

me. I closed the lid of the bureau, and got up. Reflected in the dressing-table mirror, my cheeks were pink and my eyes shone. Perhaps I could pass it off downstairs as excitement because I had tended to milady.

I descended to the servants' quarters much more slowly than I had come up. Dinner had been cleared and a game of rummy was going on at one end of the table, with Mr Craddock holding forth at the other end, closest to the fire. He paused at the creak of the door and turned his rheumy eyes on me. 'Yer back, then. Took yer time.'

I pulled out a chair and poured myself a cup of tea from the pot. 'Milady wanted dressing.'

An *ooh* of sympathy came from the women present. 'What was she like?'

I considered. 'The same as usual, really.'

'Susan says milady's a real Tartar when she's dressing to go out alone.' Ada moved round the table to sit beside me. 'What did she wear?'

'An evening dress, burgundy satin with a train and ruffles.'

Ada whistled. '*Very* nice.'

'Oh, and she said she'll be back late. I'd better tell Cookie about dinner.' I half-rose, but the gnarled hand of Mr Craddock forestalled me.

'You stay where you are, Bessie, and get your breath back. *I* will inform Mrs Harper of the change in plan.' Mr Craddock was the only person in the whole house who called Cookie by her proper name. He levered himself to a standing position, and weaved towards the kitchen.

Half a minute later Cookie stormed in, wiping her

hands on her apron. 'That woman and her bloody jaunts!' she cried. '"A special supper, Cookie, because I shall be all alo-o-o-ne!"' she wheedled, in a passable imitation of milady's honeyed tones. 'A salmon mousse, an individual Beef Wellington, and a lemon tart, and she sends word as she's going out the door!'

'Maybe it was a last-minute invitation,' I said, calmly.

Cookie's eyes bulged with fury. 'Maybe my foot! Milady plays her cards close to her chest, and well she might. Never when Sir William's at home, but when the cat's away—' Mr Craddock shot her a warning look, which bounced off Cookie as harmlessly as an india-rubber ball. 'Although of the pair of them, milady's the bigger cat by far.' Her piece delivered, she stomped back to the kitchen, muttering that *she* would have a fine supper tonight, see if she didn't.

Mr Craddock leaned across to me. 'Don't pay any mind to Mrs Harper,' he said, in a whisper that reached to the corners of the room.

'I won't, sir,' I said.

'You're a good girl,' said the butler, and winked at me. He loved to be called *sir*, and I made sure to slip a 'sir' in whenever I could.

'I nearly forgot!' Ada ran to the stove and brought me a piece of apple pie. 'I saved you this. You must be half-starved.'

I stayed in the servants' hall until fully ten o'clock, listening to the jokes and gossip while drinking cups of tea. I went up a few minutes after Susan's return, making my excuse that I would nap while I could, in case I needed to come down and open the door for milady. I wanted to be alone; and I did not want to be there when Susan discovered I had usurped her.

I lay fully-clothed on the bed and thought. Milady had said she would be late. Whatever she was doing, it clearly wasn't innocent. The special perfume meant that she was meeting a man, a secret man, but a man who had been here, if he had written the note to Effie Stanley...

How late would she dare to stay out? And this was not the first time. Did Susan know where milady went, who she saw?

I lay like a figure on a tomb, plotting errands I could invent to get out of the house and telegraph Mr Poskitt, till everything became tangled and I was running through London, chased by Cookie and her frying pan, while milady cheered her on from the sidelines—

I was woken by Ada coming to bed. 'Give up, Bessie, do,' she said cheerily. 'Milady has her own key. She won't knock you up after midnight.'

'I'll wait till then,' I said sleepily.

'Suit yourself,' said Ada, folding her apron ready for tomorrow.

I woke in the dark. What time was it? I had no way of knowing, not without waking the whole corridor. I listened to the silent house.

And through our small, draughty window, a neigh.

Milady was home.

The household stirred perhaps half an hour later. Beds sighed, boots clumped, doors creaked, and Mr Craddock's morning call advanced down the corridor.

Milady had stayed out all night. And at that moment I would have given a year of my life to know where she had been.

CHAPTER 34

The next morning I crackled with energy. Not even a thorough perusal of Sir William's abandoned newspaper could soothe me; there was nothing useful in its pages. The study, too, was as tidy and shut-away as ever. Whatever Sir William's opinion of my reading skills, he continued to be careful.

But I could write to Mr Poskitt. I had smuggled a folded sheet of paper, a stamped envelope, and my dip pen downstairs in my petticoat pocket. I composed a note in my head as I completed my chores, and when I was sure I had it right I went to the desk. I opened the lid of Sir William's silver inkwell, keeping my back to the door.

Dear M,

King in capital for weekend. Queen made unexpected move last night, wearing jasmine. Will continue to observe the game. Mercury

I hoped my simple attempts at disguise would be understood by Mr Poskitt, while if the note did fall into another's hands, it would not give me away. Only when I had the letter safely hidden did I feel the least bit calm; and how would I manage to post it?

Even with considerable caution I had managed to get ink on my forefinger. My morning duties complete, I went to the scullery to wash. I was scrubbing at my hands and nails with a stiff brush when Susan came in. 'Breakfast in bed for milady please, Cookie.' Susan's day off seemed to have done her good.

'Did milady say what she would like?'

'A boiled egg, with toast soldiers, some fruit, peeled, and a pot of tea.' Susan examined herself in the back of one of the copper pans hanging from the rack, twisting a strand of golden hair around her finger.

My fingers were irreproachable now, and I dried my hands on the rough towel. I stretched out my fingers to examine them. My nails were a little longer than when Evie had cut them, but still very short, and the skin round them was ragged. My hands looked battle-scarred. The heels of my hands were hard with callouses, and the near-constant immersion in water had made the skin crack and peel. *When I get out of here*, I thought, gazing at them, *I shall treat you so well...* I gave them a final wipe on my apron, and went back to the kitchen.

'You go up, Susan,' said Cookie. 'Bessie can bring the tray.'

'I'll wait,' said Susan, sitting on a chair near the fire and stretching her legs out.

'Did milady ask you to wait?' Cookie asked, frowning.

Susan got up and walked out, muttering to herself.

'I don't know what gets into that girl,' said Cookie to no-one in particular. 'Bessie, fill the small pan for me, would you?'

Between us we had the tray ready in a few minutes, and Cookie held the door open for me. 'No sense in upsetting it, is there?' After her outburst the night before, she seemed to have recovered her good humour. I would have loved to ask her about what she had said, but I knew a closed book when I saw one.

There was a small table outside milady's room, and I set the tray down with a sigh of relief before tapping at the door. 'I'll get it, milady,' Susan's voice rang out.

'Nonsense,' said milady. 'You'll carry on with that handkerchief.' I took that as my signal to enter and opened the door, wedging it with my foot while I steadied the tray.

Milady was in bed, wrapped in the kimono she had worn the previous day. 'Ah, breakfast. Have you brought jam and marmalade, Bessie?'

'Yes, milady.' Though milady had not asked, Cookie had put two small glass bowls of preserves on the tray, with a whole rack of toast.

'Excellent. Now, can you take the top off the egg for me? I always make a mess, and Susan is no better.'

'Of course, milady.' I set the tray on the table by the bed. I felt Susan's eyes as I tapped the top of the egg with a spoon and carefully lifted it off, separating the cooked white dome from its eggshell cradle.

'You are as neat with eggs as you are at dressing me,

Bessie.' Milady laughed. 'You shall be lady-in-waiting to the eggs.'

'Thank you, milady,' I curtsied with a smile. 'Will there be anything else?'

'That will do,' said milady. 'For now.'

I bobbed again and left the room. The look that Susan gave me slid straight off.

Cookie was sitting with her own pot of tea when I went downstairs. 'Do you need any help, Cookie?' I asked.

'Everything's in hand, thank you,' said Cookie, comfortably. 'I shall put my feet up, for no doubt something will come along to put a spanner in the works. Sit down and have a cup of tea, why don't you.'

I accepted gratefully and took a seat opposite. A hot cup of tea, and nothing to rush off to, was a luxury. I blew on my tea to cool it – everyone in the servants' hall did it. There was no time to wait, and even at comparative leisure I could not break the habit.

Suddenly Cookie leaned across the table. 'Sir William isn't happy, you know,' she said, in an undertone.

'Oh?' It seemed the safest reply.

'He never got over his first wife,' she confided.

'Ohhhhh.' I sipped my tea. 'What happened?'

'She died in childbirth; the baby too. They'd married quite late, for Sir William's mother had wanted him to find someone grander. Not that she told me any of it, you understand, but – when you live in, you see things. Sir William was heartbroken. He threw himself into his work. It was years before he'd look at another woman.'

'How did he and milady meet?' I steeled myself, in case

Cookie thought me forward for asking.

'In London, at a fundraising ball. Those were the only sort of jolly events he would go to. About seven years ago, it was.' She sighed. 'No use crying over spilt milk, though.' She poured herself another cup, and meditated silently.

Milady appeared for lunch and made a reasonable meal. After a few minutes she turned in her seat. 'Go over there, will you.' She pointed to the corner opposite her. I took my place next to the china cabinet, wondering. Why had milady asked me to move? I studied the table, but every so often my eyes strayed to milady and found her watching me, a little smirk on her face. I cast my eyes down, but I knew that she had seen me, and knew that I had seen her. I think my blushes amused her even more. *What if she has seen who you are?* Her amusement reminded me exactly of the day I had caught her stealing. It was the mischievous twinkle of a little girl who knows that she is being naughty, and that she will get away with it. I did not look again until I heard milady's knife and fork clack onto the plate. I pulled out her chair, and she rose. 'Don't forget my flowers this afternoon,' she said, and left without a backward glance.

I fidgeted through lunch, joining in the chatter as a way to distract myself from what might be going on in milady's head, and from Susan's glowering. Eventually I excused myself and went to the garden. The children were on a walk with Nanny; I had the place to myself. I was eager to see milady again.

I tackled the big vases downstairs first, pulling out the dying blooms, changing the water, and moving the flowers to make it seem a different arrangement. I had cut a spray of creamy tea-roses for milady, and I put them in a glass of water whilst I went upstairs to fetch the vase.

Milady was in her boudoir, curled in her armchair. 'Ah, here is Bessie.' Susan was sitting in the corner, embroidering a handkerchief. 'Susan, fetch my book. Oh, and I want a cup of tea. Wait, and bring it up.'

'Bessie could do that when she brings the flowers,' grumbled Susan.

'I daresay she could.' Milady's voice was a cat's paw; velvet with a suggestion of razor sharpness beneath. 'But I asked you.' Susan left without another word.

I walked to the bureau and picked up the little flower vase.

'Put that down.' Milady's voice was level. 'Open the bureau. Do you see my letter case?'

'Yes, milady.'

'Are your hands clean?'

I inspected them. 'Yes, milady.'

'In the case is a letter which I want you to post in the village. Put it in the box outside the post office; do not take it inside. If anyone asks where you are going, I have asked you to buy me a quarter-pound of lemon bonbons from the shop. Do not mention the letter. You will find coins in the dish on my dressing table.'

I opened the case and the letter gazed up at me. *Professor J. Moriarty, 45 Chiltern Square, Belgravia, London SW.* I put it in my apron pocket, then crossed to the dressing table and took a half-crown from the dish. 'I will bring you change when I return, milady.'

'Don't worry about it.' Milady watched me, narrow-eyed, from the armchair. 'The vase, Bessie. That is why you are here.'

I returned to the bureau and picked it up. 'I will leave this in the flower room and go to the village for your bonbons, milady.'

'Excellent.'

On the way back I stopped at my room. I put on my hat and coat and found another envelope and a stamp, which went into my petticoat pocket with my own letter. I stuck my head into the kitchen as I went past. 'I'm just going to the village. Milady wants bonbons from the shop,' I called, and hurried off.

I breathed easier once I was outside; but I waited until I was out of sight of the house before I pulled the letter from my apron pocket. Milady had sealed it with wax, so there was no way of opening it without the recipient seeing immediately that it had been tampered with. The seal was not the usual family seal, but a little ship. My own letter was still in my petticoat pocket – I had something new to add now.

The walk to the village took half an hour. I should have enjoyed it, for the countryside was pleasant and the road was quiet, but I was too excited and nervous to do anything but hurry.

The clerk behind the counter looked up as I entered. 'Can I help you, madam?'

'Oh you can, sir,' I said, in a flurried manner. 'I had a letter ready to post, and now I find that I have left something out of it! Could I perhaps borrow your pen?'

He grinned. 'Of course, madam.' He passed it over. I ripped open my letter and scrawled *Queen sends private letter to Prof Moriarty*, and added the address. I put it in my spare envelope, addressed it, and passed back his pen.

The clerk held out his hand and I had no choice but to give him the letter. Doing anything else would seem odd, and the last thing I wanted was to be memorable.

He dropped the letter into the bag. 'Good day to you, sir,' I said, turning to leave.

'Good afternoon, madam.'

I walked outside, waited for the door to close, and posted milady's letter in the postbox. Then I bought bonbons from the general store next door, where the assistant weighed them into a brown-paper bag. She took my money and gave change without a second glance. My heart was a little lighter, but my letter, lying in the post-bag, worried me. What if milady had had me followed, and I had been seen entering the post office? Then I shook myself, and started for home. I was seeing trouble everywhere.

'You're quick,' said Cookie when I arrived back in the kitchen. 'Susan usually takes a good half-hour longer.'

'I expect she does,' I grinned. 'Does milady like her bonbons in the bag, or a dish?'

'I have no idea,' said Cookie, casting her eyes to the ceiling. 'Leave them in the bag, and take a dish up with you.'

I selected a small glass bowl from the dresser. 'I'll just cut milady some flowers.'

When I entered the boudoir milady was reclining on the

daybed and staring out of the window, while Susan was still working on the handkerchief. 'Your flowers, milady, and your bonbons,' I said, putting the vase back on the bureau. 'Do you require a dish?'

Milady shook her head and stretched out a hand for the bag. She took one and wedged it in her cheek, then raised her eyebrows at me. I nodded, and she smiled, her eyes half-closed. 'Here,' she said, taking another bonbon from the bag. 'Open wide.'

My eyes were wide already; but I opened my mouth and bent down, and she fed me the bonbon. 'Say thank you, Bessie,' she said.

I pushed the bonbon into my cheek. 'Thank you, milady,' I said, as clearly as possible, and she giggled. I couldn't look at Susan for fear she would turn me to stone.

The rest of the day ran at half-speed. I did my chores, I helped in the kitchen, I waited at table, I was a model servant. Yet when I lay in bed that night my head was full of what-ifs. What if the clerk had opened the letter, decided it was nonsense, and destroyed it? What if Mr Poskitt did not call for the letter? What if my information was worthless? But fatigue was closing in, and my questions became fainter as they were smothered in a blanket of sleep.

CHAPTER 35

I awoke feeling stiff and sluggish. I did not want to move. To be honest, I did not usually want to get up, but after the excitement of yesterday I really did not want to drag myself out of bed and face the day again so soon.

'Come on sleepyhead,' called Ada, who was already dressed. She came across the room and I felt her warm hand on my shoulder.

She shrieked. 'Oh my!'

'What is it?' I was still half-asleep. I rolled towards her and—

Something wasn't right. My head felt . . . odd.

I ran my hand over my hair. Just below the nape of my neck, it ended. The hair at the bottom felt coarse, bristly, not like mine.

I sat bolt upright and tried with my other hand, as if it could tell me a different story, but it only confirmed the truth.

My hair had been cut off.

I scrabbled in the bed and found my plait. It had unravelled at the top. I cradled it in both my hands, as if it were an animal that had died, and burst into tears.

Ada was there at once, her arms around me, soothing. 'It'll grow back, it will, we could pin it back on and no-one would know.'

'For God's sake, Ada, everyone probably knows already,' I sniffled. I rubbed my eyes, and the plait blurred.

'You think—' Ada whispered.

'I *know*.'

Susan. After milady's teasing yesterday she had crept in, scissors in hand, while we were sleeping, and cut off my hair. What better way to get her revenge than to mutilate her rival?

'Get dressed, Bessie.' Ada dashed her face with cold water. 'We'll show her up for what she is.' She saw me glance in the direction of the mirror, and turned me gently away.

I got up, and Ada helped me into my dress and bathed my face. 'Leave your cap off,' she ordered. 'By the time I've finished, no-one will speak to her for a month.' I allowed myself to be led downstairs. I felt naked, and ashamed.

Ada flung open the door of the servants' hall. 'Look what that *bitch* Susan has done!' she shrieked, holding up my plait. 'Come in, Bessie, and show them.'

I swallowed, felt the stump of hair at my neck once more, and entered the room, my eyes on the floor.

No-one said a word. The silence grew thicker and thicker until I wanted to scream.

I heard Mr Craddock cough. 'You're sure it was Susan?'

Ada snorted. 'Who else would do such a thing?'

It was as if a spring had been released. I felt arms around me, murmured words of sympathy, assurances that it would grow, that I just looked a little different, that was all, and before long I was weeping as though I would never stop. 'It's only hair,' I choked. 'I know it's only hair, but —'

'I'm going to fetch that girl.' Cookie strode to the door, her mouth in a firm straight line. Two minutes later she marched Susan into the room and pushed her forward. 'You wicked girl!' she cried. 'What business did you have to do a thing like that?'

Susan's eyes met mine, and an incredulous, joyful smile came over her face. She began to laugh, a giggle which built and built until she was on the verge of hysteria, tears springing to her eyes. I turned away, unable to bear it. I had not seen myself in a mirror yet, and from the reaction thus far I doubted I would want to.

'You deserve a good beating, my girl,' said Ada, grimly. 'Whatever quarrel you have, that was a mean trick.'

Susan hooted once more and wiped her eyes. 'She looks so funny!' she cried, pointing at me, and that set her off again.

I stepped forward and slapped her grinning face. Susan's laughter stopped immediately and she stared at me, a hand to her cheek. Her blue eyes brimmed with tears, and she made a low crooning sound which grew into a wail, staring at me all the while. No-one stepped forward

245

to comfort her, and she wailed louder and louder, beating her fists against the table and working herself up. Perhaps I should have felt sorry; but I did not, not at all.

'What the *hell* is going on?' Milady was in the doorway with a face like thunder.

'She *hit* me!' wailed Susan, pointing an accusatory finger at me.

'Susan cut her plait off!' Ada cried, shaking my hair at Susan as if it would ward off evil.

'I see,' said milady, sitting down at the head of the table. 'Susan, do you deny it?'

Susan looked all around for a way out before muttering sulkily 'No, milady.'

Milady swivelled to face me. 'And you, Bessie? Do you deny it?'

I looked her in the eyes. 'No milady, I do not.'

'Susan wasn't sorry at all!' Ada interjected.

Milady held up a hand. 'That will do.' She turned to me. 'So you slapped her?' She didn't sound shocked. If anything, she sounded rather pleased.

I nodded.

'I would never have expected that from such a little mouse.' A little smile nudged the corners of her mouth upwards. 'I think you angered the farmer's wife, blind mouse, and she cut off your tail with a carving knife to teach you a lesson. Am I right, Susan?'

Susan, expressionless now, said nothing.

'Am I right, Susan?' Milady's voice rang out.

Susan, gulping, nodded.

'Come and stand in front of me, Susan.'

246

Susan took two steps forward. She was trembling, though milady's voice was soft again.

'So because Bessie waited on me while you were on your day off, you wanted to punish her?'

A tear slid down Susan's cheek.

'So you thought up a plan to make her more of a fright than she already is.' Angry muttering broke out behind her. 'Be quiet, everyone. There has already been more than enough noise.' She spoke with the reasonable tone of a nanny addressing her charges. 'Susan, you forgot yourself. You forgot that in this house, *I* am the farmer's wife.'

Susan looked at the floor.

'Susan, take down your hair.'

Susan's hands flew to her head. 'Oh no, milady, not that! I'll die of shame!'

'Take it down, or I shall order someone to hold you while I do it.'

Shaking, sobbing, Susan took out pin after pin until her golden hair flowed to her waist.

'That wasn't so hard, was it?' Milady stood, walked round her, and gathered her hair into a tail. 'Such pretty hair, too. Ada, fetch the scissors.'

Ada rose at once, her eyes gleaming, and did as she was told. She offered the scissors to milady, who shook her head. 'Mouse, come here.'

Ada put the scissors into my hand. 'Now you can cut off *her* tail, little mouse,' said milady.

I tested the action of the scissors before stepping forward. Susan was quivering like an animal in a trap.

'Do it, Mouse,' milady said. Was that a challenge in her

247

voice? Did she think I wouldn't do it?

And something in me snapped. I took the tail of golden hair and cut it off with one snip.

An *Ahhh,* almost of pleasure, crept round the room.

Susan flung her hands to her head, stumbling forward as if her hair had anchored her to the spot.

'I shall never ask you to trim *my* hair, Mouse,' milady remarked. 'It's longer on one side than the other. Come here, Susan, and I shall neaten it for you.' Milady motioned for the scissors. 'Sit.'

Susan stared straight ahead while milady walked around her, considering. 'I know what to do,' she said, running her fingers through Susan's hair.

The scissors flashed, and a large chunk of hair fell to the floor.

Susan clapped a hand to where the hair had been and a look of horror, and of understanding, swept over her face.

'Keep still, Susan,' milady cautioned. 'If you struggle, I shall ask Mr Craddock to shave you bald as an egg. Do you understand?'

Susan nodded. Her eyes were squeezed tight shut and tears coursed down her face.

'I am glad we understand each other,' said milady.

Humming to herself, she snipped and snipped until Susan's golden hair was a ragged crop; till it was too short for milady to run her fingers through; till only a faint fuzz covered her skull. With every snip, as the scissors crept closer and closer to her skin, Susan flinched, but otherwise she was motionless. With every snip I saw the truth of my cruelty. I tried to tell myself that someone else would have

248

done the deed if I had not, but it was no use. I had stepped forward and done the very thing which everyone had condemned Susan for. I, who thought myself superior.

And why had Susan cut off my hair? Because milady had taunted her. Had set us against each other, for her amusement. In that moment the hatred I had felt for Susan vanished, and I felt sorry for her. If anything, I hated myself, for milady had tempted me, and had made me cruel. But I hated milady more. I remembered Emmett Stanley writhing terrified in his own bed, and now I could understand why.

Without her hair Susan's features were too small for her face, and she was pretty no longer. She resembled a frightened, overgrown baby. 'Much better,' said milady, smiling as she surveyed her handiwork. 'Ada, bring a mirror.'

Ada rose, but her previous eagerness had quite gone.

'Close your eyes, Susan,' sing-songed milady. Ada returned with a hand mirror, and milady positioned it carefully in front of Susan's face. 'Now open them, and see how pretty you look.'

Susan opened an eye, shrieked, and hid her face in her hands. Her shoulders shook, and great sobs tore out of her.

'I'm tempted to dismiss you and let you fend for yourself, but on this occasion I shall be kind.' Milady stood up. 'I don't think you'll do as a lady's maid, though. Cookie, find her some work where I don't have to look at her. And a mobcap for that big bald head.' She sailed to the door. 'I shall let you have your breakfasts now. No further noise, please; I intend to sleep late. Mouse, I shall expect you in my boudoir at ten o'clock. And do something with that hair first.'

Milady's light footsteps receded. Ada and I exchanged glances, and looked away again. I felt as if I had witnessed a crime, and done nothing.

Then it hit me. Once, a lifetime ago, I had. I had watched milady steal a brooch. I could have brought her in then; I could have made sure that she was questioned, taken note of, made powerless. But I had let her go, for reasons I was still not sure of. That mercy had led to this, and to so much more, and so much worse.

'Don't cry, Bessie,' said Cookie, putting an arm round me. 'It'll blow over, it always does.'

I wiped my eyes, and tried to smile to please Cookie. But inside I was horrified at what I had done, and not done.

CHAPTER 36

Ada nudged me. 'Get your breakfast, Bessie, do. It's nearly seven. I know she doesn't need you till ten, but—' Her eyes lingered on my head.

My hand went up automatically. I had been so shocked by Susan's shearing that I had almost forgotten my own. 'Is it really bad?'

'No!' Ada's eyes were round. 'No, no, it isn't bad, just . . . it might look better if you washed it.'

I fingered the stiff little queue which was all I had left. It didn't feel much like hair. I tried to recall the last time I had washed it, and with horror I realised that it would have been at Baker Street. The rigours of our daily routine left no room for procuring enough hot water to wash three feet of hair, never mind the time to dry it.

'I shall go and deal with this,' I said, touching my head. 'I may be some time.'

'It really isn't that bad,' said Ada, as I picked up a can and went to the door. I closed it on her words. I didn't want to know how bad it was. I could imagine, and I only hoped it couldn't be worse.

In the kitchen I filled the can and set it on the hearth to heat. I thought of the plaited snake I had plucked from my bed, and which Ada had brandished as a sign of Susan's wrongdoing. It was no longer part of me. I sighed and touched a fingertip to the side of the can. What would Susan be doing? Cookie would not heap further punishments on her, she was too kind; yet she knew that milady would want Susan kept out of sight. Perhaps in the scullery, or the laundry, where she would not have to fear the gaze of strangers. I shivered at the memory of milady humming and cutting, cutting, cutting. And as I shivered, I determined that from now on, I would show no mercy to milady.

At last the water began to sing. I fetched a towel and soap, then took the can to the deep sink in the scullery. Little Janey was already there, sighing at the mountain of dirty dishes from the servants' breakfast.

'Let me use the sink first, and I'll help with the dishes,' I bargained. She assented readily, and soon I had a sink full of suds. It was such a relief to plunge my head in and rub the stickiness away, to feel the strands separating and floating freely. I ran my fingers through my hair, which was a strange, abrupt experience. I rubbed my hair gently with a towel, and wrapped my head in it.

Janey giggled. 'You do look funny, Bessie! Like a lollipop on a stick.'

'Thank you so much,' I said, gravely. 'Do you want me to help you with the dishes, or not?'

Working together, the breakfast dishes were washed, dried and put away in half the time. 'How do you think it will look, Bessie?' said Janey, gazing at my towel-wrapped head.

'I don't know,' I said. 'Not too strange, I hope.' And I hurried to my room before she had a chance to speculate further.

I gave my hair a final rub with the towel – it was merely damp already – then closed my eyes and let the towel fall.

I opened one eye and yelped. There I was in the mirror, but my new short hair was wavy, and shorter even than I had expected: around chin-length. *What on earth shall I do with it?*

I pulled my hair to the nape of my neck. I had enough left to make a tiny tail. Then I took my hands away, and it sprang back into curls.

I sighed, and picked up my hairbrush. It snarled in my hair at the first attempt. I got a comb and worked out the tangles, then tried again.

It was not the satisfying experience it had been. *At least it will be quick to deal with*, I thought. I finished brushing, pulled the hair into a tail, and tied it with a ribbon.

Two minutes later most of my hair had escaped and was hanging about my face. I sank onto my bed and clutched at it.

You could grease it down. But I thought of the pathetic little stump I had been left with, and shook my head. I got up and gathered everything that might be of use – hairpins, ribbons, a couple of tortoiseshell combs, a length of elastic, my cap – and returned to the mirror. Eventually, with combs, pins and contrivance, my hair was up, apart from a few stray wisps, and I dared to approach the mirror. If anything, it was a distinct improvement on the scraped-back greasy bun I had condemned myself to for weeks. I smiled at myself as I settled my cap on top of my new hairstyle, then went downstairs.

'Ooh!' Cookie exclaimed as I came into the kitchen. 'Show us the back.' I grinned and obliged. 'I never knew you had curly hair, dear. It takes years off you.'

I came closer and lowered my voice. 'How is Susan?'

Cookie frowned. 'I've told her I'll put her in the scullery for now. If you're to be milady's maid then Ada can be you, and she can train up little Janey to be housemaid. But that's when I can get Susan to come out of her room. I found her a mobcap, but she insisted on gathering all her hair and taking it upstairs with her. Maybe she's crying over it.' Cookie sighed. 'She'll have to come out some time, anyway. I've got a house to run.'

***

I knocked on milady's door at ten o'clock precisely. She was curled up in her kimono, reading a periodical. 'Good Lord,' she said, and laughed. 'You look almost... So much better without that muck on your hair.'

'Thank you, milady. Would you like breakfast?'

'Yes, on a tray. Toast and scrambled eggs.'

I made for the door. 'Where are you going, Mouse?'

'To tell the kitchen about your breakfast, milady.'

'Noooo,' she said, as if to a child. 'You ring, and Ada will come up. Your job is to dress me. But I shall have a bath first. Go and run it, please.'

254

I tugged the bell-pull, hoping that Ada would not resent my summons, and then went to the slipper bath which could be glimpsed through a door on the other side of the bedroom. Its taps were marked *Hot* and *Cold*, and immediately I was taken back to the first bath I had had at Baker Street after we had installed running water. And – I closed my eyes – to the last bath I had had at Baker Street, with Sherlock. Hastily I turned on the hot tap and put in the plug. A jar of bath salts stood on the windowsill, and I poured some in, mixing them round with my hand. Anything to distract myself from – oh, what would he be doing now? And was he thinking of me, too?

The bath was a third full when a tap sounded at the boudoir door. Milady did not look up. 'Come in!' I called.

'You can squeak louder than that,' said milady.

I cleared my throat and repeated the words, and Ada appeared. Milady had gone back to her magazine. 'Milady would like scrambled eggs and toast for breakfast, please.' I turned to milady. 'Would you like a pot of tea as well, milady?'

Milady nodded.

'And a pot of tea, please.'

'Tea, scrambled eggs, toast,' said Ada, and bobbed.

'Thank you so much,' I said, feeling quite distressed at having to give an order to my friend.

'You don't have to please and thank her,' observed milady, turning a page. 'She's here to do as she's told. Like you.'

'I will remember, milady.' I felt my cheeks warming. 'I will just go and see to your bath. How hot would you like

255

it, please?'

'Very.'

The water was over halfway up and steam was rising. I turned off the tap and tested it with my hand. It was as hot as I could bear. 'It's ready, milady,' I called.

'Come and put my hair up, then.' I took combs and pins from the dressing table and plaited milady's hair, winding it into a loose, high bun. She stood up and stretched. 'Will you come and scrub my back, Mouse?'

I took a step back. 'I – I—'

Milady giggled. 'Have I shocked you?' She turned, studying me. 'Perhaps you have suffered enough this morning,' she cooed. 'Go and fetch two fresh, warm towels. I shall soak until breakfast arrives.' She got up and strolled towards her bath, and giggled again as she closed the door behind her.

Ada knocked perhaps five minutes later. I was relieved to see that Cookie had added jam and marmalade to the tray. 'Is that breakfast?' called milady.

'Yes, milady,' I replied.

'Good. Towels, please.'

Ada's eyebrows shot under her cap. I shrugged, picked up the towels, and motioned to her to go, then scurried through, looking anywhere but at the bath, and put the towels down.

Milady sighed. 'Such a country mouse. Pour my tea, and bring my dressing gown.'

Milady sipped her tea and took dainty mouthfuls of toast and scrambled egg while I redid her hair. 'Now dress me.' By this point, as I knelt and laced and fastened and buttoned, I was wondering how milady kept her slim figure when she did nothing for herself.

'There,' she said when I had put on her perfume. 'Just in time for church too. *You* will have to hurry, Mouse.' She shooed me out and I hurried to fetch my coat and best hat, with its stiff artificial flowers. Holding it on, I ran down the back stairs. 'Bye, Cookie!' I called.

'Goodbye, dear,' called Cookie, who always stayed behind to superintend the Sunday dinner. She would attend Evensong later, once high tea had been served to the family.

My feet crunched on the drive. What time was it? I ran, my feet sinking into the gravel. Tom was waiting with the carriage. 'Get up, then!' he shouted, patting the box next to him.

I stared. 'What, I ride with the family?'

'You won't get there in time any other way!' I climbed up onto the box. 'Here, hold these.' He passed me the reins and jumped down.

I clutched the reins and prayed while Tom helped milady, the children, and finally Nanny into the carriage. He jumped up beside me and I gladly handed them back. 'Hold on, Bessie, we'll be setting a pace.'

I was close to vomiting by the time we reached the church. Tom helped me down and I put a hand on the stone wall, retching, while he assisted the inside passengers.

'Attend me to my seat, please, then go to the gallery,' said milady, sweeping past. I had no choice but to follow.

Heads turned as milady entered the church. It was almost full, and I had a feeling that the vicar had been waiting for the party from the Hall to turn up. He consulted his watch, then raised his eyebrows. 'Sorry,' I mouthed. Milady sailed up the aisle to the front pew and I helped her to remove her wraps, placed her hassock, and found her prayer-book. Nanny shooed the children in next, with much whispering, and I went to join the others in the gallery.

'You've been ages,' said Ada, moving up to give me room.

'I know,' I said, then fell silent as the vicar cleared his throat. I found church restful; not because of any change to my spiritual health, but because it was an opportunity to sit and think. My responses came without the need for thought, and the vicar favoured the old hymns I knew from girlhood.

At last the service was over, and Ada nudged me. 'Go on, you need to attend milady out.' I was making my way towards the staircase when my eyes fell on Susan. She was sitting at the back, in a corner, and a sparse fringe of golden hair showed under her mobcap, over which she had put a bonnet. She did not see me looking; her eyes were cast down. *So that's what she was doing in her room*, I thought. *Sewing her hair into the cap.* I imagined the painstaking needlework that must have gone into the pathetic show, the tears she would have shed over her lost hair as she stitched and stitched; and I was sorry.

CHAPTER 37

Sir William was expected back by the half past four train. It was already growing dark by the time I heard the crackle of wheels on gravel. Milady had heard it too, for she started; then she continued to wind the wool I held for her with the same lazy motion.

Presently there were footsteps on the stairs, and a tap at the boudoir door. Sir William entered and bowed slightly to milady. 'I am home, Sophy,' he said. He seemed too tired even to smile.

'Indeed you are,' said milady, putting her ball of wool into my hand and rising. She kissed him on the cheek. 'How was it?'

Sir William glanced warningly in my direction, then stared. 'Why is *she* here? Where's the other one?'

'Susan has had a little accident, and works below stairs now,' milady said smoothly, putting a hand on his arm.

Sir William's eyes narrowed as he looked at me. I dropped my gaze and sat, hands raised and wrapped in wool, feeling exceptionally foolish. 'And who is the parlourmaid then, pray?'

'Ada,' said milady carelessly, sitting down and taking back her ball of wool. 'Although I suppose we should call her Bessie.'

'What shall this one be, then?' Sir William was still looking at me, but now he seemed puzzled.

'She answers to Mouse.' Milady began to wind the wool again.

'For heaven's sake, you can't call a servant Mouse!' snapped Sir William. 'You – what is your Christian name?'

'It is Martha, sir,' I replied.

'Then I shall call you Martha.' He turned to milady. 'High tea at the usual time?'

'Of course,' she replied, her eyes on the wool.

'Then I shall go to the study.' He withdrew, closing the door softly.

'Poor Sir William has had a hard weekend,' remarked milady, not seeming particularly upset.

I felt a response was expected. 'Do you think so, milady?'

'I know.' She smiled, and wound the last of the wool off my hands, throwing the ball into the air and catching it. 'And I shall find out about it later. Bring me the latest *Graphic*, it's downstairs somewhere. The one with a painting of trees on the cover.' Her clarification made me wonder if Sir William had shared with her my inability to read.

The magazine would almost certainly be in the drawing room, but I tried the library first, then the breakfast room, hoping that the opening and closing of doors might disturb Sir William. It did not, and I did not dare to try the study before I had exhausted all other possibilities. The *Graphic* was in the drawing-room magazine rack. I took it up and went into the hall, closing the door gently.

The study door opened suddenly and Sir William stuck his head out. 'Come in here, Martha.'

I stood in front of the desk, the magazine in my hand, while Sir William closed the door, tidied his papers, and took his seat behind the desk. 'You're not in trouble,' he said abruptly. 'I want to know why Susan is downstairs and you are lady's maid.'

I bit my lip and fidgeted while I worked out how to phrase my reply. 'Susan played a prank, and milady sent her downstairs.'

'A prank, eh? What sort of prank?' He seemed relieved.

I decided an appearance of discretion might be wise. 'I would rather not say, sir.'

'Is it something to do with this?' He gestured at my hair.

I gulped, and nodded.

'What did Susan do?' His voice was kindly now, soothing. 'Tell me, Martha.'

'She cut my plait off, sir.'

'And milady sent her downstairs.'

'Yes, sir.'

'Did she do anything else?'

I nodded again.

'What did she do?'

'She cut off Susan's hair, sir. But please don't tell her it

261

was me told you, sir!'

'I see.' His face could have been carved from stone, and he seemed to gaze into the distance. Then he came to himself. 'Have you been reading, Bessie – I mean, Martha?'

I smiled, feeling on safer ground. 'I have tried a little more, sir.'

'Show me.' He motioned to the *Graphic* I was holding. 'Sit.' I went to the armchair in the corner. 'No, sit by me.'

I pulled up a chair and did as I was told, opening the magazine and looking for a page with pictures.

'Try this one.' Sir William tapped a page headed 'A Sketch from Sadler's Wells.' I stumbled through the first few sentences, with many wrong turns and much prompting from Sir William. 'Good,' he said eventually. 'I can see that you are trying, Martha.'

'Thank you, sir.' I closed the paper.

'Wait.' He scrutinised me. 'You hold your head differently, you know, without that big bun of hair.'

'Do I, sir?'

'Yes, you do. Your neck seems longer.' He reached forward and I tried not to flinch as he touched the hair above my ear. 'It's quite rough, isn't it?' His voice was a mixture of surprise and disappointment.

I stood up. 'I had better take milady her magazine.'

'Yes, you had.' He eyed the neat pile of papers.

'Should you still be working, sir?' I asked.

He smiled, wearily. 'I am a man down at present, and it is my own fault, for allowing foolish suspicion to get the better of me.'

262

He must mean Mycroft! 'Could you not make it right, sir?' I said, trying to seem politely interested.

'I could try,' he said, rubbing his forehead. 'But I think that pride will get in the way. His, or mine.'

'Perhaps you should sleep on it, sir,' I ventured.

'Perhaps I should!' He laughed. 'Go along, Martha, milady will be wanting you.'

I curtsied and ran upstairs to milady, who looked impatient. 'Where have you been, writing a new one?'

'I am sorry, milady, Sir William was talking to me.'

'Was he, now.' Milady stretched her hand out for the magazine. 'I hope you weren't pert. Do you remember what I said about pert parlourmaids?'

'I do, milady.' Something in the tone of her voice made me shiver.

'Bear it in mind.' She flicked through the magazine idly and threw it across the room. 'It's almost time for high tea. I suppose we had better have the children in, they will want to see their father. Go and tell Nanny, Mouse, and then you can get on with those stockings. The left heel is practically out.'

I fetched the darning mushroom and the workbasket, and mended until it was time for my own tea. In some ways I preferred the lighter work, but I missed the society and the good-humoured bustle downstairs.

'Here she is!' cried Mr Craddock. 'I expect you'll only require a thin slice of bread and butter and weak tea, now you're with milady.'

'I'll eat your share,' grumbled Ada. 'Up and down, pass this, fetch that… Milady's started calling me Bessie, you

263

know.'

'Better than Mouse,' I said, taking two sandwiches. 'Anyway, you're almost done, apart from bells and the front door.'

'True,' said Ada, biting into a slab of cake.

For two hours I was at leisure, and I spent it drinking tea and listening to the jokes and gossip in the servants' hall. Susan had taken a plate to her room, without a word to anyone. I had a new sympathy for her, having seen how lonely her life had been; not a common servant, but not a companion either, she had fitted nowhere. 'How is Blaze after his trip out today?' I asked Tom, who was playing dominoes with Mr Craddock.

'He's fine,' Tom considered his hand and laid a double three. 'Easier for two horses, even with six on board.'

'I suppose so,' I said, thoughtfully. 'And then he'd had a whole day to recover after his trips on Friday.'

'He's a good strong horse,' said Tom. 'London and back is nothing to him.'

'All the way to London?' I gasped. 'I had no idea.'

'Like I said, he's a strong horse. A rest and feed when we got to the theatre, and a slow ride back, and he's good as new in the morning.'

'Oh, so you took one of the other horses to fetch milady…'

Tom cursed as Mr Craddock, grinning, laid down a three-two and knocked. 'No, she was brought back, God knows when. She told me not to wait up. Aha!' He laid a two-four and knocked, then put his elbows on the table in the manner of someone who meant business.

'I'll leave you to it,' I said, and went to fetch another cup of tea, my mind churning.

Milady's bell sounded earlier than usual, at nine o'clock. I found her sitting at the dressing-table, waiting for me. 'You are early tonight, milady,' I said, beginning to take the pins from her hair.

'Yes.' I looked at her in the mirror as I worked a pin from her hair. On each cheek was a high spot of colour. I resolved to be especially careful. 'Three hundred, please.' She relaxed as I brushed, counting each ten aloud. When I reached one hundred, she said. 'The bottom drawer on the left, open it.'

I put the brush down and did as I was told. The bottom drawer was deep, and held nothing but a bottle and two crystal tumblers. 'Pour me a drink – a finger-width.'

I poured a measure into the glass. I couldn't tell what the drink was; the name meant nothing to me. Milady laughed. 'It won't hurt you, you mouse!' She picked up the glass and held it out to me. 'Try it.'

I sniffed the liquid as I raised it to my lips. It was definitely a spirit, and strong. I was no drinker, and I prayed as I drank that it would not cause me to let my guard down. I almost choked as the drink hit the back of my throat. It was harsh, brutal, burning; liquid fire.

Milady took the tumbler from my hand and drank it down in a gulp. She gasped, and giggled. 'I feel as if I could conquer the world. Never mind Dutch courage,' she grinned. 'Irish whiskey is better.' She set down the tumbler and motioned towards the bottle. 'And by God I need it. You may carry on with my hair.' When I had poured another finger of the whiskey I resumed my brushing, although it seemed to take much longer to reach each ten than it had before. 'Put it half-up,' she said, looking at herself in the mirror. 'Pin the top and sides back, and leave the rest loose. He likes that.' She picked up her glass and drank half. 'Aaah.' She sat back, and giggled. 'Have you ever eaten an oyster, Mouse?'

'Of course, milady.' I began to pin her front hair up.

'Have you ever taken one out of its shell?' Milady was not laughing now. She was watching me in the mirror, eyes bright, pink lips parted.

'No, milady, my husband always did it for me.' It was half true; while I liked cooked oysters, the sight of raw ones hunching in their barnacled shells revolted me.

'Oh, there's an art to it.' Milady set down her glass. 'First you need a good glove, a mail glove if you can get it, and a sharp, sharp knife. Then you have to judge your oyster, and slip the knife in in exactly the right place, and give it a little wiggle, and then a little twist, and voila! The oyster opens like a treasure chest, ripe for plundering.' She smiled, her almond eyes closing. 'Men are oysters. You just need to know where to slip your knife, and when to twist. And then they spill all their precious secrets.' She spoke as if it were the most natural thing in the world. Then she downed the rest of her drink and stood up, wobbling a little. 'I shall clean my teeth. Then I need lip salve, and perfume, and a little rouge, and you can help undress me. And then you will go and tell Sir William that I wish to see him upstairs.' She giggled again. 'You must be as silent about what awaits him upstairs as an unopened oyster.'

I felt sick to my stomach, and I suspected it was not the whiskey making me nauseous. Yet I had no choice but to prepare milady, and hide the bottle and glasses, before going downstairs to convey her message to Sir William.

CHAPTER 38

For once I was up before Ada the next morning. 'Come along,' I laughed. 'It's not like you to be a slugabed.'

'Another bloody morning.' Ada leaned on her elbow and blinked. 'You don't even have to be up yet, Bessie.' Exasperation crossed her face. 'I've that to get used to, as well. Ada isn't my favourite name, but at least I'd got into the habit of it.'

'What's your real name?' It was a shock to think that Ada was only Ada by chance.

She darted a look at me. 'Rebecca. My name is Rebecca Davies.' She gave me a shy smile. 'You?'

'Martha Platt.' I almost wished I could tell her the truth. But then, what *was* my real name? I had had so many. 'You can still call me Bessie, if it's easier.'

'Same. It's been so long since anyone but family called me Rebecca, I doubt I'd answer. Go on, you can have first go at the hot water.'

We scrambled down to breakfast together. It was a

grumpy affair, after the comparative ease of Sunday, and everyone seemed to have the weight of a week at work on their shoulders. Even Susan was at table, her mobcap pulled well down, nibbling at her toast.

'Well, those rooms won't air themselves,' said Ada eventually, draining her mug and standing up.

'Do you want any help?' I asked. 'I could do the flowers.'

Ada sighed, heavily. 'Best not. I need to learn how to do them myself, horrid prickly things.' She was the first to leave the table, and gradually, in ones and twos, the others followed suit.

'Susan, the scullery, please,' said Cookie, a trifle sharply. Susan shot her a look and slunk off.

I poured another cup of tea. 'Is there anything I can help with, Cookie? I can't really get started till the family are up and about.'

Cookie shook her head. 'Take your ease while you can, Bessie. Pour me another, it'll be bedlam soon enough.' She slid her cup and saucer across the table, and frowned at the menu she was working on.

I sipped my drink and toyed with another piece of toast, but I was working on the problem of how to get at the newspaper. It usually came between half past six and a quarter to seven. Perhaps if I listened out, and then when I heard it land, I made up an excuse to go into the reception rooms… I glanced at the clock on the mantel, which said twenty past six. I took a tiny bite from the piece of toast, and yawned. I began to see why Susan had rarely appeared at breakfast when Ada and I were there.

At last my patience was rewarded by a rattle and a thud. Cookie seemed to have heard nothing. 'I think milady left her embroidery in the drawing room,' I said. 'I'll go and see.'

'Fetch my recipe book down on the way, would you?' I lifted the book off the shelf and put it on the table by the menu. 'Thank you, dear.' I felt a sudden rush of affection, and guilt for lying to her. *But it's necessary*, I told myself.

The newspaper was still on the mat, and I could hear Ada humming in the drawing room. I crept forward and secured it. Where to take it? My eye fell on the breakfast-room door. That seemed safest. I did not trust the study or the library since my unexpected encounter with Sir William. I hardly breathed as I turned the knob, but it opened with the softest of clicks.

I riffled through the paper for the personal column, trying not to rustle too much, listening all the while for footsteps which might mean discovery. I found it, and scanned the newsprint for *Mercury*; and I gasped at the message.

Queen— Send any further letters to me. Do not let them pass. Mercury.

Did Mr Poskitt know what he was asking? Milady's letters would be expected, surely. If they were missed enquiries would be made, and the finger would point at me. My heart sank as I remembered my recent encounter at the post office. The clerk would remember me, and then – I shuddered to think what my punishment would be. I turned to the news section. The first headline said *Disaster in the East*, in huge letters. Our forces had fallen victim to a surprise attack. *Slaughter . . . a serious setback . . . enemy intelligence...* I closed the paper, and sat down without thinking. Was this the result of milady's letter? The thought made me feel ill. But it also made me resolute. I had to obey the message, and do what I could to avoid the consequences. And from what milady had said to me last night, I would probably get the chance to do so very soon.

I smoothed the paper, refolded it, and got up. I was about to replace it on the mat when the drawing room door opened. 'Oh!' Ada and I both jumped. 'What are you doing with the newspaper, Bessie?' She sounded surprised.

'I was looking for milady's embroidery, and then I heard the paper and went to get it.' I handed it to her. 'I forgot the newspaper isn't my job any more.'

Ada put it on the table. 'I'll get to it when I've finished opening the rooms. You didn't find the embroidery, then?'

'I'd only gone into the breakfast room when the paper came. I didn't want to disturb you. It isn't in the drawing room, is it?'

'Not unless she's hidden it.' Ada smiled.

'Oh well, in that case I must have made a mistake. Sorry I made you jump.' I went back to the connecting door, and took a moment to compose myself before returning to the kitchen.

Cookie was busy with breakfast and Susan was standing in the scullery doorway, drying the dishes and staring at me. I could not stand to be in the room with her, and especially not in my current state. 'I have a stocking to mend,' I said. 'I will do it upstairs, out of your way.'

There was a little cold water left in the bedroom jug. I washed the traces of newsprint from my hands, and bathed my face. In the mirror I looked the same as ever, except that there was a touch more colour in my cheeks; but inside my mind was racing, my heart was banging in my chest, and blood sang in my ears. I felt as if I might faint any minute. I sat on the bed and leaned forward, and gradually the fog ceased to churn around my brain.

Once I intercept milady's letter, I thought, *I must leave before it is missed.* Having seen what had happened to Susan, I did not dare to imagine what milady might do to someone who interfered with her own plans. Once I was back in London and respectable Mrs Hudson again I would be safe, so long as no-one tracked me to Baker Street. I needed enough time to get to London before the hue and cry was raised. In fact, probably the best thing to do with the letter, once I had it, was to get on the next train to London and deliver it personally. That would give me the start I needed. I sighed with relief that I had a plan, and hunted for a stocking to darn.

I had mended my stocking before I heard Sir William's heavy tread on the stairs. There was no clock in the room; but I estimated he was a full half-hour later than usual. Had milady opened her oyster? I put away my mending. Perhaps it was time to offer more help in the kitchen.

I found Ada sitting over a cup of tea with Cookie. 'Aren't you waiting on?' I asked, as I took a seat.

Ada shook her head. 'Sir said not to. He only wanted tea and toast, anyway.'

Cookie tutted. 'It's not right,' she said, shaking her

head.

Ada frowned too. 'He didn't look best pleased to see me,' she said. 'I think he was expecting someone else.'

'I suppose they get used to things, just as we do,' I said.

'Yes,' said Ada, watchful. 'I suppose they do.' She smirked. 'Tom'll be bored of waiting. He had the trap out at the usual time and Sir William's a good forty minutes behind.' She was addressing Cookie, but glanced sidelong at me.

'A gentleman's time is his own perogative,' said Cookie, sternly, and poured herself another cup.

Ada sniggered when the breakfast-room door opened, then closed with a sharp snap. 'There he goes,' she said. 'I'd better go and help him put his coat on.'

Cookie leaned over to me once she had gone. 'Don't pay attention to Ada,' she whispered, although as Cookie was rather deaf it was a loud whisper. 'She likes things regular.'

'Yes,' I said.

Cookie sighed. 'I'll be glad when things are back to normal, that I will. It's been too topsy-turvy lately for my liking.'

We listened to the rattle of the front-door bolts. Outside Blaze neighed, impatient to go. Sir William was on his way to London again.

And milady's bell rang not two minutes after the carriage had left.

CHAPTER 39

'Good morning, Mouse,' sang milady. 'It's a beautiful day, isn't it? Lay out my pale-blue silk, with everything to match, and run me a bath.' Her eyes sparkled, and the two high spots of colour I had seen on her cheeks the evening before were still there.

'Would you like a breakfast tray, milady?' I asked. 'Shall I ring, or go down?'

Milady held up a finger. 'Not yet. I'll get ready first. It wouldn't be fair of me to disturb the other servants so early, would it?' She wagged the finger, and laughed.

'Is it a special day, milady?' I opened the wardrobe and drew out her blue silk, running my hand down the luxurious folds. It must be, to wear silk in the morning.

'It is now,' said Milady. 'I am going to London to do some Christmas shopping, and you will attend me.'

'To London, milady?' I gaped. 'Me?'

'Yes, London, Mouse. You shall be a town mouse today and carry my parcels, so you had better put your best frock on too when you have finished with me.'

'Yes, milady,' I said, and went to run her bath. As the water gushed, I thought. Milady, clearly, *had* opened her oyster, and discovered a pearl which she planned to deliver in person. There would be no letter to intercept, as per Mr Poskitt's instructions, but what could I do instead?

The answer wafted from the rose-scented water. *Get away somehow, and intercept her.*

I bided my time until I was applying milady's jasmine perfume, while she admired herself in the mirror. 'Milady, I hope you don't mind me asking, but could *I* do some Christmas shopping too?'

'You, Mouse?' she laughed. 'Well, I suppose so. I have private business to attend to first: a very particular present. A *special order.*' She laughed. 'You may do it then, Mouse. You can hardly expect me to attend you round the slop markets.'

'Thank you, milady, you are very kind.' I pinned up a last stray curl. 'Shall I ring for your tray now?'

'No, go downstairs and tell them, and at the same time you can ask them to keep the carriage waiting when it gets back. Oh, and bring the Bradshaw – the red train timetable. You'll find it in Sir William's desk.' She patted her back hair and smiled at herself in the mirror.

'A breakfast tray, at this time? What's got into her?' Cookie banged the tray onto the kitchen table.

'The Christmas spirit,' I said, smiling. 'Milady is going shopping in London. Can someone ask Tom to wait the carriage when he returns, please?'

'I'll see to it.' Cookie began to cut bread. 'Will you wait

275

for the tray?'

'Could someone bring it up, please? I have to get ready too.'

'What, are you going as well?'

'Yes, to carry the parcels.'

Something clattered on the scullery floor. 'Susan!' bellowed Cookie. 'If you break another plate it'll come out of your wages!' She sighed. 'I thought Janey was careless.' She turned back to me. 'Milady'll have you loaded like a pack mule on the way home.'

I found the Bradshaw in its usual place in Sir William's desk and I took it up to milady. 'Good,' she said, patting it. 'Now go and get ready. You have until I finish breakfast.'

I fled to my room, removed my apron and cap, changed into my black dress, and pinned on my 'best' hat with the artificial flowers. Then I took my small stock of money from the toe of the stocking I kept in the drawer, and put it into my bag. I took my coat from the nail, and looked at the room – the two iron beds, the foxed mirror, the photo of my 'husband'—

A tap at the door, and Susan entered.

'What are you doing here?' I snapped, then felt a pang of guilt.

Susan said nothing, and sat on the bed. 'I saw you,' she said.

'I beg your pardon?' I stared at her. Her mobcap was slightly askew, her fringe crooked. 'I don't have time to listen to nonsense, I have to go to London with milady. I can't believe you have the nerve to come up here, after—' My hand went to my hat.

'I saw you reading the paper through the breakfast-room keyhole.' Susan's blue eyes met mine. Yet they were not accusing, but clear as a child's. 'Milady told me you couldn't hardly read.'

I imagined the pair of them giggling over my stupidity. Now here I was, caught. 'I was trying to read it—'

'No you weren't. You was reading properly.' Susan paused, studying me. 'I'm not stupid,' she said. 'And if you pretended not to be able to read, what else are you pretending?'

My mind was spinning, trying to find a way out. I was so close, so close, and Susan could bring it down with a few words. 'Susan, do you hate milady?'

'*Yes.*' Susan's mouth twisted and her eyes were the hard, bright blue of sapphires. 'I thought she liked me, really liked me, and she didn't care a bit. She played favourites with you, and made me mad, and when I paid you back, she did – she did this.' She touched the edge of her mobcap, carefully. 'So yes, I hate her.'

'I'm sorry, Susan,' I said.

'It's all right for you,' she said. 'At least you've got some hair. But that isn't why I'm here.'

Milady would be breakfasting by now. 'I must go soon,' I said. 'I can't keep milady waiting.'

'You ain't really a maid, are you?'

Susan's expression seemed guileless. I decided to gamble. 'Susan, what do you want most in the whole world?'

'To have my hair back as it was.' She fingered one of the straggling locks stitched to her cap. 'And to pay back milady for what she did to me.' The sneer which spoilt her pretty mouth showed me that the old Susan was still there.

'Then if you keep quiet, Susan, and tell no one that you have seen me reading, or that I'm not really a maid, then I shall send you a golden wig from London, the best I can find.'

She motioned me closer. 'If you ain't a maid, what are you?' she murmured.

My heart was thumping so loud that I feared milady would hear it. I swallowed, and looked at Susan. Would my bribe be enough? I cupped my hand carefully to her ear and whispered. 'A Government spy.'

Susan was silent for a moment. 'On milady?'

I nodded.

'Then you'd best know this.' And she cupped her hand to my ear, and whispered.

**

Milady was halfway through a piece of toast when I returned. 'About time, Mouse,' she said, and put the half-eaten toast down. 'Help me on with my things.' I could hear the excitement in her voice. I obliged, hoping that any trembling on my part would be put down to my own anticipation of the treat. Milady's eyes sparkled as I fastened her cloak, and she almost panted to be gone.

'Where are you going?' she asked, as I went towards our part of the house.

'To the back stairs, milady.'

'Today you are attending me, so the *front* stairs, Mouse. Take my bag.' She sailed down the steps, and I followed, the thick carpet like a feather bed compared to the hard treads of our own stairs.

'We shall be back by tea-time,' milady called in the direction of the servants' quarters, and waited for me to open the door. Ada was hurrying to do it, but milady waved her off and she stood back, her hands clasped before her, looking straight ahead. She made me uneasy; but once we stepped outside and I closed the door behind us, the feeling vanished. I had left the house, perhaps never to return; I had a little money, and had secured some free time; and I had information from Susan which I could not have hoped for.

'No need to rush, Tom,' said milady as he helped her up. 'We have half an hour to catch the train I want. Mouse, do you have the Bradshaw for the journey back?'

I patted my bag. 'Yes, milady.'

'Good. Sit up front with Tom.'

Tom winked at me as he climbed up. 'Let's see if we can get there without you turning green, eh?'

'That would be very kind,' I smiled, but inside my stomach was doing somersaults. We were going to London; milady was going to betray her husband; and I would betray milady.

CHAPTER 40

Any advantage I had gained from Tom's gentler journey to the station was soon lost on the train. I was crammed into third class, without a seat, hanging from a leather strap under the stink of the lamp, and buffeted by draughts from the sides of the carriage. Milady, of course, was in first class. I just hoped I would be able to fight my way out of the train in London and find her, or this whole trip – and possibly my whole mission – would be a dead loss. A man standing near blew a cloud of cigar smoke into my face.

The houses outside were getting closer and closer together, and I began to elbow my way to the door with the aim of escaping as quickly as possible. A few people swore at me, but I did not care.

'Paddington!' called the porters. I gripped the door handle as the train slowed, and almost fell onto the platform as people pushed behind me.

I stumbled out of harm's way and looked about me. The first-class carriages were at the head of the train, and I

walked towards them, seeking milady's fur cloak and blue dress. She descended carefully from her carriage, waving away the porter who had leapt forward to assist her. 'I am here, milady,' I said, hurrying to her side.

'Of course you are, Mouse,' she said, completely unruffled. 'Go and hold a cab.'

I chose the steadiest-looking horse I could see, and presently we were moving again; but away from the main shopping thoroughfares, round the edge of Hyde Park. 'Where do you plan to shop, milady?' I asked, as innocently as I could.

'Not here,' she replied with a short laugh. 'I have my special order to deal with first.'

We seemed to be in Belgravia. Cool, smooth, white townhouses, and the occasional tree or church. No costermongers yelled, no hawkers knocked on the doors. The cab rolled to a decorous stop.

Milady handed me a sovereign. 'Pay the cabman, Mouse, and give him a tip.' I did so and then helped her out. She settled her skirts and looked up and down the street. 'Am I disarranged, Mouse?'

'Not at all, milady.'

'Thank you.' She consulted her watch. 'Now, Mouse, you may have two hours to buy whatever hideous things your heart desires, so long as you can still carry my parcels. This is Chiltern Square. You see the church clock there?'

I nodded.

'What time is it, Mouse?'

'Half past ten, milady.'

'I want you back here – exactly here, by this lamp-post – by half past twelve. If I am not here, you will wait. I think your needs will be best satisfied – certainly for your limited means – in Pimlico, which is that way.' She waved a dismissive arm. 'Be off with you!'

I bobbed a little curtsey and set off in the direction she had indicated. I looked back once, and milady was still standing where I had left her. She flapped a gloved hand at me impatiently, and I hurried on. I did not need to see which house she entered. The address was seared into my brain.

If I was in Belgravia – which I must be, since Chiltern Square was there, I knew that much – then I was a good two miles from Somerset House. Even in a cab, assuming a Belgravia cab driver would let me on, I might be delayed by traffic. What if Mr Poskitt were out? Or they would not admit me? I glanced at my worn boots, and sighed my exasperation. Two hours was not enough.

I would find a post office and send a telegram, but not in Belgravia. I had already been given a suspicious look by a young man in spats, strolling in the direction of Green Park. I kept my pace until I was on the outskirts of Pimlico, then I ran, seeking a pillar box or a sign for a post office. A flash of red a few yards further on – oh, let it be – yes, it was! I paused, gasping for breath, before going in.

There was a queue of two in front of me. I composed and recomposed in my head the message I would send, and checked my bag for money. At last it was my turn, and I stepped forward. 'I need to send an urgent telegram.'

The clerk passed a form over the counter, with a pencil.

'Come back when you've filled it in, madam.'

I took the form to a nearby ledge. *Mr Poskitt, Somerset House, Strand, WC1*, I wrote in the *To* box. *From* was more difficult, and I decided to leave it while I wrote my message.

Urgent Queen has secrets STOP With Moriarty 45 Chiltern Square till 12.30 STOP At—

I took the form back to the counter. 'Which post office is this, please?'

'Belgrave Road,' said the clerk crisply.

'Thank you.' I added *Belgrave Road PO STOP Please advise*, and wrote in the *From* box *Queen/Mercury*.

The clerk took the form and counted. 'One shilling. Is an answer required, madam?'

'Yes please,' I said, sliding a shilling across the counter to him. 'I'll wait.'

A couple of minutes later the clerk was back behind the counter and serving the next customer. I tried not to fidget. When the customer had gone, the clerk flashed me a kindly smile. 'Your telegram will have been sent by now, madam.' I nodded my thanks and looked at the clock above his head. Ten minutes to eleven already. Milady would be with Professor Moriarty, smiling her slow smile. She had spoken of a special order; what would she get in return for her gift?

I started at a cough from the desk. The clerk was eyeing me. 'Excuse me, madam, but do you answer to – *Queen Mercury*?' He pronounced the words as if he might break them.

I came to the counter. 'I do.'

'Then I have an answer for you.'

I took the piece of paper, on which was scribbled *Wait outside coming now P*. 'Thank you, thank you!' I cried, and almost fell over my own feet in my haste to leave.

I scanned the street. How quickly could they reach me? And how would they come? I remembered Mr Poskitt's plain carriage – would he take that, or jump in a cab? I watched every fast-moving vehicle, but none stopped. I knew that it would take even the fastest cab fifteen minutes to come from Somerset House, and that assumed Mr Poskitt could hail one right away.

I looked through the glass pane of the post-office door at the clock. Five minutes past eleven. I willed the horse through the streets, and if wishing could have given it wings at its heels, it would have flown. I longed to move, to pace, to get rid of my surplus energy, but I dared not. I could not move from the spot.

A cab was coming at great speed. Suddenly I panicked. What if it was a trap? What if milady had had me followed, and the cab took me to Chiltern Square? I remembered Emmett Stanley screaming and writhing on his bed, and turned away. Milady would show no mercy.

'Whoa, whoa there!' The cabman hauled on the reins and the horse almost lifted off the ground. The cab jerked to a stop just past the post office. The blind flew up and Mr Poskitt stuck his head out. I stepped forward, more thankful than I had ever been to see him. He was looking up and down the street. 'Madam, have you seen—'

'Mr Poskitt, it's me. Nell Hudson.'

Mr Poskitt stared for a second, and his brow furrowed

as if trying to make me out; then he smiled broadly. 'Of course it is!' He opened the door. 'We'll talk on the way.' He helped me in, taking hold of my ungloved, battered hand as if he might break it. 'Chiltern Square,' he called to the driver, and we set off.

'What is going to happen?' I asked, pulling the shade back down.

'As soon as I got your telegram I wired Scotland Yard. They are sending their best men down, and we shall take the pair of them in for questioning.'

'In that case,' I said, 'there are some other things you should know.' And leaning forward, I told him what I had seen, and what Susan had told me that morning. Mr Poskitt maintained his composure; but his hand gripped the top of his cane until the knuckles were white.

'I see,' he said. 'I see.'

'Will it be enough to clear Mycroft Holmes?'

Mr Poskitt managed a smile weak as January sunshine. 'More than enough.' He tapped his cane on the panel. 'Stop here, driver, and wait.' He leaned over and drew up the blind.

'Will my name come into this?' I felt an icy hand squeezing my heart. What if, somehow, milady walked free? She would find me, and kill me, and it would not be an easy death.

'Possibly.' Mr Poskitt peeped out. 'Ah, here we are. Now listen.' Mr Poskitt knocked a rhythm on the side of the cab. 'You will stay here. Lock yourself in, and do not open the door except to my knock. You may peep, if you wish, but do not raise the blind.'

I caught a glimpse of another vehicle, further down the road, as he opened the door. It was not a cab, and that was all I could make out before the door slammed. I locked the doors, and raised the shade a quarter of an inch. I was scared to look; but not to look would be worse. I could see policemen now, some in uniform, one or two in plain clothes. Mr Poskitt was advancing towards one of them, signalling to the door, and as he turned I saw the profile of Inspector Lestrade. He knocked, the door opened, a badge was shown, and half the group, including Mr Poskitt, stepped in. The door closed behind them.

I waited, my breath loud in the silent cab. Occasionally the horse harrumphed, and each time I started as if a gun had gone off. What time was it? How long had the policemen and Mr Poskitt been in there? I could not see the church clock from either side of the cab—

A scream made the hair on the back of my neck stand up. Another, and another. I knew it, though I had never heard her scream. I closed the blind. I could not be seen, I *must not* be seen.

The scream turned into a gurgling laugh. I moved the blind a fraction and glimpsed a flurry of blue silk. Milady was between two policemen, one on each arm, who were half-carrying, half-dragging her down the street. 'Take your damn hands off me!' she shouted, struggling.

As they neared the other vehicle, a policeman went ahead and opened the door, and two more came forward, lifted milady's feet from the ground, and put her into the vehicle. The door slammed shut.

But there was someone else; a tall, broad man with a

high forehead, who walked unrestrained, talking to a stooped white-haired man in striped trousers. He reminded me a little of Mycroft save for his eyes, which were deep-set and dark. His expression seemed benign, amiable; but his gaze roved about the street. His eyes seemed to find the sliver of space I was peeping through, and I dropped the shade at once. I did not dare look again, and shrank back against the leather seat, panting.

Professor Moriarty...?

At last Mr Poskitt's knock sounded, and I opened the door. 'We have them,' he said, smiling. 'I shall go along with them, but I have an escort you will know.' He stepped back, and Inspector Lestrade appeared in the doorway.

'Inspector!' I cried, holding out a hand. 'It has been a long time since I saw you.'

'And I you.' Inspector Lestrade smiled; but I had already seen the flash of dismay in his eyes. 'I should not have known you, Nell. And it seems that your hard work has paid off.'

'Am I so changed?' I knew it was not what I should be concerned with at this moment, but the reaction of both men to my appearance had shocked me.

'It is superficial, I am sure,' said the inspector, soothingly. He banged on the roof, and the cab began to move.

'Where are we going?' I asked.

'To Scotland Yard, Nell. You look as if you need a cup of tea, and I need a full statement from you before I take you back.'

'Back?' I raised my eyebrows. 'To Baker Street?'

287

'Hardly,' said the inspector, stretching his legs out. 'Back to Chambers Hall. You have a job to do.'

CHAPTER 41

I stared at Inspector Lestrade. 'I'm not going back,' I said flatly. 'I *can't* go back.'

'But there may be more to find out! You are in the best position to do it by far, Nell. Who else could we put in, at this point?' Then he grinned. 'The only alternative, really, would be to arrest you as a possible accomplice to milady.'

I glared at him and he held his hands up. 'For the record, only.'

'You'll take my statement at Scotland Yard, and then I am going home,' I said firmly.

The inspector said no more until the carriage drew in under the familiar archway. I, however, thought a great deal, and marshalled my arguments in case they were needed. Going back to the Hall was both futile and dangerous, even assuming that Susan had not shared what she knew. Sir William would question me, and quite possibly suspect me. Ada, I felt, had noticed my interest in the newspaper, and it would not take her long to put two and two together. Everyone else would hate me for what had happened, and blame me for not taking better care of milady. And if she was somehow exonerated, and came back…?

At Great Scotland Yard I gave as full a statement as I possibly could, hoping that would count in my favour. 'Excellent,' said the inspector, blotting the last sheet and replacing the cap on his pen. 'It isn't absolutely conclusive, of course – your analytical eye will see that, Nell – but Lady Chambers' remarks, as well as her actions, are most suggestive.' He squared off the sheets. 'Now, about what we discussed earlier—'

'There is nothing to discuss,' I said. 'I have done what I was asked to do, and my employer – who is Mr Poskitt, not you – is satisfied. Going back would put me in danger, and achieve nothing.' I got up from the table and opened the door. 'Good day to you, Inspector.'

'Nell, wait—'

I stepped into the corridor and almost collided with Mr Poskitt, hurrying along with a policeman and—

Sir William.

'Oh, er, do excuse me,' muttered Mr Poskitt.

'What is *she* doing here?' exclaimed Sir William. 'Martha, what has happened? Why did you leave your mistress?' His face showed more anger than confusion. *This is what I can expect if I return*, I thought.

I heard footsteps behind me, and Inspector Lestrade joined us. 'Well, Martha, what do you have to say for yourself?'

Mr Poskitt caught my eye, and shook his head almost

imperceptibly.

'I have told the inspector everything I know, Sir William,' I said.

'And now you can tell me,' he replied, drawing himself up.

It was my turn to shake my head. 'I'm sorry, Sir William.'

'What do you mean, you're sorry?' His voice rose. 'How dare you, a servant, speak to me like that? I've a good mind to—'

'I am not your servant.' Oh, the effort it cost me not to shout back at him. 'I was engaged to pose as one.'

'What?' exclaimed Sir William. 'That's ridiculous.' He began to laugh. 'What's the point of that? She can barely read!' he said, turning to Mr Poskitt. 'Who in their right mind would engage her?'

'Who, indeed,' murmured Mr Poskitt, looking exceptionally ill at ease.

'I can read perfectly well, thank you, Sir William,' I said. 'I merely pretended I couldn't when you caught me with the newspaper.'

There was a distinctly unpleasant glint in Sir William's eye. 'So you lied to me, Martha, and you are a spy.'

I met his eyes. 'Yes, I am; and so is milady. But unlike her, I am on the right side of the law.'

'I never heard such rubbish!' scoffed Sir William. 'My wife wouldn't hurt a fly!'

Inspector Lestrade coughed. 'Excuse me, Sir William, but does the address 45 Chiltern Square mean anything to you?'

Sir William shook his head. 'I don't recall anything. Should it?'

Inspector Lestrade's face was expressionless. 'A man named Moriarty lives there, and your wife visited him today. We suspect that the purpose of her visit was to pass on classified information which she had obtained from you.'

Sir William reeled backwards as if he had been punched. 'Oh my God.' He put a hand on the wall to steady himself. He looked utterly stricken. 'Last night—'

'What happened last night?' Lestrade prompted gently.

Sir William's dazed expression changed, and his mouth was set firm. 'I shall say nothing further about the matter without a lawyer present.' He frowned. 'Does my wife have access to a lawyer?'

'She has not been arrested, Sir William,' the inspector said smoothly. 'She is merely helping us with our enquiries at present.' He paused. 'So you did not know that your wife was planning to go to London today?'

'Of course not, man,' said Sir William. 'She was probably buying a present for me. Of course she wouldn't tell me!' His tone, though, was not exasperated, nor indignant. It was bitter, and defeated, and cornered.

'If you'll take a seat in here, Sir William,' said the inspector, 'I have some questions which I would prefer to ask you in private.'

'I should hope so,' muttered Sir William. He glared at me. 'You ought to be ashamed of yourself.'

'Ought I?' I faced him square on. 'I have cleaned your house, prepared your food, and waited on you. I have borne your wife's rudeness, and suffered at her hands. But through it all, I have done my duty.' I glared at Sir William. 'You, Sir William, have not.'

Mr Poskitt appeared ready to faint. 'Gentlemen, if you will excuse me.' I nodded to him and to the inspector, and walked down the corridor with my head held high.

It is over, I thought, as I emerged into the vestibule of Scotland Yard. *I can go home.* I saw myself, in my best parlourmaid's dress, knocking on the door at Baker Street. Yet I could not imagine what anyone would say, how they would look. Surely they would be pleased to see me? I shook the thought out of my head, and walked into the sunshine.

I blinked, once, twice.

Outside the entrance a man was loitering, watching the world go by. He had a stoop to his shoulders, and under his hat white hair stuck out. Moriarty's servant. I looked away hurriedly, but fear made me look again, and when I did, he was staring right at me.

***

How many stooped old men must there be in London? I asked myself, as my boots pounded the street. I glanced back once, and glimpsed him sauntering behind. *If it isn't him, it's his twin brother.* He leered at me, and it was all I could do not to break into a run.

I could not go to Baker Street now, for it would draw Professor Moriarty there. He would know where I lived, and I would put Sherlock in danger, as well as myself.

Where can I go? Where will I be safe?
What would Sherlock do?

293

He would find an advantage.

With every step I took my brain jolted. I longed to stop, to compose myself, but there was no time.

How could I lose him? I had but a few pennies left; not enough to get to Petticoat Lane, never mind buy a fresh disguise.

I was on the Strand. Somerset House was out of the question; it would link me to Mr Poskitt and Mycroft Holmes. Charing Cross station loomed to my left and I plunged in, darting among the knots of people seeking their platform. He was not in the station yet…

What is my advantage?

I ran to the ladies' conveniences and dashed in.

The bright lights did me no favours in the mirror, but I did not care. I snatched off my hat and ripped the flowers off. 'Do you have a pair of scissors?' I asked the attendant, who was staring at me.

She nodded, eyes wide, and handed a pair of small, sharp scissors to me. 'Thank you,' I said, and began to cut off the brim.

She found her tongue. 'What are you doing?'

'I'm being followed by a man,' I said, 'and I'm scared. I'm trying to lose him.'

'*Oh*,' she whispered. She opened the drawer of her little stand and pulled out a red woollen shawl. 'Here, someone left this—'

I seized it gratefully, took off my coat, and settled the shawl in its place.

A young woman dressed even less smartly than me came out of a cubicle as I changed. 'You leavin' that coat?'

she asked, not looking directly at me.

'You can have it,' I said.

She grinned, slipped it on, and left hurriedly, I suspect in case I changed my mind. I would have felt guilty except that she was nothing like me, being dark-haired and buxom. The coat fitted her better, anyway.

I washed my face, recalling how many times I had been excited to transform into someone else in the secrecy of a ladies' room. Now it could mean life or death. A few minutes later I put two of my remaining pennies in the attendant's dish, took the Bradshaw from my bag, and strolled out, pretending to look up a train. I peeped around the edge of my book many times; but as far as I could tell, Moriarty's man had gone. And yet I still did not dare to go to Baker Street.

I took a roundabout route to my destination, though it was far away. I walked down side-streets, I cut through alleys, criss-crossing the district as the light faded. My mouth was so dry I could barely speak. At last it was fairly dark, and I dared to approach the place I sought; Portland Road.

The rookery was just as I remembered, but quieter; it had not warmed up for the evening yet. I walked into the court, took a deep breath, and whistled as Sherlock had done. Someone leaned out of a window and swore at me. A dog barked. My eyes were wet. Had I come so far, to fall now? I took a shaky breath and whistled again. This time there was more shouting; but at last a door opened. I walked towards the sound; no light came from within. Whoever had opened the door did not step forward. They were waiting for me. As I approached, a small shaft of light appeared, and behind the dark lantern I glimpsed Wiggins.

'*You* ain't Sherlock.' He laughed, then peered at me, frowning. ''Oo are you? 'Ow do you know the code?'

I came closer, until the light shone on my face. 'I remembered you, Wiggins, not so long ago. Don't you remember me?'

Wiggins's face changed. He knew me, I could tell. 'Bloody hell, ma'am,' he whispered. He shut the dark lantern, pulled me into the doorway, and bolted the door behind us.

CHAPTER 42

Once the door was closed, Wiggins opened the dark lantern and took my hand. 'Up the stairs, ma'am, to the top. Watch where you're walking.' I stumbled after him, up stairs which were missing pieces, and grew more crooked as we climbed, until we reached a bare room with a mattress on the floor. The room I had shared with Ada was a palace by comparison. Wiggins took off his coat and spread it on the bed. 'Get some rest, ma'am, you look all in. I'll go and scare up food. You'll be safe here; I'll lock you in.' I was about to protest that I did not want to be locked in when I remembered my first reaction to the slum. Wiggins I trusted; everyone else was an unknown quantity, and if Wiggins thought I should be locked in, perhaps I should. I sat on the mattress, wrapping my shawl around me.

'Wiggins…' He paused on the threshold. 'Don't tell *anyone* where I am.'

He leaned on the doorframe. 'Why not, ma'am?' His

voice was perfectly reasonable.

'I'm worried someone might have followed me. I want them to think they've lost the trail.'

'Like I said, I'm only going for food.' And he was gone. The key grated in the lock. I curled up on the mattress, and sighed.

I was woken by a gentle shaking. At first I thought it was Ada. 'Not time to get up,' I murmured.

'It's morning, just,' grinned Wiggins. 'I looked in on you, but you was snoring fit to bust.'

'I'm sorry.' I rubbed my eyes and sat up.

Wiggins put a paper bag on the bed. Inside I found an orange, a large piece of cake and some cabbage leaves. 'I washed 'em best I could.'

'Have you – have you seen a man with white hair and a stoop? And striped trousers?'

Wiggins shook his head. 'No ma'am.'

I began to peel the orange. 'What do I owe you?'

Wiggins chuckled. 'I didn't get these with *money*.' He wiggled his fingers. 'I gotter go. Got work to do for a friend of yours.' He grinned.

I was wide awake in an instant. 'How is he?'

''E's well enough,' said Wiggins. 'Although he'd be better if he knew you were safe.'

'Has he said anything about me?'

Wiggins snorted. 'He's had me hunting for you for weeks. Can't I drop a hint?'

'No!' The word came out more forcefully than I had meant, and Wiggins looked at me as if I had slapped him. 'I mean, I'm not sure I am safe, yet. And if I'm not, he

298

isn't either. If no-one comes sniffing around, I'll go later. If I can stay for now,' I said hastily.

'I ain't got no objection,' said Wiggins, 'but you'll have to stay up here. People round here don't like strange faces, and if they decide to ask questions you won't like it.'

'I'll stay here,' I said.

'Yes, you will.' Wiggins pointed to a tin can in the corner of the room. 'If you gotta go, go in that. Tip it out the window if you need to. But don't let anyone see you. Make that food last, there's no more till I get back.'

I spent the day turning the events of the previous days and weeks over in my mind, and peeping out of the grimy window. I longed to return to Baker Street, but what sort of welcome could I expect?

Wiggins came back mid-afternoon, as far as I could judge, with a hunk of bread and some bacon. Once he had cooked it on the fire outside, we made a small meal. I asked how his day had gone, but Wiggins shook his head. 'Reckon I'm getting good at keeping quiet,' he said, stuffing a large piece of bacon into his mouth.

'I don't *want* to—' I began.

Wiggins swallowed his mouthful. 'Where've you been, then?'

'I can't tell you.'

He gnawed at a chunk of bread. 'Zackly.' He swallowed, with an effort. 'You'll be able to get off soon, ma'am,' he said. 'I've seen nuffink unusual out there, and believe me, I oughter know.'

'You're sure?'

'Sure as I can be.' He scrutinised me as he chewed.

'You scared?'

I nodded.

''Ang on.' He went to the corner of the room, lifted a floorboard, and returned with a small bottle wrapped in a dirty cloth. 'Brandy.' I uncorked it, took a sip, and gasped as the spirit burned my throat. It was like the burn of the whiskey I had drunk with milady. I corked the bottle hastily and handed it back. 'He's missed you, you know. You've no need to be scared of that.'

It was not the brandy that made me unable to speak.

'Time to go, ma'am,' said Wiggins. He gave me a hand up. 'The light's fading, and the gas-lamps will be on soon.'

I put my mangled hat back on. 'Thank you for looking after me, Wiggins.'

He shuffled his feet. 'S'all right, ma'am. Any friend of Sherlock 'Olmes…'

I pulled the brass ring from my finger. 'Here, see what you can get for this. I don't need it any more. Wait—' I rummaged in my bag. There were still a few coins left. I divided it in two, and put half into his grimy hand. 'It isn't much, but—'

Wiggins's jagged grin lit up his face. 'It's 'preciated, ma'am. Now go on home. Keep to the back streets.'

'I will.'

Wiggins saw me down the ramshackle stairs and into the street. I looked back once, before I turned the corner, and while Wiggins had retreated into the doorway, I knew he was still there.

I walked quickly, my feet slipping in my boots. I wanted to run straight to Baker Street, but it was too dangerous. A running woman in poor dress would be seen as in trouble, or up to no good, and I would probably find a policeman chasing me in no time. So I walked quickly, eyes down, but with every step I drew nearer to Baker Street. To home. My mind kept straying to what everyone might be doing at this time. Billy and Martha were probably preparing dinner. Dr Watson might be returning from work at Barts Hospital. And Sherlock – where would he be? I found my pace quickening, and reluctantly pushed him away.

It was only a few minutes' walk. I was coming to streets I knew like the back of my hand – although given what my hands looked like now, the streets seemed more familiar. I huddled into my shawl, in case I saw anyone I knew. My heart thumped in my chest, and sweat ran down my back.

And here was the alley that led into the maze of pathways near Baker Street. I felt as if I had not breathed until I entered its welcome darkness. My steps echoed on the cobbles. I ran my fingers along the cool, rough brick wall. I could barely keep from running.

One more turn, and the familiar back view of townhouses rose before me. 221B was twelve houses down. I could bear it no longer. I ran the last few yards to the back door, rang the bell, and hammered on the door.

Martha opened the door with a face like thunder. 'What do you mean by making such a noise?' she snapped. 'What do you want, anyway? We've no scraps.'

I took off my hat. 'Martha, it's me.' I tried to smile, but her stare unnerved me. The enormity of what I had done hit me. I had left everyone without warning, with no clue of my whereabouts. What must they think of me? My knees trembled, and I put a hand on the door-frame to steady myself. 'Please let me in.'

Martha's jaw dropped. She grabbed my arm and pulled me inside so swiftly that I almost fell, then slammed the door. 'She's home!' she yelled at the top of her lungs. 'She's come home!' I buried my face in her shoulder, and her hug was ferocious in its strength.

Billy came charging over, and his expression changed from welcome to something like alarm. 'Good God, ma'am! Begging your pardon, but—'

'Never mind that!' Martha cried. 'Go and get the master!' She helped me to a chair and I sat down gladly. 'I'll put the kettle on.'

Billy sped off, bellowing 'Mr Holmes! Mr Holmes!' Martha mentioned Dr Watson, but I had no ears for her. I only cared about what was going on two storeys up. Then footsteps clattered downstairs, and Sherlock burst into the room.

'Nell!' Somehow I was standing up, though I felt myself wobbling, and before I knew it I was in his arms. I could scarcely breathe, he held me so tightly. 'Where have you – what have you—' He lifted my chin, and kissed me, and then held me close again. 'It doesn't matter. You're back.' He rested his chin on the top of my head and sighed, a long, shuddering sigh. 'You're back.'

'We'll just go and see about something,' said Martha. 'Come along, Billy.' She took Billy's arm and led him away, closing the kitchen door.

Sherlock pulled back a little to look at me. 'You're shaking.'

302

'I need a hot bath.'

'You do,' he said, running a fingertip over my cheek. 'Certainly before dinner.'

'Oh, *dinner…*' I sighed with pleasure. 'With proper cutlery, and napkins…'

'And all dressed up?' He smiled. 'Where did you get these clothes?' He took my hand and examined it, holding it gently, exploring the callouses, the rough places, my ragged nails. 'What have you been doing to your poor hands?'

'Hard work,' I said. 'It is over now.'

Sherlock studied me for a long time. 'And – this?' He ran his hand over my hair.

'It's a long story.'

'One that you'll tell me?'

'Yes, but not yet. Not until I'm clean, and wearing my own clothes, and feeling more like myself.'

'Yes. You look . . . different.'

'That was the point. You didn't even see the worst of it.'

Sherlock touched my face again, and I couldn't read his expression. 'Would you have known me, if I had passed you in the street?' I asked, and my voice sounded small even to myself.

'I don't know.' He met my eyes. 'I looked for you every day. On the street, in places where I thought you might be. I know you told me not to try and find you, but every day I wondered where you were, what you were doing. Sometimes I thought I saw you . . . but it never was.'

'I'm so sorry,' I whispered. 'I wish I could have told you.'

303

'I know.' He bent his head to kiss me. 'But you're home now.' He kissed me again, and again, until we were both gasping, half-laughing, on the verge of tears. 'Come along.' He opened the kitchen door, and scooped me up in his arms. 'Let me look after you. We'll start with that hot bath. I'm sure you're absolutely filthy underneath.'

I rested my head on his shoulder. 'Will you ask me lots of questions?'

Sherlock shook his head. 'When you're ready, Nell.' He carried me up the stairs as if I weighed nothing at all, and after so much time away, so many worries, so much trouble, my heart felt as light as a feather.

CHAPTER 43

A tap at the door. 'Nell?' Sherlock's voice came softly. 'Martha is waiting dinner.'

'Just a moment,' I called. I knew she was; the clock said it was well past the usual dinner-time. But still I was not ready.

'May I come in?' Sherlock asked.

I tried to fluff up my still-damp hair, and sighed. 'Yes, come in.'

'Dr Watson is home, and we have told him the good news—' he began, then stopped. 'What is it, Nell?'

'Nothing fits.' I plucked at the loose bodice of my dress. 'My dresses look wrong. I – I don't feel like myself any more.' I sat on the edge of the bed and buried my face in my hands. 'My hair—' I pulled at the curling strand that had fallen forward, 'everything.'

Sherlock sat beside me on the bed. 'Then we'll get you things that do fit, and you can get a wig, if you wish.' He stroked my hair.

The tale poured out of me; Mr Poskitt's telegram, the proposition, the interview, milady, the house, Sir William and the newspaper, the servants, the incident with Susan, the letter, the trip to London… I had not realised what a relief it would be to tell the story, to let it go. Sherlock took my hand early in the narrative, and his grip tightened at certain parts of the story; then he would recall himself, and slacken it.

When I stopped speaking he was silent for a while. I glanced across; his face was inscrutable. 'What are you thinking?'

He looked up, and smiled, but it faded quickly. 'I am not sure I could have done it.'

'Of course you could. It was mostly about working hard and putting up with things.'

He smiled, and this time it stayed. 'Exactly.' He touched my cheek, and his hand strayed to the nape of my neck. 'How does it feel?'

'My hair?' I reached behind, and our fingers joined. 'Odd. Light. I can put it up, just.' I shivered as I remembered Susan's cropped skull. 'I must buy a wig tomorrow.'

'It really isn't that bad—'

'Not for me!' He raised his eyebrows. 'I made a promise to someone.'

'Very well,' he said, laughing. 'Tomorrow you may buy whatever you like; but tonight you must have dinner with Dr Watson and me, and be waited on.' He lifted me to my feet. 'Now put your hair up and make yourself respectable, young lady.'

I combed, and pinned, and put on earrings and a necklace, and found my little slippers. 'Something is missing,' said Sherlock, eyeing my left hand.

'Oh!' My other hand flew to it. 'I sent it, in my letter—'

'You did.' Sherlock slipped his finger inside his collar and drew out a fine chain. My ring was suspended on it.

I slid the ring from the chain. It was warm, from him. I kissed it, read the inscription, and slipped it onto my finger. It fitted a little more loosely than before, but it still fitted. Sherlock touched the ring. 'There,' he said softly. 'Now we are complete.'

***

Everyone was pleased to see me downstairs, and very complimentary, to the point where I wondered if Sherlock had briefed them. We began with drinks in the parlour, and I asked Martha and Billy to join us. Dr Watson beamed. 'A toast!' he cried. 'To the safe return of Mrs Hudson!'

I grinned. 'I haven't been called that for a while,' I said, as we clinked glasses.

'Pardon me asking, ma'am, but what have you been doing all this time?' Billy's eyes were like saucers, and I knew that he was anticipating a good yarn.

'I went undercover, and I was a servant in a big house.'

'You were a servant, ma'am?' Martha looked suspicious. 'What sort of servant?'

'A parlourmaid, Martha, and I was a lady's maid for a short while.'

'So you opened doors, and dusted, and did the silver, and – did you wait at table?'

'I did. I even ironed the newspaper.'

'Good heavens,' Martha said no more, but once or twice I caught her studying my hands.

We went through to dinner. 'Ah, excellent,' said Dr Watson, lifting the lid of the soup tureen. 'May I offer you soup, Mrs Hudson?'

'Please.' It was an effort to eat slowly, daintily, for I was so used to slurping up with the rest of the servants. 'What have I missed?' I asked.

Sherlock held up a hand while he swallowed. 'Firstly you have solved a mystery for me. Mycroft called yesterday to apologise.'

'Has he got his job back?'

'He has, and all suspicion wiped from the record. He thought I had something to do with it, which was a little embarrassing.' He grinned. 'I must admit I did wonder whether you were behind it.'

I grinned back. 'Mr Poskitt deserves much of the credit.'

'Yes, and he will be rewarded. In fact Mycroft told me, in confidence' – Sherlock gave me a significant look – 'that they have been asked to consider a promotion.'

A tap at the door. 'Are you ready for the lamb chops?' called Billy.

'I am,' I called.

We were quiet while Billy brought the dishes. 'Have you been busy, Dr Watson?' I asked, helping myself to a sizeable chop.

Dr Watson sat back. 'I have been working at the hospital, and also attending on Mr Stanley.'

'Oh! How is he?'

'Much improved. I prescribed rest and quiet, combined with electrotherapy, and he is sitting up and taking in his surroundings. He recognises his wife, and he can speak a little. He is easily tired, though; the nurse tells me that he still sleeps most of the day.'

'That is a great improvement.'

'It is; but I doubt that Mr Stanley will ever make a full recovery.' Dr Watson sighed, and helped himself to a chop. 'He will never be able to tell us what happened; the shock would either send him back into full catatonia, or kill him outright.'

I shivered. 'And you, Sherlock, what have you been up to?'

'This and that,' he said, airily. 'Nothing of note, really.' The conversation petered out, and we addressed ourselves to our food.

After dinner we did not separate, but all went to the parlour. I took a novel from the bookcase – what a pleasure to be able to read openly! – and curled up on the sofa, and as I did I recalled milady. Where would she be now? I remembered her words when I had caught her stealing: *I should be sent away for a rest cure.* Her insolent, privileged face came between me and the pages, and I closed the book.

I looked up, and met Sherlock's eyes. 'Would you like anything?'

'Perhaps some tea?'

'I shall go down.' He sprang up and went out.

I waited until I was sure he was out of earshot. 'How was Sherlock while I was gone?' I asked Dr Watson, in an undertone.

'Frantic, at first.' Dr Watson's voice, though low, had the same professional detachment as when he had spoken of Mr Stanley. 'I had to stop him from reporting you missing.'

'Did he—?' I looked up to the consulting room above.

Dr Watson shook his head. 'I threw away his syringe and told him that if I even suspected him of taking anything stronger than brandy, I would have him admitted.' He sighed. 'We got through.'

'Thank you, John.'

He studied me for a long moment, then bobbed his head in a funny little bow. 'As for you, Nell, I prescribe good food, fresh air, idleness, and time with your friends.'

Footsteps sounded outside – rather loud footsteps – and Sherlock came in. 'Tea is ordered,' he said, sitting down. 'Have you two been catching up?'

'We have indeed,' I said, exchanging glances with Dr Watson.

I jumped as the doorbell pealed. Sherlock saw it. 'You don't have to see anyone, Nell, if you'd rather not.' He moved to sit by me, and took my hand.

We heard voices at the door, and Martha came in. 'Mr Poskitt,' she announced. 'What shall I say to him?'

I shifted closer to Sherlock. 'Is he alone?'

'He is, ma'am.'

Sherlock squeezed my hand. 'Then show him in, Martha, please,' I said. I would have to face him some time, and it might as well be now.

'I thought I might find you here, Mrs Hudson.' Mr

Poskitt had an unaccustomed twinkle in his eye. 'I came to update you on proceedings.'

'Tell me.' I leaned forward, and I could see that Sherlock and Dr Watson were as curious as I was, but any revelations Mr Poskitt had were postponed by Martha, with the tea-tray. She poured out for us, adding milk and sugar as required, and perhaps I was mistaken, but she seemed to do it more carefully than usual.

'So,' said Mr Poskitt, sitting back composedly with his teacup. 'After we left you, Mrs Hudson, Lady Chambers and Professor Moriarty were taken separately for questioning. Moriarty refused to speak without a lawyer present; but Lady Chambers told us everything she knew.' His mouth twisted a little. 'Everything. I shall not go into it all, but we went to find the man Lawrence at Wandsworth Prison, as a result of her information. We found him dead, poisoned, and a smell of jasmine in the air. Moriarty's networks move quickly, and with fatal effect.'

I shuddered. 'Milady's jasmine perfume…'

'Quite,' said Mr Poskitt. 'We could never have connected Mr Stanley's abduction and the military leaks were it not for your observation, Mrs Hudson. Lady Chambers told us that the perfume was a gift from the Professor for services rendered.' I blinked. 'As it turns out, Moriarty has interests in Asia which go far beyond jasmine…' He gave me a sharp glance. 'I am saying more than I ought.'

'What happens now?' asked Sherlock.

'We are in the process of working that out,' said Mr Poskitt, and I got the impression that his 'we' was of a

311

royal nature, and possibly included the entire Cabinet. 'Nothing will be public, of course.'

'Is that because of Sir William?' I asked. I could imagine what the papers would make of the scandal.

'Partly, though he has already resigned,' Mr Poskitt said quietly. 'No, there is another factor to consider. What Professor Moriarty knows would probably bring down the government, if the case went to trial. He is one of us.'

'One of us?' Sherlock was on the edge of his seat, his eyes wide.

Mr Poskitt nodded. 'He is a mathematician by profession; the best of his generation. We have used him for many years, mainly to calculate probabilities and forecast trends. He began at the Ministry for Agriculture, but his remit widened until he was privy to the secrets of many departments. I dread to think what he has been doing over the years; but at least we can stop the rot.'

'Will he go to prison?' I asked, shivering as I thought of the deep-set eyes which had sought me out, even in a closed carriage.

Mr Poskitt shook his head. 'I doubt any prison could contain him. But we have other ways.'

'And milady?'

'Lady Chambers has been examined by a doctor, declared of unsound mind, and removed to a private nursing home, where she will remain.'

I shivered as I imagined milady pacing in a room like the one where I had been confined, long ago. I had been there for only a few days, and it had nearly broken me. Milady, I suspected, would never leave. I wondered what she had told Mr Poskitt, but my mind could not go into such dark places, and perhaps it was as well.

Mr Poskitt's voice cut into my thoughts. 'And the other reason for my visit.' He drew a leather purse from his inner pocket. 'I hope you don't mind coin; we cannot pay you in banknotes, since they may be traced.' He leaned across and put it into my hand, which sank with the weight. 'It is what we agreed, plus the information bonus and – ah – a little extra. Thanks to you, a force for evil has been curbed.' He drained his teacup, and got to his feet. 'When you are ready, Mrs Hudson, I would be very interested in discussing further assignments with you. But for now, I wish you a good evening.' With a little bow to the three of us, he left.

I looked down at the purse in my lap, and when I looked up again both Sherlock and Dr Watson were watching me. 'What terms did you agree?' asked Sherlock. 'Is it heavy?'

'A pound a day.' Sherlock whistled. 'How long was I away?'

'Twenty-nine days,' he replied at once.

'Then I suppose it is twenty-nine pounds and . . . something.' I opened the drawstring and tipped the bag into my lap. A cascade of golden coins poured out. 'Oh my… I need a table.'

Dr Watson brought a small table to me and together we counted. I reached fifty; I reached one hundred; and there were still coins in the folds of my dress. 'One hundred and fifty.' I laid the last coin down and looked at the little golden columns. It was enough to pay our living costs for a year, and more. I had never seen so much money in my life. And all of it, every penny, belonged to me.

CHAPTER 44

Sherlock was waiting by the front door when I came downstairs. I could feel his eyes on me as I put on a smart little hat. 'You don't have to come, you know,' I said. 'I wouldn't have thought that shopgirl talk would interest you.'

'Perhaps I shall learn something.' He took my hand as I was about to put on my glove and ran his thumb over the gold band. 'It's good to see it in its proper place.'

'It's good to have it back.' I smiled. 'Billy, we are going out,' I called.

'Will you be back for lunch, ma'am?'

'We shall.'

'Good.' He grinned. 'Make sure she doesn't go disappearing again, sir.'

Sherlock took my arm. 'I shall hold on to you for that very reason.' He opened the door. 'Cab, or walk?'

I took in a deep lungful of smoky, dirty London air. 'Let's walk. You have no idea how much I missed this.'

We weaved our way along the busy streets. I was glad of Sherlock's arm, for though I had been gone but a short time, the noise and bustle of London was overwhelming. Smells and sounds and sights crowded in on me until my brain sang.

'Are you sure you're all right, Nell?' Sherlock's voice brought me to myself.

'Yes, yes of course.'

A few minutes later we were standing in front of the department store. I gazed up at the building; the pillars, the lights, the air of prosperity oozing from it. 'Are we going in?' Sherlock asked.

'Yes.' I said. But I did not move. What would Mr Turner say? I had deserted my post and left him to manage without a detective. Would he throw me out? I found it hard to imagine the plump little manager doing anything so physical; but I braced myself.

'Hey!' Alf was waving at me. I hurried over, glad to see a friendly face.

'Good morning, Alf,' I held out a hand and he pumped it up and down.

'Where've you been? The boss was beside himself!'

'Oh dear.' I disengaged myself. 'Perhaps I shouldn't come in.'

'Don't be ridiculous, ma'am. Come along now.' He practically marched me into the shop.

'Look who it is!' Alf bellowed to the nearest counter. Gladys squealed, abandoned her customer, and ran towards me.

'Nell! We thought you'd gone for good!' She hugged

me and then drew back, inspecting me. 'I like your hat.'

'Thank you. Is Evie about?'

'Yes, she's – oh, you won't know!' Gladys tried to hide a smile behind her hand. 'I'll go and track her down.'

I wandered to the display of silk scarves. I wanted to buy them all, take them home, spread them on the bed, and roll in them—

'Nell!' Where I would have expected Evie's tall, elegant uniformed figure was a lady in a camel-hair coat and a cloche. She rushed over and folded me up in a bear hug. 'You came back! And just in time!'

'Just in time for what?' I laughed, wriggling in her grasp. 'What are you up to, Evie?'

'I'm getting married next Saturday!' she cried. 'In your blue dress.' She drew me to the side, talking nineteen to the dozen. 'I'm being you at the moment. When you vanished, not that I've said a *word*, Mr Turner was furious, and I said why don't we girls go on patrol? So we've been taking it in turns to play detective, and you wouldn't believe the things I've seen!' Her eyes were round and bright as sovereigns, and I watched them shift from me to Sherlock. 'Aren't you going to introduce me?' she said, with a significant look.

I grinned. 'Miss Marchant, may I introduce you to Mr Sherlock Holmes. Mr Holmes, Miss Evie Marchant.'

'Pleased to meet you, Mr Holmes,' said Evie, stressing the surname slightly, and giving her hand to Sherlock. 'Will you be accompanying Mrs Hudson next Saturday?'

'If she will have me,' said Sherlock, bowing over Evie's hand.

317

'Where are you getting married, Evie?' I asked, in an attempt to turn the conversation.

'At our local church, St Mary's in Bow,' Evie said, promptly. 'The wedding is at eleven, and then we will have a little breakfast in the church hall. It won't be fancy,' she added, hurriedly. 'Sandwiches and cake and lemonade.'

'I'm sure it will be lovely,' I said. 'We would be delighted to come. Are you all ready, Evie?'

'I think so,' said Evie, still looking at Sherlock with curiosity. 'Something old: my grandmother's ring. Something new *and* something blue: my dress. Something borrowed: my mother is lending me her pearl earrings.'

'Then you are ready,' I said, smiling.

'I don't feel ready,' laughed Evie. 'But I don't suppose you ever do.'

'No, I think you're right.'

'Just think, next Saturday I shall be Evie Smith! How funny!' Evie clapped her hands to her pink cheeks. 'Anyway, I must get back to work, or Mr Turner will be coming after me.' She clasped my hand. '*Do* come next Saturday. Both of you.' She smiled shyly at Sherlock.

'Will you carry on working once you're married?' I asked, remembering my own adventures in that department.

Evie's laugh was short, sharp and mirthless. 'I don't have a choice! Not if we're to afford a flat of our own. We've scrimped and saved for all we're worth, really we have, but I can't afford to play the fine lady just yet. Saturday, don't forget!' She scurried off, and I caught sight of Mr Turner peeking from behind a stand of hats.

'Can we go now?' Sherlock muttered.

'Not yet.' I put my arm through his and led him to the wig section. 'I have a promise to keep.'

***

'How does it go?'

We were sitting in the parlour. No, that description was not entirely accurate. Sherlock was sprawled on the sofa, and I was leaning against him, my head pillowed on his chest. Dr Watson had gone to bed already, claiming fatigue and an early start in the morning, but the sly look he had cast at us on leaving the room had roused my suspicions.

'How does what go?' I said. Sherlock's face was a study of innocence.

'Something old, something new…'

'Oh! Something old, something new, something borrowed, something blue.'

'What does it mean?'

'You mean you don't know?' I should have been used to Sherlock's occasional ignorance of things which I considered common knowledge, but I could not stop a note of incredulity from creeping in.

Smiling, Sherlock shook his head. 'Somehow it has passed me by.'

'It's just a little rhyme. Brides are supposed to have one of each when they get married. That's all it is.'

'Oh.' Sherlock stroked my hair, absently. 'Something old…' He touched the gold band on my ring finger. 'Something new . . . these curls are definitely new…' He ran his hands through my hair, dislodging several pins. 'Something borrowed – wait…' I felt him shift behind me,

319

and presently I felt the slither of silk around my neck as he dropped his necktie over my head. 'Something blue – your dress!'

I twisted round to look at him, and as I did his expression changed from merriment to a look so tender that I had to hold myself from crying. 'Marry me, Nell. You have no idea how much I missed you. I couldn't bear to lose you again.'

My heart leapt for joy. But my brain, my stupid careful brain, caught it and brought it crashing down. 'What about . . . what about Jack? I thought we agreed we would wait.'

'I don't care about Jack. I can't wait another – what – three years? For all I know, you could run away tomorrow.'

Sherlock put his arms round me and I revelled in the warmth. *It would be so easy,* my heart whispered. *Isn't this what you've dreamed of?*

'Do you really want me to marry you, Sherlock?' I blurted it out, and felt foolish immediately.

'What, must I get down on one knee?' He laughed. 'Very well, I shall do it.' And with a great upsetting and wriggling, he extricated himself from beneath me and knelt beside the sofa. 'Nell Hudson, will you marry me?'

My heart screamed yes. My soul shrieked the word. But my cold, hard brain held back. 'Sherlock, you know how much I want to say yes. When I left you, to go undercover, it was one of the hardest things I have ever done.' I took a deep breath. There did not seem to be enough air in the room to fill my lungs. 'But doing what I did – the drudgery, the deceit, the spying – it was one of the great moments of my life. And I did it not as your assistant, but as myself. On my own.'

Sherlock frowned. 'I thought you hated it.'

'I did, often. But it was still worth doing.' I stroked his cheek. 'Sherlock, if I marry you now, knowing that Jack is still alive, I am no better than him.'

'He isn't coming back, Nell.' His eyes narrowed. 'But this isn't about him, is it?'

I swallowed. 'No. I love you, Sherlock. But if I married you tomorrow – much as I would love to – I would find myself keeping house, and planning meals, and working as your assistant. All those things you have laughed at me for, and chided me for, when I have been frustrated.'

'But how is it different, Nell?' His glance fell on my hand. 'You wear my ring, we live together, we share a bed…'

'If it would be no different, why are you asking me to marry you?' My smile faded as I saw the unshed tears in his eyes.

I reached out to him, and held him close. 'One day perhaps I shall want to be what people call a "proper wife", and run the house. But not yet. I want to be my own person, first, with my own work.' I brushed away a tear of my own. 'So my answer is – not yet. Not no; but not yet.'

We held each other and wept, hot salt tears on our cheeks, our necks, our shoulders. Yet even as I cried I felt tension leaving me. I had said it. 'I love you,' I whispered.

'I love you too.' Sherlock's voice broke on the words.

We held each other all night, clinging, scared to let the other go. I knew that I had risked my happiness, perhaps

321

risked everything – and for what? For a dream of a career that was possibly not even within my grasp. An opportunity such as the one I had had might not come again. Sherlock might not ask again. But as I drowsed in his arms, our tears dried, comforting each other in our exhaustion, I knew that I had made the right choice.

CHAPTER 45

I treated myself to a new outfit to attend Evie's wedding, visiting a dressmaker for the very first time. I chose a rose-coloured silk with ruffles, a matching jacket and little hat, which she assured me was 'à la mode, especially for someone as elegant of figure as you, madam.' I took that to mean that I was skinny.

Sherlock whistled when the boxes arrived, and demanded to see me in it. I was quite ready to try on my new treasures and pose like a fashion plate. 'Very nice,' he said, kissing me, 'you can wear it for—'

'For what? It's for Evie's wedding.'

'That's what I meant.' He picked up the newspaper.

I twitched it out of his hand. 'You're up to something, Sherlock Holmes. What is it?'

'Nothing,' he protested, laughing. I swatted him with the paper, but it had no effect.

Evie's wedding was beautiful. I wept a little as they exchanged vows, remembering, as every married woman does, their own wedding day, and hoping the very best for their marriage. Sherlock saw me dabbing my eyes, and put an arm round me. 'Are you all right?' he whispered.

I nodded.

'My offer still stands, you know.'

A woman in the pew in front turned round with an angry shush louder than any noise we had made. That sent us both into fits of laughter which bent Sherlock almost double in his effort to suppress them, and the disapproval around us made it worse, until we sneaked out to the churchyard and had our laugh in peace. We had recovered by the time Evie emerged, radiant in her pale-blue wedding gown, and she kissed me warmly. 'I saw you laughing with your young man,' she grinned. 'Pair of lovebirds, you are.'

I gave her an envelope. 'I wasn't sure what to get you, so I hope this is all right.'

She peeped inside, and gasped. 'Oh!' Then she grinned. 'I take it your job went well, then.'

I smiled back, glad that my sore red hands and my painful feet were well-covered.

'Next time, go undercover somewhere you can have nice clothes. That would be fun.' She winked and passed down the line to the next guest: the woman who had shushed me. Sherlock snorted, and I nudged him.

We returned home to find that my mother had called half an hour ago. 'That's odd,' I commented. 'I always go to her. She's never visited me here.' I had dashed off a short note to let her know that I had returned, and in it I had said that I would visit in the next day or two, so I was mystified. 'What did she say, Billy?'

Billy looked up from the boots he was polishing. 'She said either you or Mr Holmes would do, but I said you were both out.' Martha, darning a sock at the other end of the table, frowned at him.

'Did she, now.' I went upstairs and found Sherlock unknotting his necktie in the bedroom. 'Sherlock, why would my mother call on you?'

'I have no idea,' he replied, poker-faced.

I unpinned my hat. 'So while I was away, you had no contact with my mother?'

'I didn't say that,' he replied, throwing the tie on the bed.

I rolled my eyes. 'Just tell me.'

'All right, all right!' He took off his shoes and sprawled on the bed. 'I might have written to ask if she knew where you were.'

I bit my lip. 'You didn't.'

'I did. Your mother called at Baker Street the next day. I think she was a little surprised, particularly as she said she had been given to understand that Dr Watson and I were two elderly bachelors.'

'I didn't say that.'

'You implied it, then.' Sherlock's grin was wide as the Cheshire Cat's.

I sat down on the bed. 'What else did she say?'

'Not very much. She left shortly afterwards, because she was rather cross with me for not being an elderly bachelor. But I thought it over, and decided I should call on her to explain myself.'

'Oh God.'

'It went very well. Your mother reminds me rather of you, in fact.'

'Don't say that.'

He grinned. 'At any rate, she decided that I was not so bad after all, and neither were you.'

'Does she know that we—'

'Good God, no!' Sherlock sat up and put his elbows on his knees. 'I said that we had a deep mutual affection.'

'She knows, then.' I flopped backwards onto the bed and hid my face.

'If she does, she doesn't mind.' Sherlock gently moved a hand aside and kissed my forehead. 'She regards me as a steadying influence.'

'*You?*' I gaped at him, then giggled. 'Remind me to share that with Dr Watson tonight.'

'Am I forgiven, then?' Sherlock kissed me on the mouth. 'I only wrote to her because I was trying to find you.'

I sighed. 'I suppose. So long as you don't have any other nasty surprises for me.'

'No nasty surprises.' He leaned on an elbow and looked at me, smiling. 'I do like that dress,' he murmured.

'Wait a minute,' I said, scrambling up to face him. 'You said something . . . you said I could wear it when, and then you stopped. What did you mean?'

'Nell, have I ever told you that you are a very suspicious woman?'

'Never mind that. Out with it.'

'I want to take you to visit my parents, at Christmas.' Sherlock's voice was steady. 'Mycroft will be there too.

He's looking forward to seeing you.'

'Your parents?' I stammered. 'For Christmas?'

'Yes, for Christmas.'

'What about Dr Watson?'

'He won't fit in my suitcase.' Sherlock rolled his eyes. 'Nell, Watson can look after himself.'

'I didn't think you liked Christmas.'

'You do, though. Perhaps I shall like it better with you.'

'Where do they live?'

'In a village in the countryside, thirty or so miles away.'

'It isn't in Berkshire, is it?'

'No, no.' He stroked my cheek. 'There will probably be snow, and there's always lots of food, and carol-singers, and a tree with candles.'

'It sounds lovely.' I imagined waking on Christmas morning to church bells ringing, and looking out onto snowy fields. It would be like waking up in a Christmas card. 'What have you told your parents about me?' It came out a little more baldly than I would have wished.

Sherlock considered. 'If you take your outfit off now, and hang it up, the creases will probably drop out.'

'Sherlock…' I said in my best warning voice.

'It's true, though.' He rolled onto his back and put his hands behind his head. 'I haven't said much. I have hinted that I am very fond of someone . . . a most intelligent, accomplished, attractive woman…'

'Why, thank you.' I mimicked his pose, dislodging my back hair in the process.

'Entirely deserved. I just haven't mentioned that I happen to live under your roof.'

'No, I don't suppose you have.' I sat up and began to unpin my hair. 'Ow.'

'Here.' Sherlock sat up too, and carefully took the back pins out.

'Thank you.' He leaned in and kissed the nape of my neck. 'Don't think you can soften me up.'

'Can't I?' He kissed me again, and eased my little jacket from my shoulders. 'Let me help you with those creases…'

Later, much later, I lay in the crook of his arm. We breathed together, slow and deep, as the sky outside the window grew darker and darker. 'I should go and see about dinner,' I said.

'No you shouldn't.' Sherlock put his other arm over me. 'It is all in hand. Stay here, with me.'

I closed my eyes, and stayed. The sheets and the patchwork quilt pinned me down, warm and heavy. Evening noise was beginning: a barrel organ cranking out a new tune, shouts, calls, whistles, hurrying footsteps. I had been prepared to miss Sherlock, and I had – but I had missed my home too, more than I had ever thought I would. I wondered how long it would be before I grew bored with my present life, with whatever I felt was holding me back; how long it would be before I visited Mr Poskitt, and wrote Sherlock another note. *Perhaps*, I thought as I drowsed, *meeting Sherlock's parents, seeing where he grew up, spending Christmas with them, is just a different sort of adventure.* I smiled to myself as I remembered Evie's words. At least this time I would have nice clothes for it.

ACKNOWLEDGEMENTS

First of all, thank you to my wonderful beta readers – Ruth Cunliffe, Paula Harmon, and Stephen Lenhardt. Apologies that I kept you waiting so long for a sequel! Also many thanks to my indefatigable proofreader, John Croall, who as ever did a fabulous job. This wouldn't be the book it is without you all.

I'm also going to thank the internet, without which I would know far less about what parlourmaids do, and would have fallen down far fewer research rabbit holes. Swings and roundabouts! I won't even attempt to cite all the websites I've visited in the course of researching and fact-checking; but the Victorian Web (http://www.victorianweb.org), Victorian London (http://www.victorianlondon.org/index-2012.htm), and of course Wikipedia were incredibly useful.

I'll admit now that this book was a tough one to write, and particularly to edit. I wrote the first draft back in 2017 and let it mature – or gather dust – for some time before plucking up the courage to reopen the file and peek from behind my metaphorical sofa. One of the reasons I did was the gentle but tenacious nudging of my husband, Stephen Lenhardt. 'But what about Mrs Hudson 2?' So big thanks to him for making me face up to my first draft.

And of course, thank you for reading! I hope you've enjoyed *In Sherlock's Shadow*, and if you could leave the book a short review or a star rating on Amazon or Goodreads I'd be very grateful.

FONT CREDIT

Title page and chapter heading font: Libre Baskerville by Impallari Type: https://www.fontsquirrel.com/fonts/libre-baskerville License: SIL Open Font License v. 1.10.

ABOUT THE AUTHOR

Liz Hedgecock grew up in London, England, did an English degree, and then took forever to start writing. After several years working in the National Health Service, some short stories crept into the world. A few even won prizes. Then the stories began to grow longer . . .

Now Liz travels between the nineteenth and twenty-first centuries, murdering people. To be fair, she does usually clean up after herself.

Liz's reimaginings of Sherlock Holmes, the Pippa Parker cozy mystery series, the Caster & Fleet Victorian mystery series (written with Paula Harmon), the Magical Bookshop series and the Maisie Frobisher Mysteries are available in ebook and paperback.

Liz lives in Cheshire with her husband and two sons, and when she's not writing or child-wrangling you can usually find her reading, messing about on Twitter, or cooing over stuff in museums and art galleries. That's her story, anyway, and she's sticking to it.

Website/blog: http://lizhedgecock.wordpress.com
Facebook: http://www.facebook.com/lizhedgecockwrites
Twitter: http://twitter.com/lizhedgecock
Goodreads: https://www.goodreads.com/lizhedgecock
Amazon author page: http://author.to/LizH

BOOKS BY LIZ HEDGECOCK

Mrs Hudson & Sherlock Holmes series (novels)
A House Of Mirrors
In Sherlock's Shadow
A Spider's Web

Maisie Frobisher Mysteries (novels)
All At Sea
Off The Map
Gone To Ground
In Plain Sight

Caster & Fleet Mysteries (with Paula Harmon)
The Case of the Black Tulips
The Case of the Runaway Client
The Case of the Deceased Clerk
The Case of the Masquerade Mob
The Case of the Fateful Legacy
The Case of the Crystal Kisses

Pippa Parker Mysteries (novels)
Murder At The Playgroup
Murder In The Choir
A Fete Worse Than Death
Murder in the Meadow
The QWERTY Murders
Past Tense

The Magical Bookshop (novels)
Every Trick in the Book
Brought to Book
Double Booked
By the Book

Sherlock & Jack series (novellas)
A Jar Of Thursday
Something Blue
A Phoenix Rises

Halloween Sherlock series (novelettes)
The Case of the Snow-White Lady
Sherlock Holmes and the Deathly Fog
The Case of the Curious Cabinet

Short stories
The Secret Notebook of Sherlock Holmes
Bitesize
The Adventure of the Scarlet Rosebud
The Case of the Peculiar Pantomime (a Caster & Fleet
short mystery)

For children (with Zoe Harmon)
A Christmas Carrot

WHITE
RHINO
BOOKS

.

Printed in Great Britain
by Amazon

16411282R00195